The Dual Path is a wonderful a[nd] story with strong lessons for young readers. A summer with her Aunt Joy pulls Zelia into a magical world teeming with magical creatures, talking animals and trees, and a cast of inspiring travelers on a journey that takes her to the stars.

The characters are exuberant and, believe me; you will want to live your life as purely as Zelia comes to experience it, filled with a sense of wonder and a sacred joy no one can steal from you. It's a powerful book that shows readers the possibility of a world that exists alongside ours. It is entertaining and utterly inspiring.

 Review by Jose Cornelio

AnnaMariah Nau delivers a highly engaging fantasy novel that delves deep into a colorful and interesting magical land where trouble brews just beneath the surface.

I would not hesitate to recommend this novel to anyone who enjoys entertaining fantasy books and unique and quirky characters.

 Review by K.C. Finn

The Dual Path is an exciting story, a wonderful tale for young adults (and older ones) to lose themselves in. A well-written tale, the story flows well and shows great imagination. The way it is written will entice readers to use their own imaginations as they travel to a magical world that may just exist in parallel to our own – how would we know it didn't? But this is more than just a tale of magic and mystery. It is a story of self-discovery, a lesson in facing new challenges and experiences as they arise and taking them in our stride, facing them head-on. An engaging story with wonderful characters, this is a magical adventure no reader can fail to enjoy.

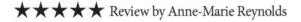 Review by Anne-Marie Reynolds

The Dual Path

AN EARTH TO STARS ADVENTURE

AnnaMariah Nau

The Dual Path – An Earth to Stars Adventure

Cover Illustration Copyright ©2021 by Joyous Heart Press

Logo & book design by Patrise Henkel

Editing by Carol Burbank, Storyweaving www.storyweaving.com

Published by Joyous Heart Press
P.O. Box 5467, Central Point, OR 97502

info@joyousheartpress.com

Be part of our magical adventure -sign up for mailing list -

Promos, News, Quizzes, Events & Offers:

www.earthtostarsadventures.com

I dedicate this book
to all who've inspired me and all who are drawn to read these tales from my heart

This book is for all young or old who've felt there is something more. You may have been touched by that sense of magic and wonder that lifts your soul and draws you to search past what you've been told is real. You peek into the dark places, and in doing so, you bring out the light.

This book is for all who have struggled to fit into this reality, who've felt something is missing. You've longed and searched for that elusive something.

When the goddess/angel/fairy/aunt opens the way in and invites you to "live the world," and you feel a tingle or a longing deep inside, you don't need to know what it means, just that there's something in you that responds deeply.

This book is for all the misfits, optimists, and dreamers who've sometimes given up because it seems the world you seek to live is not the world that is today. You often feel on the verge of giving up because what's the point of being the only one holding this dream.

Read with the eyes of your heart, allowing in the possibilities, the magic, and the love, and feel your inner knowing come to life.

Learn to "live the world," and as you do, you'll discover that you're not the only one who feels these things.

May you discover small awakenings that speak to your heart's knowing and allow you to realize that you can live the world of the dual-path, walking both in this reality and in the realms of spirit – magic – love – the Universe, that which speak to your joyous heart.

Please join our Crystalline Heart Family and be part of the ongoing adventure www.earthtostarsadventures.com

May you live the world with love and joy in your heart,

AnnaMariah

CONTENTS

CHAPTER 1:

Meeting Joy, Definitely Not a Maiden Aunt

I couldn't wait to get off the Greyhound bus. The absolute worst way to travel! Not sure why I was happy to get off; I had nothing to look forward to but a boring summer with an eccentric aunt and in the middle of nowhere to boot. I would have been much happier with my parents in the Amazon looking for lost temples. I get why I couldn't go; I didn't relish the idea of getting jungle sickness again, but it might be better than being babysat for the summer.

I might as well get this boring summer started. I couldn't believe my eyes when I saw this wild-looking woman cavorting down the road, waving her arms and shouting in my direction. I stopped so suddenly my backpack slapped against me with a thud. Under my breath, I prayed, "Please, God, don't let that be her!"

Excitement, dismay, and shock warred in my heart when I realized I might be with this odd woman for the entire summer. I couldn't believe she was even a distant relation, let alone my mother's sister! My mother had described her sister as eccentric. I was expecting something entirely different, maybe one of those stuffy spinster women who tend flowers, iron doilies, and feed the neighborhood cats. I couldn't have been more wrong.

Because there she was, a sight to behold. Her dress was so puffy, she looked like a cross between a gaily striped circus tent and a hot-air balloon – not the slightest hint of the expected maiden aunt, and no sense of decorum, as she danced, careened, and hooted in my general direction!

It was difficult to know where to look first as she zigzagged towards me. She defied linear thinking. I could not be rational in the face of such creativity.

I still can't adequately describe her, and when I first saw her – well, bear with me. The sight of her fantastic outfit addled even my usually steady wits.

If this was her, I was pretty sure this wouldn't be at all like the summer I'd been anticipating. As she got closer, I could see that what looked chaotic at first glance was a beautifully tailored, flowing dress. The silky fabric moved as she twirled, her enormous floating skirt curved in diagonal stripes of brilliant yellow, orange, and red, separated by tiny strips of bright green. Her gigantic puffed sleeves seemed to defy gravity. I wanted to reach out and pinch them to see if they were stuffed or starched. One sleeve was a bright purplish pink, a color I'm pretty sure had no name, the other lime green. Her skirt billowed and waved in the breeze, making me dizzy as the vertical stripes moved, creating optical illusions. Tied around her waist were silken scarves of every imaginable color and hue, even a few I'd never dreamed possible. Tassels and bells and all manner of things hung at different lengths from the various scarves, and some of the ends flapped wildly in the wind.

For a last, desperate minute, I hoped I was mistaken, and this wasn't her at all, but just a woman passing by on the road. I looked around for a boring spinster or an approaching car with renewed hope, but no one else was in sight. We were on an empty stretch of road miles from town. The only thing here was the tiny bus shelter, not even a proper station.

Maybe I got off at the wrong stop? I guess I should have paid better attention to my mother's many instructions. I admit I'd been angry and pouting about being babysat for the summer. After all, I was twelve and fully capable of taking care of myself.

There was something vaguely familiar about her that niggled my brain. I dismissed it; she was *nothing* like my mother! Finally, the woman stopped, her skirts gathering around her ankles, and I took a few cautious steps towards her.

"Zelia?" she smiled quizzically.

I tried to smile a polite greeting but failed. The shock was just too much. This outrageous woman *was* my mother's sister. I wavered between excitement and absolute horror. Eccentric was an understatement.

I couldn't meet her eyes. The items dangling from her waist glittered and clanked, so I was distracted trying to see each one. I could only make out a few things as they peeked in and out of the billowing skirt as if playing hide and seek. I saw a small pair of opera glasses, a golden wishbone, a tiny ballerina, a purple parasol, red satin dancing slippers, and a small silver dagger encased in a jeweled sheath. She shook a little and laughed. I saw a tiny bottle filled with iridescent purple liquid, a spinning top, a mirror framed with what looked like real daisies, a pointed hat, an antique door key, a kaleidoscope, a thimble with a needle and thread, and hanging from the central scarf, was a book.

The book and the words on it appeared to shimmer and change colors. I could not take my eyes off it. The letters refused to stay still, changing too rapidly for me to read. The book entranced me, and I dropped my backpack on the side of the road without a thought and moved closer.

Her laughter, deep, full, and unexpectedly gay, brought me out of my reverie and kept me from touching the book. To my surprise, I started laughing, too, still staring as I looked up into the most beautiful blue eyes I'd ever seen. Her eyes reminded me of a bright spring sky, the blue and cloudless kind that makes you feel that anything could happen.

Time ceased to exist. The world dimmed, and there were only the two of us, laughter and the most intense joy I've ever felt. Tears streamed down my face. I gasped for breath. I felt so light and buoyant; I wasn't sure if I would burst or simply float away. I didn't care what happened next, as long as I could keep laughing like this.

A delightful shiver went through me as she stepped forward and placed her graceful hands on my shoulders.

Our laughter slowed, and finally, we were quiet. Her gaze made me feel as if she'd seen through to my core with the good and the bad of me exposed to her sight. But she loved and accepted all that she saw. I didn't feel like a misfit anymore, continually starting over because we moved so much, longing to make new friends but afraid to try because I knew we would leave again soon. I didn't feel like a chameleon, trying to do/be/say everything expected of me, sometimes succeeding, sometimes failing so massively I wanted to give up. For the first time I could remember, it didn't matter if I was less than perfect or didn't fit in under her feathery touch. She wouldn't judge me for anything I could do, be, or say. I straightened my back, feeling strong and secure in a way I'd never experienced or thought possible.

We laughed again, and this time I was laughing because of myself, not despite myself. For the first time, I was perfect, just the way I was. She took my hands, and we twirled and danced in circles, right there on the side of that dusty road. I didn't even stop to be embarrassed though my actions weren't at all fitting for a girl my age. I was surprised to look down and see my feet still touching the Earth. I was sure we must have levitated and left the ground. Then we sat side-by-side, right there in the dusty road in the middle of nowhere. Strangely, it felt like a perfectly natural thing to do.

She put her arm around my shoulders. I compared her in my mind to my mother. She was so different it was hard to believe they were sisters. My mother always wore a T-shirt and jeans, hair pulled back in a ponytail, and smelled slightly of the solvents she used to clean artifacts. My aunt's fragrance was of lemons and something flowery, her hair curled and bounced, and her dress was a long way from a T-shirt and jeans! It seemed as if colors were more brilliant, and sounds seemed clearer and crisper than I'd ever perceived. I tried to wrap my head around everything that had happened in the last five minutes and looked at her in wonder.

"Welcome to the real world, Zelia," she said with a gentle smile.

"What?" It was the first word I'd said aloud since I saw her in the distance.

"I know, you think your life has been real. So far, only a shadow of truth has come through; there is so much more to discover. When we danced with joy and delight, you removed your blinders and awakened to the world you came to live."

"Don't you mean 'the life I came to live?' How can I 'live' a world?"

"Ah, now, that's a great question. I *meant* to say the 'world you came to live.' I'll explain. You 'live' a world when you drop the illusion that you are separate and know that you are part of the whole and that the whole is part of you. You came into this world completely connected to the Earth, all its inhabitants, in harmony and love with all that is. As you grew, you began to doubt and feel unworthy and lost that connection. You've been living a half-life, feeling alone; you against the world. That's not the way it should be. Now you feel aware of, and one with the magic and love all around you, and anything seems possible. Does it not?"

"Yes!" I cried as that affirmation washed through me. It was as if my 'yes' was an acceptance of a whole new life as I realized her words' truth. I felt

4

free and light, as if I could dance forever. I couldn't wait to learn more. But if I had known then how dramatically the course of my life would alter, would I have stayed or run back to the bus stop and waited all night for the next bus to take me away? I like to think I would have been brave enough to leap without hesitation.

But suddenly, I pulled back from her. I must have had some idea that something big was happening because even though I wanted to take off down the road or fly into the sky, straight into my new life, something held me back. How could everything have changed so quickly? Even though all looked the same, nothing was the same.

I put my head between my hands, knees on elbows, and I think I even closed my eyes, trying desperately to figure out what I should do. As if in a dream, I pictured us walking down new roads, entering towns I'd never seen before, meeting new children, animals, and a few wild-looking adults as we went. I desperately wanted it to happen, and I could hardly breathe.

I'd been searching for my purpose all my life. I know, I know, I'm only twelve. It never comforts me when adults continuously say there's plenty of time to figure things out when I'm older. Even worse, they condescendingly ask what I want to be when I grow up. So, which is it? Should I leave the question until I'm older, or did I need to know the answer when I was in kindergarten? Maybe it's all a game to adults.

My nomadic life with my archaeologist parents sometimes made me want to map out a clear and settled future. We'd barely settle in a new town when some opportunity would come up to explore, and off we'd go, completely changing direction. I had never been in one school for longer than six months! We mostly traveled and lived around the world. My parents called it "tent schooling" when they were on a dig.

The last time I'd been to public school, I'd enjoyed being with other kids, but I was bored stupid by the classes. Learning from my parents and my natural curiosity had pushed me ahead of most kids my age. Tests showed I was already doing some college-level work. I longed to be a normal kid but always felt I didn't belong with kids my age. Being out of the country and with adults so often, I didn't watch the same TV shows, didn't know the slang, and in many cases, I didn't enjoy the same things. I always ended up feeling a complete dork. Most adults acted like I was a stupid child.

For now, though, I just felt confused. "If you're my aunt Joan, who are you? Gee, that doesn't make sense! What I'm trying to... Oh, I don't even know what I mean!" I stammered, face reddening in frustration.

"I am the Story Lady. I help you see the story that is yours to live."

"But you *are* Joan, aren't you?"

"I was, but I don't use that name anymore," she said with a smile.

"Why? What is your name now?"

"Why is simple. Joan describes the girl I once was, but I am no longer that scared, angry, cautious person. I can't relate to that name or even relate to the *me* I was before I became the me I am now. As for my name now, well, I resist taking on a permanent name. My name changes with each person I meet."

"What?! That's crazy! How can each person you meet have a different name for you?"

"A name boxes you in and defines you. Why would I want to be pre-defined? When I meet someone, I look deeply to see what their experience of me is, and I either give myself a name or sometimes let them choose it for me. What would you call me?"

"Joy?"

"Joy, I am!"

"Isn't it weird to be called by different names?"

"No, every name chosen is a part of me. I can continue to change and evolve and not get trapped." She looked at me for a long minute. "Have you ever felt that your name defines who you are? Does it limit other people's expectations of what you will do or be?"

"I never really thought about it; it's just the way things are," I mused. "But my mother calls me by several names. When she is pleased with me, she calls me 'Lia,' and I know that I can be happy and excited about things. If I've done something wrong, or she is disappointed in me, I am 'Zelia.' As Zelia, I have to act quieter, more thoughtful. When I'm in deep doo-doo, I am 'Zelia Maria Magdalena.' As soon as I hear that name, it's like I freeze, afraid to do or say anything."

"What does each of those names make you feel about who you are?"

"Lia feels loved and accepted, playful, laughing, but sometimes irresponsible and forgetful, and I don't worry about cleaning my room or doing homework."

"What about Zelia Maria Magdalena? How does she feel?"

"She feels like she must be perfect and always on task. It's hard being Zelia Maria Magdalena. I can't relax and have fun. I have to do everything right; I feel dull, depressed—eventually, I kind of break down. I need to have fun again, and I become Lia. But it's like I get carried away with the sheer relief of it all. I never seem to find a balance between these parts of myself."

"What about Zelia? Isn't she somewhere in between?"

"Maybe she's the balance between the two, but I feel like a poser when I'm her. Zelia is the responsible one who picks up after herself and does all the assignments and chores without being asked. She is serious. Adults like her. When I feel unsure of myself, I become Zelia and do things to get approval. But I always feel pulled in two directions like I'm putting on a false show. Lia and Zelia Maria Magdalena feel real. Zelia is my pretend self that isn't sure if she should be playful or solemn. I end up being Zelia a lot of the time, but I don't like the pretense. I don't even have words to explain it; it's as if I'm not completely there."

"I see. Which one do you think of as the 'real' you, the core of who you are?"

"I don't know if there is a 'real' me! I'm always reacting to what I think other people – my parents, my teachers, and my classmates – want from me, knowing that I'm not living up to their expectations. It never seems to make them happy either. I think I've lost myself." I said, exasperated.

"That's how most people go through their lives, bounding between one little part of themselves and another little part of themselves, never tapping into their larger, whole self. Now is your chance to 'live the world,' not just live in it. You can be fully in touch with everything and everyone around you, but most of all, you can live from your core. Do you see how the names you've carried tend to separate you into bits of yourself? Why don't you choose a new name that encompasses everything real about you?"

We were still sitting in the road; luckily, there weren't any cars. But even so, shouldn't we move? I couldn't seem to get up. I put my head between my hands, closed my eyes, and thought and thought.

"You're thinking way too hard," Joy laughed. "Your brain only knows what you've put into it before. Free yourself from your thoughts and let them go, to be in the world."

"How do I do that?" I blurted out with frustration.

"It's easy if you stop trying or forcing it. Do you know about meditation?"

"I've heard about it, of course. I think my mother meditates. But what's that got to do with me?"

"Meditation is a good way of getting out of your head and letting the Universe guide you. Are you willing to try?"

I nodded, dubious.

"Good. Relax your body, breathe deeply into your belly and chest. Follow your breath in and out, in and out. Feel it coming in through your nose or mouth, then going out, either through your mouth or your nose. Whatever feels right. That's good." Her voice was calm and smooth, like a hypnotist in one of those old movies. In a way, it made me want to unwind and rest.

What the heck, why not? I decided to give it a try and began following her voice as I breathed. Slowly but surely, I got the hang of it. Of course, my mind was still whirling with questions. "What's my name? What's my purpose? Why am I here?" and on and on, my brain chattering away.

"Allow your breath to expand beyond your body. Feel your breath touching the trees, the grass, expanding into the sky. Good, keep opening. When you feel you've reached out as much as you can, ask for your name."

My mind kept going in circles. I tried. I honestly tried. And I'd breathe again, asking silently, "What's my name?" My mind's persistence to keep playing round and round like a video loop, never stopping, was frustrating.

"Breathe. Expand."

I took another deep breath and concentrated on following my breath in and out, as she'd suggested. Suddenly, a shimmer went through me, and I relaxed fully. It was as if my breath touched the trees; I was lighter and freer. Another breath and I reached the sky! Bluebirds were miraculously flying through me, darting in and out in delight. The sun was warming me, filling all my dark corners with beautiful light.

"My name is Zemma!" I announced with an assurance that astounded me. What kind of name was that, I wondered?

"Hello, Zemma. It's nice to meet you."

I was surprised when I just blurted out this answer, "It's a combination of my other names, and yet it's new. It comes from what I was, and yet it's also what I'll be, a confident girl, then a strong, amazing woman."

"How does it feel to be 'Zemma'?"

"It feels right. It's as if now I'm wholly me if that makes any sense."

"It does. All the parts of you have become one, with your new name. Zemma, are you ready to see what this day has to offer?"

"Yes!"

My feet tingled with anticipation, and I felt ready for nearly anything. It was going to be a glorious summer!

CHAPTER 2:

Adventure Begins – Learning to Live the World

"Well, Zemma, what do you propose we do with ourselves this summer?" Joy looked at me expectantly.

"Aunt Joy, you're the adult! I figured you had all that planned out. Aren't I staying with you at your house?"

"We *could* do that."

"I'd rather hoped it wouldn't be *that* boring," I laughed nervously. Oh gosh, what if all we did was hang around in her living room and talk? I'd so hoped for something slightly more interesting. Could my first impression of her have been wrong? Was she just a regular adult disguised in kooky clothing?

"There are always choices, Zemma. We can make our time and our lives into anything we choose. If you want a nice quiet relaxing summer, we can go back to my place. You can help in the garden and hang out with the neighborhood kids, who I'm sure will be happy to show you the swimming hole, play video games, or whatever else girls your age do these days. I'm sure it would be a perfectly acceptable way to spend your time." Somehow the way she described it made summer sound decidedly dull.

"Do you have a TV? And is there a movie theater in town?"

"Oh, yes, all that's available." I could almost hear a sigh in her voice as she spoke.

Ordinarily, I would have jumped at the chance to spend a regular summer vacation like other kids. "Okay, Aunt Joy, I'll bite. What other options might there be?"

I waited for her answer but dived into my thoughts, suddenly longing to take a journey with this magical woman and really 'live the world.' But wasn't I supposed to be staying at her little cottage? Could we do both?

I turned toward her. She was smiling and nodding her head. "Yes."

That was all she said, but I knew she knew.

"Did you hear? Dang, I'm not making sense. Did you see my vision of us taking a trip together?"

"Yes!"

"How? How did you know?"

"You will see that when you 'live the world,' we can feel things together and have a sense that all is in perfect order. You will easily find your way as you live moment by moment in joy. So, we could go on a little adventure for a week or so and see how it goes, then decide if we want to keep going or come back to my cottage. We could easily stay there for all or part of the summer, and you can relax and enjoy all the regular summer activities for a change."

I thought about this for a moment, torn between a typical type of summer, maybe even hanging out with other kids, but the idea of an adventure was much more appealing. "Both are tempting. I like your idea of deciding after a week or so. What do you have in mind as far as traveling? Are we talking a big trek or a slow meander down the road?"

Joy laughed, "Somewhere in between, definitely not a big trek. I love to backpack. We can camp along the way—nothing strenuous, no endurance hikes, or anything like that. I prefer taking the time to wander down the backroads, seeing the countryside at leisure. It can be a delightful experience. You meet people as you go and see nature up close and personal, very up close and personable."

She giggled, honestly giggled when she said that. "I especially enjoy spending nights in the stars." Her eyes twinkled merrily. "Oh, and who knows what can happen when you just throw yourself at the mercy of the Universe and go where it leads. You may even discover your destiny."

"Did you say *in* the Stars?"

"Hmmm, yes, I did. We'll talk about that later if you don't mind. I think you have another question."

"Ummm… Did you say my destiny? I've been trying to figure out why I'm here…not here, here, but *here* on this planet? What's the purpose of my life? I sometimes feel like I've got a specific something I'm supposed to do, but I haven't got the slightest clue what it is. I've studied, I've read, looked for some flash of inspiration. I thought I'd follow in my folk's footsteps. Their jobs and lives are intriguing and interesting, but it just doesn't have that special spark that I feel when I know something is right."

"Zemma, at your age, it doesn't take a genius to know that you're not only curious but starting to get worried about your calling and what the future holds in store for you."

"That's just it; people keep asking what I want to do or be when I grow up," I shouted, exasperated. "There's so much pressure at times; I want to explode. I don't have a flipping clue about any of it!"

"I get what you mean. It's so unfair of adults to assume you have an answer, but they don't do anything to help you uncover your own heart's desire and make a decision."

I slapped myself in the head, red-faced. "I'm sorry for yelling at you. You must think I'm a real nut case. I've known you for an hour, and already I'm hollering at you."

"No worries. Perhaps, just perhaps, this summer, you can discover the answer to both the little and the big questions."

"Little *and* big? I thought there was just one question, what am I going to do, and who will I be when I grow up."

"Well, first off, do and *be* aren't always the same thing. *Do* is a job you take on. That job can change and shift over time. You might decide to play one role for a time and then feel pulled to try something else."

"That's lame. Don't most people choose one career and stick with it for their lives?"

"Usually, but that doesn't always bring happiness. A good number of people stay stuck in a rut doing the same thing year after year, long after it's lost its appeal. They feel trapped, as if they had no other options. I don't believe we are predestined to do one thing forever. Sometimes one job evolves naturally into another and then another, in sometimes strange and surprising ways. After ten, twenty, or even thirty years in one career, I know people who have gone back to school to learn a completely new profession and have been thrilled with the changes in their lives. Others discover that they can use the skills they've gathered in new ways."

"I get that, I think. But you said *being* is different than *doing*. What's that about?" I said, an edge of sarcasm sneaking into my voice. I wondered if perhaps she was just a bit of a nutcase.

"*Being* is about who you are, the inner you. What are your values and your character? What are the philosophies, passions, and rules that guide your actions? Are you a compassionate, caring woman, or are you just out for a profit or fun? Do you believe in magic, love, or a higher power, and do they guide your life and actions? What brings you joy? I'm not talking about *being happy*. Too many people think that if they can just do so and so, get rich, famous, fall in love, get married, etc.., then they'll be happy. I'm talking about finding an inner joy that goes beyond merely happy, underlying everything you do. When you feel that, you know you're on the right path."

"I feel like I just stepped into a philosophy class or something. Isn't that the kind of stuff you ponder when you're older? I mean, I'm just a kid."

"Yes, you're a kid, but perhaps not '*just*' a kid. Now is a good time to ask these questions, especially if you want to know your purpose and destiny. When you ask big questions about being, the smaller issue of doing will come into focus as a natural occurrence."

"But how can a backpacking trip through the dirt roads and the countryside possibly make any difference to the rest of my life? Isn't that what school is supposed to teach me?"

"Unfortunately, most people expect the school to provide those answers. But in most cases, school is about details and facts, not inspiration. It's about learning the rules and following them, not discovering who you are and the dream of your inner soul. It's difficult to follow all the rules and still find the freedom to explore the edges of yourself and the possibilities of the world. If you expect that information to come through your teachers or counselors, you will assuredly be continually disappointed."

"But do *you* have those answers?" Cynicism was sneaking into my voice again.

Joy shook her head. "Nope, I can't give you a single answer."

"Then why are we having this talk?" I yelled, at the end of my patience.

"I don't have the answers; no one does. They're inside you, waiting for you to discover them. I can point the way and maybe lead you to some adventures that will lead you to your answers."

"Wow, for once, an adult who isn't going to tell me what I *should* do."

"Exactly. I don't think anyone can know that for you or anyone else. Zemma, are you up for an adventure, one that may change the life you create for yourself?"

"Create for myself?! I thought there was a kind of pre-set destiny, and we all 'fill in the blanks' as we go through our lives."

"Destiny and fate are funny things, hard to explain, and even more tricky to pin down. Some think everything *is* fated, and we don't have any actual influence on our lives' events. I find that viewpoint to be depressing. If that's true, why bother?

"I subscribe to the other school of thought. My personal view is that there are various possibilities set in place for us from the beginning. We always have free will and can make new decisions and change course as we go. Each time we do this, a whole new range of potential futures opens out before us, our 'what ifs.' Life isn't one single road, going along a straight line from birth to death. Our lives are meandering pathways. Sometimes we go straight, but we often zigzag our way from one 'what if' to the next. The roads crisscross, and we go down a different path. Eventually, we get to the same place in the end. I prefer that kind of adventure. Frequently you can't see around the bend at all. We take each step one at a time, then the next step will be revealed. The next corner can be a huge surprise. Isn't that a more exciting way to live?"

"Okay, I'm sold. Let's go!" Oddly enough, I think I thought I knew what was going to happen. There was no way I could have known my answer was about to alter the course of my life and change me forever. Even today, after all these years, I still wonder. I'd like to think I would have said 'Yes' regardless.

CHAPTER 3:

The Book Opens to the World

We walked for a time in silence. Communication in ways I cannot explain filled our silence. It seemed like we were telling our lives' stories and exchanging our hopes and dreams, but without words. I may sound daft, but it was as if we could share so much because we were quiet. For the first time in my life, at least as much of it that I could remember, I did not question what was happening. I had decided to go with it and see where the road was taking us.

It was unusual for me not to be trying to pre-plan everything. I liked to look ahead so I wouldn't be surprised or at a loss about what to do or say. Of course, time and time again, I'd get it wrong and be disappointed. I took a deep breath. I was walking down an unknown road with an unknown person into an unknowable future, and yet, I was utterly at ease. I felt alive!

I don't believe my feet were touching the ground. No, I take that back. They did hit the ground but in an oddly new way. Instead of feeling the thud of each foot as it hit the road, it was like I was one with the road. My steps were smooth and even as if I was walking on air. The rubber of my scuffed-up tennis shoes and the warm asphalt of the road seemed to hug one another, to enjoy the coming together and parting of ways. I stretched out my arms, feeling as though I was embracing the wind, and it was embracing me at the same time. With joy and delight, I laughed. I danced, and I cried. I was myself and the world at once! I was Zemma!

I wanted to ask Joy why she and my mother didn't see each other and why I hadn't met her before. But I was afraid to ruin the moment by bringing up what might be bad memories. I wanted this moment to be all mine, nothing to do with my mother. Don't get me wrong, I love my mother, but sometimes I just need to be me, not who I think I'm supposed to be. I wanted to distance myself from the past, so I kept quiet and tried to ignore all the questions that kept bubbling up in my mind.

We turned off the road and crossed the lush, emerald-green meadow filled with wildflowers. I stopped to smell the orange poppies and brushed the white and yellow daisies as we passed. These were always my favorites. Their smell was sweeter than I remembered.

The meadow ended at a cliff overlooking a small valley surrounded by gentle hills rising into even higher peaks. A tiny village nestled by a sparkling ribbon of river below us, looking like a storybook picture in a children's fable. I couldn't believe we were in the same country, let alone the current century! The houses had thatched roofs, flower boxes, and their doors stood wide open, welcoming. A hand-made stone wall with a sturdy-looking wrought-iron gate bordered each yard. Somehow, I knew the walls and gates were to keep children and pets inside rather than to keep anyone out.

There were plenty of kids, dogs, cats, even a pony or two everywhere I looked. Boys and girls filled the yards and paths, dogs barking happily at their heels. Mothers were hanging wash on the line, coming out of houses with pitchers of icy lemonade, gardening, or talking to each other over the fences. Fathers were mowing lawns or fixing roofs or chatting with neighbors. Some parents joined in the children's games, playing like kids themselves. I saw one man with a bouquet walking with a carefree step towards a young woman smiling broadly. Though I knew we must have been over a mile from the village, every detail – the sounds, the colors, the expressions on the villagers' faces – was as plain as if I were standing in the middle of town.

I looked at Joy with the question in my eyes, "How can this be?"

"You'll get used to it, eventually. When you are living the world, no part of it is separate or far away from you. It's possible to be both far away, over-looking a place or situation, and within it at the same time."

"But how?"

"In the past, when something was happening, you tended to get involved in your own experience, losing perspective. Now you'll be able to see things from several points of view at once. It will probably be disconcerting at first, but over time, you'll learn a lot. You may even wonder how you ever lived life from a tiny perspective."

18

"Doesn't it get confusing?"

"Sometimes it does, especially in the beginning. You'll learn. Let's practice!"

"Okay. I think." Fear crept in, my stomach tightened, and my heart beat just a little more quickly.

"Ha! Do I hear Zelia Maria Magdalena trying to come back!"

"Ouch! Will I ever lose her?" I murmured.

"No, not entirely. With time and practice, Zelia Maria Magdalena will integrate with Zemma, and you'll no longer fear new situations."

She reached down to her dazzling assortment of scarves and objects. Her slender fingers touched the magnifying glass, and she shook her head. She likewise passed over the parasol, opera glasses, and various other items of indeterminate origin and purpose. When her hand rested on the book, she smiled and nodded. "Yes, this is just the thing."

The book was about the size of my hand, bound in black leather. The title was in gold, but the words and colors began changing moment to moment through a rainbow of iridescent hues. It was like watching a movie or the headlines racing along the bottom of the TV screen when my parents watched CNN. I breathed deeply, willing myself to be Zemma and not Zelia Maria Magdalena. Fear was an old companion, firm even in the presence of Joy. I focused my attention on the book's cover and concentrated on the titles as they flashed by. Although I paid close attention to this day, I cannot tell you exactly what I saw. As I peered even more closely, the words stopped moving and settled into "The Path." Just below the title was a picture of a gravel road curving slightly through green meadows.

I stared at the words and the picture. I tried to breathe calmly, but the world seemed to twirl around me, the wind brushing softly against my skin. I shivered and briefly closed my eyes in a vain attempt to get back in focus.

When I opened my eyes, Joy and the book were gone. The village was gone. The cliff where we had been standing was gone. I was standing on the path I'd seen on the cover of the book! I turned round and round. The trail stretched out in both directions as far as my eyes could see. I felt pulled forward and back. I was surprised to realize; I didn't want to follow the path. I wanted to make my way! I turned and started walking across the expanse of meadow. The ground was smooth and soft, the grasses and flowers gently brushing against my jeans. I kept walking across rounded hills. Briefly, I got scared as random thoughts crept into my mind: "Where am I going? Why didn't I stay on the path? What if there's nothing here but more meadow? What if I get lost?"

I concentrated on feeling my feet and the warmth of the sun on my head and shoulders as I breathed in the delicious scents rising and swirling all around me. My fears fell away. I was elated with the sheer beauty of life. It felt good just to be here.

Then I was going up a steep hill, beginning to tire. It was tempting to go back where the walking had been effortless. The grade was rapidly becoming rockier, but I kept going. I practically scrambled on my hands and knees as the way narrowed, and the rocks on either side of me made climbing increasingly tricky. I kept going – driven by a sense of purpose I did not understand. Without warning, I was standing on top of a mountain.

I caught my breath, taking in the magnificent vista. A smooth road wound its way up the more gently sloping side of the peak, opposite the arduous route I had chosen. It would have been much easier to come that way. I looked behind me; there was no path. I felt a surge of pride and achievement. I'd done it in my own time, in my way. I sat on a large, smooth boulder and looked out in all directions.

I flung out my arms and embraced every possibility, singing loudly, until I was hoarse: "I am Zemma. I am Zemma. Welcome to my life. Welcome to my life. No more strife! Welcome to my life!"

I remembered when I was little; I had often stood by a well in a park near our house and looked down into its depths, wondering what secrets hid there. Somehow, I knew those secrets now. I could feel myself spiraling down into the dark stillness of the well, letting the cool waters surround me. I surfaced, opening my arms to the sky, back on my rock at the top of the mountain.

All my life, I'd heard, 'Keep your feet planted firmly on the ground. Come back to Earth, don't be such a space-case or dreamer.' But I knew right then there was no difference; they were one, and I was one with them and all things. I expanded and kept expanding.

Then a small doubt crept in. "What if I'm just making all this up?" Whoop! I was back in my body, firmly outside the book sitting next to Joy.

All my excitement was gone. Depression settled over me like a black cloud. I covered my eyes with my hands and cried. It dawned on me that I hadn't cried in a long, long time – not a cool thing for a gal to do. Now the tears flowed, sobs racked my chest, and I felt more alone than I ever had before.

"I had it all, and it left me!" I shouted, deep red fury replacing my dismay. I was angry at the Universe for letting me down.

Joy put her hand on my shoulder. "It didn't leave you. You left it. Your doubt caused you to disconnect from the oneness. It's OK."

I looked into Joy's soft, compassionate eyes. "But I finally felt at home. Now I'm back here, stuck where no one understands me! And it's my fault!? Are you telling me that I'm the only one who held myself back?"

Joy held my eyes. "I'm not telling you anything you don't already know. You are responsible for everything that happens to you, for you, with you."

"I don't know if I want to take responsibility for my life. That's pretty huge!"

"But, Zemma, you've always had responsibility; everyone does. The only change is that you're consciously aware of it now and can make new choices. You can learn to hear the voice of doubt and ignore it."

"If it's that easy, why doesn't everyone do it?"

"Did I say it was easy?"

"No, you didn't. Are you saying then that it's hard?"

"No, not that either. It's a choice, one that you get to make in each moment, in each situation. Awareness and willingness are the keys to changing how you live and opening to the wondrous possibilities that lie before you. Are you willing?"

"Yes! Standing here on this mountaintop, I saw a purpose and a meaning to my life before I got so sad. I've always felt I had something important to do, but I couldn't figure out what it was. I just felt right and wonderful. I knew at that moment that it was the reality I truly desired."

"What did you see?"

I looked down, feeling exposed and childish. I knew this was one of those moments I had to decide if I was willing to take the chance and move forward or allow my fear to take over and hold me back.

I took a deep breath and looked Joy straight in the eyes. "I saw myself journeying with you, not just for a week, but all summer. Sometimes we traveled, just the two of us. Other times, there were others. We seemed to have no set path, and yet I felt we were always arriving at just the right place at the perfect moment in time."

"Yes, Zemma. I've seen that too. What do you feel when you see it?"

I felt peace flood through me and remembered those scenes in my mind's eye once again. My entire body tingled, and I grinned. I tried to stop, but I couldn't. Laughing, I said, "Well, I guess from the feeling in my body and this crazy grin, I feel pretty happy about it."

"I see you're used to understatement. Looking at you, I'd say you're ecstatic!"

"Yes! Yes! The world seems completely amazing. I feel so good! And to think I thought you were going to be boring and just babysit me for the summer! Well, you're not anyone's maiden aunt, and I don't think boredom is going to be a problem."

"Welcome to our journey, Zemma." Joy took my hands, and we were back on the mountain, whirling until we were dizzy. Then we followed the easy path down the other side, through pine-scented shrubs dotted with delicate rose-colored flowers. We reached a small pond filled by a gurgling waterfall and stood for a moment, reveling. After drinking from the waterfall and cooling our faces and hands with the clear water, it was time to go on.

"Which way do we go?" I asked.

"Why don't you choose this time?" Joy replied.

"What if I choose wrong?"

"You can't. There is no wrong way, simply different experiences. Close your eyes and feel the pull."

"The pull of what?"

"Life, the path, experience, destiny. It's all one. Just choose."

I closed my eyes, self-conscious at first. I took a deep breath. I felt the unmistakable urge to move to my left; I did so and took one step, then another. I started running.

"Zemma, where are we going?"

I stopped and turned back to her. "I don't know. I just know that this is the way."

"Perfect. Lead on!"

She caught up to me, and we ran, then trotted and finally slowed to a walk. We kept on, up, down, over hills, through streams, climbing over fences, always pushing on in the same direction. At first, I wondered where we were going. After a while, the steady pace and the rhythm of our steps took over. I quit thinking about the future. I began to see, really see, where I was. Everything was beautiful in ways I never noticed. Even barbed wire was fascinating, wrapped artfully around a fence post. I'd get swept away by the scent of a flower as we passed, wanting to take it all in.

There seemed no need for words. The world felt whole and complete with every stick, leaf, and rock arranged perfectly for our pleasure.

Perhaps I should have known that as soon I became that sure of myself, something would burst through my complacency. I didn't have an inkling that things were about to change. Funny, it's always been like that. When I worried, I was continually on the alert for the next catastrophe. But when I was happy, I was convinced the world would always remain calm. So, breezily, I walked on, seeing everything around us as a splendid extension of my perfect self, right into the craziest place I'd ever been.

CHAPTER 4:

The Juggler & the Dead-Eyed Unmaker

We walked companionably at a leisurely pace. It seemed the valley was alive, wildflowers, birds, rabbits, even a few deer peeking out from behind trees. Everywhere I looked, there was more to see. The green landscape, clouds shading the bright blue sky, the warm sun, and the light breeze felt magical.

We topped a hill and were surprised to see a flash of many-colored tents, a great fair with people milling about, music, voices, and smells of fried food rising towards us, inviting us to join. We looked at each other, nodded, and without a word, picked up our pace.

It was a market fair. The tents abounded with goods of all kinds, fresh fruit and vegetables, clothes, bags, toys, and other handcrafts. There was a cacophony of sounds, colors, and activities that made me feel quite merry.

I was so busy looking at all the goods on display as we strolled that I hardly paid attention to where I was walking. A juggler who was tossing balls in a circle overhead as he went nearly ran me over. Balls flew everywhere, and I landed flat on my rear in the dirt. I looked up warily, expecting to see anger on his face, but instead was met with a gleeful smile.

The juggler was around sixteen and taller than me by about 8 inches – making him about 6'0 and with that crazy jester's hat closer to 6'3". He had dark hair, a little on the long side and a bit mussed, laughing hazel eyes, and a bright smile. He didn't seem to be a jock type despite his athletic build. He wasn't handsome exactly, but good-looking in a boy next door kind of way.

He grasped my hand and pulled me to my feet, laughing.

"You've got to pay attention to your surroundings, my girl. There's a lot of activity today, and not everyone understands and forgives as I do. I wouldn't want you to run afoul of *him*."

"Him? That sounds ominous. Who is he, and why should I avoid him?"

"I don't know his name, I've kept as far away as possible, but I see what he leaves behind and wouldn't want you to suffer."

"Suffer how?" I asked. Joy was standing just off to the side, watching us but not saying anything.

"It's hard to explain. I didn't understand or trust what I saw at first, but after watching it happen several times, I had to admit that something dark was happening."

"This sounds grim."

"I believe it's much more than that, possibly even a threat to all of humanity if it spreads. I don't know if the man even has a name. He came about a week ago and started gathering people around to hear him speak. He seems to be a preacher, telling people that he is a prophet, sent to share news of a great future. But there's something dark and hidden within his words. I cannot figure out what's wrong with his message, it seems to be okay, something to be welcomed, but something unsettling happens to those who listen for any length of time."

"What happens?" I said as foreboding traveled down my spine in icy waves.

"His energy makes something happen to people. They become slow, kind of depressed, almost sleepy, almost like they're too bored to care. Even animals seem to lose some spark. People who come in contact with him seem to have no willpower or desire to connect; they give up their life's passions and dreams to this deadening energy," said my friend with intensity. "Be careful. I'm sure this is a vile threat. He is the antithesis of who and what we are."

"He steals their passions and dreams?" I said, not sure if I was starting to feel scared.

"Yes, and he's incredibly good at it. Most of the time, his victims never realize anything has happened. They simply no longer feel the drive to do anything much. They are happy to live day to day in what I'd call a gray existence. I know it's only been a week, but the change that has come over them is profound. People's eyes change from bright and curious to dull and dead! I cannot bear to look into them. In the past, I've seen those I'd call evil, and there's a glint in their eyes that warns of malicious intent. That's something I can protect against and fight. But this is much different. It's insidious. I cannot find a way to confront it. It's as if those under his spell are sure in their minds that what they remember of the old way was wrong and silly, and they're better off now. They think they are at peace," said my juggler friend.

I wanted to ask his name but didn't want to break into his story. I glanced at Joy, and her usual smile was gone, her face grim and focused. She nodded at him to go on.

"I'm trying to get my head around all this," the juggler continued. "I think he gets people to believe that sameness, constant compatibility, and harmony might be progress. It sounds a lot like the heaven we're taught by the priests. But there is something in me that recoils from the very thought of this. Wouldn't we lose our wonder, our magic? Those are the things that keep us going, pulling us through the hard times, pushing us, and even nourishing us. It's a terrible sight to see people in whom the fire is dead."

I looked imploringly at Joy and back to the juggler. "Is this a threat? Is there a way to prevent it from spreading?"

Joy stepped forward and finally spoke. I was relieved, sure that she'd have an answer.

"I am Joy, and this is my young niece Zemma. We will do what we can to help. May I know your name?" She reached out her hand.

He grasped her hand tightly. "Joy, I am Justin. I've never thought of myself as a hero or one who would battle evil. I want nothing more than to entertain and make people smile. But I cannot deny what I've seen and feel compelled to do something, but I have no idea what that could be. It's hard to fight what I can't explain. It's as if he brings a grayness that blankets people's energy. He seems to gain strength with each encounter. I wonder, would it be easier to fight if we knew his name?"

Joy responded thoughtfully. "That may help. It would give our thoughts a clearer focus. What you describe makes it seem he is an *Unmaker*."

Justin exclaimed, "That's a perfect name. The Unmaker. It *is* as if he is unmaking their dreams and desires. He's the opposite of Creation as if somehow he is unraveling everything that matters."

"Justin, I think you've gotten that exactly right," said Joy sadly. "The only thing I can think of that might help for now is to hold firmly in your mind the person you know someone to be, or who they were before the deadening."

"How will that help?" Justin and I asked at the same time.

"I've seen this a time or two. In the past, it's happened more gradually. This time it sounds and feels different and much more insidious. As I see it, what's happening is a disconnection from Source, the truth of who they are. But if someone can hold an image of them in their wholeness, then perhaps seeing that reflected back will allow them to remember and choose again to return. The followers who chose to become their old selves return because it's like they have been gone."

Joy continued thoughtfully, "The drawback is that you would have to know them already. So, it's a long way from a perfect solution. But it's at least a start while Zemma and I see what else we can discover. I'm sure there are other ways, and we'll keep looking while we travel."

"Are you coming back in this direction?" Justin asked.

Joy looked at me, and I nodded. She turned back to Justin, "Yes, when we have more answers, we'll come back and share them with you, or if that's not possible, we'll get a message to you."

"Thank you. I'm so glad we met. I don't feel so alone now. I've tried to explain to others, and they're not listening to me at all."

"I know how frustrating that can be. This Unmaker, dead-eye concept can seem pretty unbelievable. I can't blame people for not taking you seriously since it's so far beyond their previous experiences or comprehension. Let's hope it stays that way. Justin, as much as we'd love to stay and talk, we're going to go on our way. We need to search out a solution."

We hugged all round, and Joy and I turned towards the tents and all the wares displayed. I had a sense of something urging me towards a particular stall halfway down the aisle. I started in that direction, only slightly surprised that Joy seemed to have the same idea. We looked at each other and grinned.

Gemstones of all colors and shapes filled the stall. There was one table of beautifully handcrafted gemstone jewelry. It was clear this was the source of the pull we'd felt.

I've never been one to believe too much in the power of stones. However, I have had some memorable experiences in ancient temples and dig sights with my parents. My most memorable experience was the E Tū Ake Maori stone, named Hine Kaitaka by the Maori in New Zealand. It was a "touchstone" meant to connect the life force in all things, living and inanimate, a sizable green stone. Each person entering touched the stone.

I casually touched it and felt a pulse of energy move from my head through my feet and into the earth. Before I could gather my wits, I looked up into the eyes of an old Maori woman who had the oddest expression. I could swear I heard her say, "Welcome; we've been waiting for you." But her lips never moved.

I asked my parents and other members of our group if they'd felt anything. No one had. I dismissed it as my imagination. Fascinated by the display, I wondered if I may have been too quick to reject my experience. I felt a palpable vibration from the booth in general, but several heart-shaped stones seemed to keep pulling me to them.

"Is it okay to touch?" I asked the older woman tending the stall. She smiled and nodded. I swear my hand had a mind of its own and instantly reached out to touch a small clear pendant. I assumed it must be quartz crystal. It wasn't entirely clear. When I looked closely, I could see slight imperfections, tiny bubbles that looked like they wanted to break through the surface. It wasn't as intense as the touchstone, but I felt warmth in my whole body. My heart seemed to grow within my chest. It grew more intense, yet I didn't want it to stop.

I picked up the heart and held it in my hand. It fit perfectly in the center of my palm. I couldn't stop smiling. I wanted to keep it with me. I was surprised to see the price was low, well within my budget. I pulled the money out of my pocket and handed it to the shopkeeper. When she started to wrap it, I stopped her. I would just wear it on the leather cord that came with it. I put it on and continued looking at and touching various stones – amethyst, jade, carnelian, amber, Lapis Lazuli, turquoise, chrysocolla, and many others I couldn't name at the time.

I was so thrilled to touch and connect with all these beautiful stones; I didn't give Joy a thought. She gestured to me that it was time to go. I didn't notice the bag she was securing in one of her inner pockets until she spoke.

"We need to find Justin. I have something to give him," she said and started back the way we'd come.

We found him quickly. Joy didn't waste time with explanations. She opened her palm and showed Justin a pendant just like mine except that it was purple. Joy confirmed later that it was amethyst.

"Justin, I want you to wear this always. It will protect you and provide you with wisdom and protection when you need it. I will share others with the people who want to join the fight. I have energetically connected all the stones to help us stay in close communication. Each stone is different, with specific qualities to the wearer. They'll act as personal touchstones and as a symbol of our alliance."

I could tell by the skeptical look on Justin's face that he wasn't sure about this idea. But he reached out his hand and took the amethyst heart Joy was offering. His face lit up in wonder the moment he touched it. It seemed he was experiencing something as I had.

He put it on and smiled, seemingly lost for words.

Joy touched the brilliant amethyst that hung over his heart. I swear it glowed for just a second. Without a word, we shared a group hug. This hug seemed different than the one only a short time ago. Is it possible that something had changed?

CHAPTER 5:

Tent Skirts & Endless Protein Bars

Joy and I quietly walked away from the village. Questions were rushing through my head, but I was overwhelmed by what we'd heard and worried that we had no idea of the Unmaker's influence. We didn't know if there was just one or many. Would the pendants help? How many did she buy? What did each do? How would we know who to give them to? Is gemstone energy real? We must have walked for hours in silence, but my mind was anything but quiet.

I was relieved when Joy started talking. "Zemma, I believe our one-week trip has just expanded into something a lot bigger and more far-reaching, but I'm unable to make any decisions at the moment. I'm sure you must be as tired as I am. Let's stop here for the night." She settled back against a tree and closed her eyes.

I looked around wildly. There were only meadows and forests around us, no motels in sight. I was incredulous. We could have easily stayed in town and found a comfortable place for the night. We hadn't brought a tent. We were in the middle of nowhere out in the open, and she wants to spend the night here?

"And just where are we supposed to sleep? It gets cold and damp at night. We'll freeze if we sleep without a roof over our heads."

"Do you think I'm completely unprepared? You have a backpack, do you not?"

"Yes, but all I have is some clothes and a flimsy sleeping bag. I wasn't planning on wilderness camping. Couldn't we have stopped at a motel or inn or at least something with a roof? It's not warm enough for the open meadows yet."

"Don't worry about those little details."

"Little details! You call proper survival equipment little details?" I said more sharply than I'd intended.

"Didn't you liken my skirt to a circus tent when you first saw me?"

Embarrassed, I looked at the ground. "Hey, how did you know I thought that? I'm sure I didn't say it out loud! I'm sorry…"

"I think I said this before. I know many things. It's kind of hard to see this outfit and not make that comparison, silly. You were right; it *is* a tent, although not usually a circus tent!" She undid the ribbon encompassing her waist and pulled her skirt off. I closed my eyes, afraid to look. I wasn't ready to see her in her underwear. I slowly opened just one eye and was relieved that she was wearing another skirt underneath it. It was gold and shone gently in the softening evening light. Joy held her tent skirt up and flicked it as one does with a towel that's just come out of the dryer. Before I could blink, we were standing inside a small bright tent. It was remarkably cozy, and its stripes glowed in the waning light.

Whoever heard of a skirt that becomes a tent without even poles or stakes? I set my backpack down. "Joy. I hadn't planned on camping. I don't think my lightweight sleeping bag is going to be warm enough."

"Silly girl," she laughed. "I'm sure you'll learn to trust that I've got it together better than that." She pulled one of her scarves off her waist and snapped it like she had the skirt. It grew wide and puffed up to be a comfortable-looking mattress as it settled to the ground. She did the same with another scarf, and it became a thick, fluffy blanket.

"Wow, those were great little tricks. Where did you get your scarves; in the witches' magical camp-out store?"

"Of course not! I'm not a witch."

"Then what are you? Normal women don't go around turning scarves into mattresses and blankets."

"I am just a woman who has discovered the true nature of being and that things are not always what they seem. There's nothing magical about it."

Tired and confused, I turned away. My stomach growled loudly. I was shocked to realize I hadn't thought about food all day and didn't remember the last time I'd eaten. I pulled a protein energy bar out of the depths of my backpack. I unwrapped it quickly and prepared to take a frantic, hungry bite. Then I remembered my manners, tore it in half, and offered half to Joy. She smiled and thanked me. I admit I was disappointed that she accepted. I'd hoped she'd refuse my offering and conjure up some magical feast. But, instead, she started eating *my* energy bar! *My* energy bar!

Angrily, I began eating. I wanted to eat slowly and savor each bite, but I was too hungry. I took huge bites chewing quickly. With the hungry bites I was taking, that bar should have disappeared in three bites. But, somehow, I kept eating. It began to dawn on me that I had already eaten enough to make up not only a whole bar but two, at least! I looked down – I was still holding half a bar!

Joy slapped her knees and laughed out loud.

I glowered at her. Sheepishly, I began to see how childish and unimaginative I'd allowed myself to be. I began to chuckle; then laughter bubbled up from deep inside until there was simply no room for anger or doubt.

The best I could do was a sort of mock bow. I apologized. "Forgive me, my lady, for doubting you. I regret my childish anger. Thank you for providing for my nourishment even though I was an ungrateful brat."

"Nicely said. You were acting the brat! At least you admit it! It's so easy to get caught up in anger. It's even harder to admit to the possibility that you were idiotic. A sincere apology goes a long way toward making up for misbehavior. Thank you. Let's talk no more tonight. I believe it's time for some sleep."

Joy pulled two more scarves off and turned them into a mattress and blanket for herself. In a blink, she was inside her little bed and appeared to be asleep at once.

I crawled into my sleeping bag. Despite the comfort and warmth, I was unable to relax. My mind kept replaying the events of the day. Had it only been just one day? It seemed at least a year had passed. I wondered if time worked differently in Joy's world than in the real world where I used to live. I tried breathing deeply, following my breath as she'd shown me, and still, sleep eluded me.

I heard a light, tinkling laugh. Opening my eyes, I saw something glittery float gently over my blanket. Finally, I slept.

CHAPTER 6

Talking Trees, Fairies & Possibilities of Monsters

The next morning, the darkness and my anxiety had lifted. We skirted a cedar forest. The trees were tall and magnificent, so different than evergreens in the "real" world. I reached out and caressed a few near the path. Their soft fernlike needles wafted a warm green fragrance over me.

I wanted to enter the forest but shrugged that feeling off as being silly. After all, walking in the woods could be dark and treacherous. Surely we should stay on open ground. So, we only walked close to the trees over loamy, dark rich earth covered with needles and tiny cones. The surrounding scents were spicy and intoxicating.

Then, Whoomph! I landed flat on my face in the dirt. My backpack flipped up over my head, adding to the indignity. I looked back to see Joy slapping her knees in a most unladylike fashion. I wasn't sure why or how I'd landed on the ground. I jumped to my feet, looking around. Despite my close inspection, I still couldn't see anything that might have tripped me. Puzzled, I looked where I'd fallen, kicking the dirt. Nothing. Had Joy tripped me?

I brushed myself off and resumed walking. In less than three strides, I found myself lying face down in the grass again.

I jumped up in classic fighter stance, balled fists, feet planted apart for stability. "Okay, who did that? Come on out and fight me like a man!"

Joy was standing off a bit, serious now but struggling to keep from laughing. I was thrilled to give her such merriment. Not!

"Okay, Joy, did you trip me?"

"Gee, Zemma, I don't know. Look around, why don't you."

I could tell from the twinkle in her eye that she did know but thought it would be fun not to say. I scuffled along, angry that she wouldn't just tell me.

"Ouch!"

"Who said that? I don't see anyone."

"It was I." The voice came from the grove of trees to my left.

"Who's there?" Fear crept in, replacing the anger in my belly; I couldn't see anyone at all.

"Me, you silly goose. Don't stand with that absurd look on your face. Don't tell me you haven't seen a talking tree before!"

I looked closely at the tree and saw through the shadows. The whorls and scales on its trunk seemed to form a face, complete with eyes and mouth. One small branch reminded me of a nose. I shook my head. "The last time I looked, trees don't talk."

"Really? How do you know? Did you ever try?"

I was sure I'd seen the tree's mouth moving. "Well, no. I've never talked to a tree, and I don't know anyone else who has." Had I stepped inside one of the old cartoons I loved watching?

"Oh, you're one of those," said the tree, in what I'd swear was a disappointed voice.

"One of what?" I let my anger show.

"Oh, you know, one of those people who are sure that just because no one else does something, it's not worth doing. I'll bet you do everything your friends do. You're just one of the crowd, a mindless fool. The problem with that is that you only see the same things everyone else does, and you miss out on most of the magic around you. It takes a brave soul to risk seeing what nobody else sees."

"Why would that take bravery?"

"Well, what if you see things and nobody else does, and they make fun of you?"

"Then it would be their loss."

"Hmmm. So, you're telling me you'd think the ones who see what everyone else sees are right?"

"Yes, of course."

"Not so fast, my little twig. How about the time when you were four and saw a fairy in the flowers?"

"I didn't really see a fairy. I was just making up stories."

"Do you believe that? Don't you remember how excited you were when you first saw her in that pansy?"

Cautiously, "Yeah, I remember. I told the other kids, and they laughed at me, saying it was just a trick of the sun and shadows, and my crazy imagination filled in all the rest. Everyone knows there are no fairies."

"Really. Don't you ever wonder what the world would be like if there were fairies for real?"

"Well, yeah, sometimes. But I sure wouldn't let anyone else know I have lunatic thoughts like that. I mean, it's not normal."

"Ah, normal. Look around you at everyone who is considered normal. Normal thinks the same, dresses similarly, eats the same type of foods and acts consistently, and dies the same. It seems pretty boring to me."

"No, it's not like that!"

"If it's so wonderful, why aren't you there now, with everybody else?"

"Well, I met Joy and decided it was time for an adventure."

"Did you not set out for an adventure and then meet Joy?"

"Well, yes, actually, I did start on a quest to find my purpose in life. Then, Joy and I started on this journey."

"Well, girl, if you're on an adventure, as you are, then open your eyes and ears. The world is much more than you have thought. That fairy was genuine, and Gena, that's her name, was extremely disappointed and hurt when you turned away and refused to see her."

"Refused to see her? After everyone laughed at me, I looked back, and there was just a shadow, no fairy. That's when I knew they were right. I'd made it all up."

"Au contraire. You simply closed down so that you would no longer be bothered with seeing the unexpected or unexplainable."

I sat down right where I was. Hearing this sucked the air right out of me! Had I, indeed, seen a fairy? Had I honestly let bullies trick me into not only believing that I hadn't seen her but into never, ever seeing fairies again?

I swear that tree looked at me with a compassionate and friendly expression. "My little friend, don't worry. You made a choice based on the evidence you had. Very few children or adults, for that matter, have the self-assurance to believe their senses when everyone else says they're wrong. You may now make a new choice. But I warn you. If you ask to see fairies, you'll also be able to see all the other beings in the "unseen" world."

"Okay, that sounds wonderful!" I practically squealed with excitement. "I can't wait to see things that I've always thought were, well, fairy tales."

"Yes. But remember those stories. Some of them have monsters."

"Ha. Everyone knows monsters aren't real."

"Is this the same 'everyone' who knows that fairies aren't real?"

"Well, yeah." I paused. "Does this mean…" I couldn't finish the sentence; my mind was spinning with pictures of both the good and the horrible that could then be part of my until-then-unseen reality.

I tell you, that tree reached out a branch and touched my shoulder, chuckling in a friendly way. "Yes. Many of the fables, myths, and fairy tales have truth at their core. However, you'll be both relieved and disappointed to know that some of them are simply imaginations gone wild and nightmares passed down as true stories. Others are a combination of truth, lies, and make-believe. The problem is if you decide you want to 'see,' you don't get to decide only to see happy, magical creatures like me or fairies. You'll also see the actual, scary monsters."

"Okay. I accept. I would rather go through life seeing the truth, both good and bad. I don't want to block my eyes any longer. Besides, I've been learning quite a bit about gaining perspective." I glanced at Joy and grinned at the tree. "Somehow, I know that's going to help me if I do run into your scary monsters."

"Hey, they aren't MY scary monsters. They're just monsters. And you may be right about that perspective thing. But what if you're not?"

"Well, here I am, inside some kind of storybook, talking to a tree. My life is already starting to get bizarre. I'm beginning to enjoy the outlandish adventure of it all. Bring on the fairies and the monsters!"

The tree waved all its branches at me in a menacing manner. Even though we'd been having a pleasant conversation, I came close to fleeing. I could imagine myself running and running and never stopping. I didn't like that picture at all. I decided to stand and face whatever fate had in store. "All right, do your worst...or is that your best?... Oh, just do it!"

The tree waved and shook. Two branches reached out and touched me on both sides of my face. It held me still for a minute, as if blessing me, then passed its soft needles across my eyes. "Awaken from your dream and see."

I snapped to attention. "I don't feel any different...." The words stuck in my throat as I looked around. There were dozens of tiny fairies flitting around me, frolicking in the beams of sunshine at the edge of the forest. They were all colors and sizes, and each exquisitely delicate. Their colors would have made any rainbow blush. I swear there were colors I'd never experienced anywhere, even in a box of 144 crayons! The pictures I'd seen didn't begin to show how beautiful they were. Each tiny fairy had a perfectly formed, little, human body with wings so delicate it was hard to believe they could fly.

They played all around me, landing on my nose, my ears, and my shoulders, taking off quickly before I could touch them with even a fingertip. It was hard to imagine I'd ever allowed myself to believe these gorgeous creatures didn't exist and hadn't been open to the magnificent beauty of the world.

I walked over to the tree, put my arms as far around it as possible, and rested my head against its scaly trunk. "Thank you. How can I ever show my gratitude?"

A fierce, grumbling voice answered back, "You can quit kicking my roots and never, ever carve your initials in a tree again!"

"How do you know about that? That was years ago -- when I had a crush on Joe. We both carved our initials in a heart."

"Yes, Zemma, we remember. Second grade. You are discovering that the world is a much different place than you'd realized. Each tree feels the pain, sorrow, and joy of every other tree. What you've done to one, you've done to all."

"I'm so deeply sorry. I didn't know!" I cried, meaning every word, wishing I could take back the carving I'd done and wincing as I felt in my toes all the trees I'd kicked in anger over something that happened in my life.

"Don't worry, Zemma. We forgive you. You didn't know any better. But now that you do know, you won't get off so lightly in the future. As you continue your grand adventure, remember to be kind to all living things."

"I promise." I wanted to bow down and do penance to make up for all my years of thoughtlessness. I started to drop to my knees.

"Don't do that! It's not necessary. When I told you we forgave you, I spoke the truth. The past is just that, the past. From now on, the best thing you can do is live a life conscious of others' feelings. And share your experiences so more people will begin to see the world around them in a new light."

"I will. I will!" I touched my head to the tree's trunk and thanked it once again. I felt the pull of the path, drawing me on my way.

Suddenly, I realized I hadn't seen Joy for a while. I looked around wildly, afraid I'd lost her. I didn't see her in front of or behind me. I was beginning to panic when I heard a tinkling laugh from above. Joy was high up above me, swinging from one of the branches of the tree. A dozen or more fairies roosted on her head and shoulders. Like magic, the tree branch lowered her back to the ground. She turned and bowed ceremoniously to the tree. She kissed her finger, touching each fairy on the forehead. The fairies flew off, blowing kisses back to us.

"Well, Zemma, are you ready to brave a world that really does have fairies AND scary monsters?"

"Yes. I just refused to see it. It won't be that different, will it?"

"I wouldn't count on it." With a mysterious smile, Joy skipped ahead.

I felt smugly satisfied with myself and with life in general. It was comforting to know that fairies were real. I wasn't so sure about how I felt about a world where scary monsters were also real.

I hoisted my backpack up to its usual position and followed behind Joy at a sedate pace.

CHAPTER 7:

Hair, Stars & Magic Wand Gardens

I was exhausted, and it was only noon. I couldn't seem to put one foot in front of the other. I stumbled about, probably looking like a drunken sailor. With each step, I swayed and stumbled. I felt like I was about to fall over at any moment, trying to be aware of everything around me. I might kick a tree root! Being aware was going to be hard work. I wouldn't be able to muddle through life blind to the damage I might cause.

Joy turned and caught the thoughtful frown on my face. "What's the matter, kiddo? You look like a girl who just figured out that with new abilities come new responsibilities."

"Uh, yeah. How do I manage to pay attention to trees and fairies and watch out for monsters and keep my balance all at the same time?"

"It's like everything in life. At first, it feels strange, and you struggle through it. Eventually, it's second nature, and you don't even think about it. Remember how it felt when you first started to ride a bike. In the beginning, you had to remind yourself of the rules and consciously maintain your balance. Eventually, muscle memory takes over, and you don't have to think about it at all; it's automatic. I'll bet soon you'll be walking easily over tree roots and watching for fairies in flowers, naturally and without needing to overthink it." Perhaps taking just a bit of pity on me, she winked. "Why don't we sit and take a load off? We could rest and get a cool drink at that spring over there."

I fell into step slightly behind Joy, and we walked companionably toward the bubbling spring.

"Zemma, now that you can see what's here, fairies and monsters included, we need to talk." Joy said.

"Okay. Why do I have a feeling I'm not going to like this?"

"You may not, but I'm sure you've been thinking about what Justin told us as much as I have. I still don't know what we need to do, but I'm convinced it was no accident that we met Justin. We need to come up with a plan."

"How do we do that? I don't have even the glimmer of an idea about what's needed to combat something that leaves deadened eyes and hearts in its wake."

"I think what we need is a new perspective. If we can look at things from a higher vantage point, that might help. I admit to feeling as clueless as you right now."

As Joy talked, she filled her canteen with clear, cold water and motioned for me to do the same. She sat down again, taking a thoughtful sip of her water, absently twirling her hair as she did so. Well, it seemed like an unconscious gesture then, but in retrospect, I'm not so sure.

My eyes were drawn irresistibly to her hair. I must confess that I hadn't taken a good look at her hair initially because her dress and collection of extraordinary objects enthralled me. I got closer and saw that the curls tumbling down over her shoulders were a wild mixture of every possible color; blond, brown, red, brunette, copper, white, black, silver, and many colors. I was at a loss to name. No single color stood out from the rest. Even more peculiar than the unique color mixture was that every strand appeared to shimmer and twinkle as if covered with tiny diamonds.

"Your hair … it's sparkling!" I blurted out before I could catch myself.

"Oh, thank you. I quite like the effect."

"Are those diamonds in your hair, as in gemstones?" I asked, a bit surer of myself now that I knew she wasn't offended by my query.

"Diamonds? Good heavens, no. Those are stars."

"Oh, you mean like the glitter stars you sprinkle on?" I queried.

"No, my dear. I mean, stars, real, honest-to-goodness twinkling stars."

"Joy, I may be gullible, but I know better than that."

"Yes, Zemma, but you also 'knew' fairies didn't exist, didn't you?"

"Well, yes, but that's different. It's impossible to have stars in your hair."

"Really? Why are stars in my hair more impossible than fairies or books that let you enter the stories or talking trees? Don't you think that perhaps you aren't the best judge of what's possible and what's not?"

"Okay, you got me there," I conceded, not altogether convinced. "But real stars would be huge."

"But they are huge! It's another one of those perspective things. I can't explain without going into quantum physics, so I won't begin to try; we'd just get all caught up in the science and miss the good stuff. Come closer, look at this little bunch here." She pointed to a curl that had come loose from her combs and was dangling over her right ear.

Cautiously I moved closer. The sun shone brightly on her curl as she turned her head to give me a better view. The light coming from her hair was almost blinding. In particular, one star seemed to glow in the sun, its color changing from blue to green to purple and back again. Curiosity overcame caution. As the delightful scent of her light perfume rose into my nostrils, I moved closer until my eyes were almost right up against her curl.

With a spiraling whirl, I completely lost my footing and went swooshing through the blackness, past twinkling stars, moons, and suns. I didn't seem to be having any difficulty breathing. How could I be breathing? I thought there was no air in space! I was having a real struggle getting used to accepting the seemingly impossible.

Relaxing into it, I felt lighter than ever and leaned back to enjoy the show as stars sped past at ever-increasing speeds. I put my feet out in front of me, pushing as if to stop myself by braking in the air. My arms flailed as I spun. My actions did not affect the situation except to throw me off balance and start me spinning even more wildly through space.

"Aurrrrrgh. Help, Mr. Wizard [(Appendix A)], take me home! I mean, Joy, help! What's happening to me? Where am I going?" Panic and a slight feeling of motion sickness started to rise in my stomach. Again, I wondered if too many cartoons in my younger days had addled my brain and caused me to imagine something. Is it possible cartoons sometimes told the truth?

"Relax, relax." I looked over, and there was Joy, floating calmly alongside me as if this were an everyday occurrence for her. Who knows, maybe it was. I took a couple of deep breaths, slowing and gaining more control over my spinning. Dizzily, I began to laugh. I'm sure I sounded more crazed than amused. I couldn't help myself. I knew I was becoming more than a bit hysterical. I tried, honestly tried, to stop. I kept on laughing. Wheezing, crying, guffawing with hilarity, I came to a thudding halt as I hit the ground. Stardust puffed up around me.

You ask how I knew it was stardust. Well, the first reasoning was that I was on a star. I could tell that because when I looked back, I could see the Earth, moon, sun, and thousands of other stars or planets around me. It must be stardust because it twinkled and glowed, just like stardust does on every cheesy movie or cartoon I've ever seen. Even in fantasy video games, some fairy godmother comes along and sprinkles stardust on someone or something and causes magical things to happen.

"Oh, my goodness, we're on a star!" I know I squealed like a very little girl, but I was feeling positively giddy by that time. I'd always thought, or been taught, that stars were hot, glowing astral bodies. What kind of stuff are they teaching in schools these days, anyway? It wasn't hot, or cold, or anything other than incredible.

"Yep, that pretty much sums it up! So, what do you want to do first? Wish on a star? That is since you are sitting on a star. How about carrying moon-beams home in a jar? If so, we can take care of that on the return trip. I'll bet you've wondered what a star is made of and recited that silly little twinkle, twinkle poem and meant it. Well, here's your chance to find out."

"Forgive me if I don't answer right away. I'm in shock, I think. In the world I come from, one doesn't look at someone's hair and go flying through space and land on a star. Things like that just don't happen! I know, I know. They *do* happen. I just always thought they were dreams."

"Oh, so you do remember?"

Cautiously, "Remember? Remember what?"

"Why, having been here before."

"Oh, sure! I'm sure every little girl makes trips to the stars and then forgets to remember them."

"Well, yes, that's pretty much true. Think back to some of your more memorable childhood dreams. Do you remember a woman in them? She may have appeared as a fairy godmother, witch, or just a kindly lady along the way."

I thought for a few minutes with my eyes closed to concentrate. My eyes flew open in shock, "Joy, you were in my dreams! Is that why you seemed familiar when I first saw you?"

"Yes, you and I had many nighttime adventures."

"How could I have forgotten something like that!?"

"It's normal. Most of us don't expect to see the characters from our dreams in real life. Even those who do remember their dreams quickly learn not to talk about them. They certainly never talk about their magical trips or who was there because nobody believes them anyway. There isn't much outside verification that such experiences are valid because no one, but no one, admits to having had them. Well, at least they only mention it once or twice, get laughed at, and then forever after keeping their experience to themselves. After a day or two, your night-time dream trip recedes into memory, and you've convinced yourself it was just a marvelous dream. Sound familiar?"

"Uh, yes. So how many other 'dreams' weren't?"

"Gee, Zemma, I can't tell you that. But you'll be getting those answers on your own eventually."

"I'll try. Somehow the way you say that makes me nervous."

Laughing merrily as only Joy could, she twirled her hair. I got dizzy as I watched. I couldn't look away from her hair and the whirligig of stars, oh my, the stars! I was off again, spiraling through galaxies.

I landed with a plop and a pouf of stardust. I looked around, expecting to see the Earth and the moon. They weren't there! It was one thing to be in outer space sitting on a star, but it was a whole different matter to be in outer space sitting on a star in some distant galaxy or wherever I was, but far, far from home!

"Joy, what happened to Earth!" I shrieked.

"It's right there," she said, pointing at a barely visible blue and green planet.

"We're a lot farther away than I thought. Why are we here? I know you said getting a new perspective, but wow!"

"Zemma, you can be such a delight. We've come this far so we can take a look at what's going on for the whole galaxy, not just Earth. We're on the edge of the Milky Way right now. We can't see everything, but we can see a lot."

"We sure can!"

"For the last few hours, I've been 'hearing' from my intuition that the Unmaker may be putting the entire fabric of the Universe at risk. Everything is connected, and if enough people and animals lose their connection to their Source, there will be actual holes in the fabric of the all-that-is. If there are enough holes of substantial size, it may cause things to begin to unravel. Justin, unfortunately, was correct when he suspected that."

Looking at Zemma seriously, Joy talked haltingly as if thoughts were forming as she spoke. "Zemma, you can see fairies, scary monsters, and other usually unseen parts of Creation. I'm hoping that together we can see the overall patterns in the fabric of the Universe."

"How can we do that? I wouldn't even know what I'm looking for."

"If we both ask to see the truth, I believe we'll be able to see tears in the patterns or just dark spots. That could give us a clearer idea of how serious this menace is. With your ability to see, even though this is something new for you, between us, we'll have a clear enough picture to give us some insight."

"Hey, I'm game to try. What do I need to do?"

"Close your eyes and ask to be shown the true fabric of the Universe. I'll be doing the same."

I closed my eyes and took several deep breaths, allowing my mind to soften its focus to encompass all of Earth and everything between Earth and where we sat. I sat for quite a while and was about to give up when I started noticing that there were indeed dark spots, some were small, but some of the larger ones appeared to be growing. In my mind's eye, it was as if a very dark cloud was blocking out the light, and it was spreading slowly but steadily.

Suddenly there was a flash at the edge of one of the smaller dark areas, and the dark receded before it, and all around it lightened up. Zemma's eyes flew open at the same time as Joy's.

"What was that, Joy?"

"That was something I did. I had an idea, and it worked to some extent. Not as much as I hoped, but it's a good sign. I know it's something we can push back. We may not be able to erase it entirely, but I am positive we can shrink it back down to a point where it's not an imminent danger."

"What exactly did you do?"

"I felt into the area of darkness, and what I sensed was that there was no magic or love within it. Some people call this the darkness as if it's an actual force, but in reality, it has no substance; it's just the opposite. It's the absence of magic and love that makes it dark. To protect against it, we must reinforce the love, the magic, and all that is kind and positive in the world. I filled it with love."

"We can't fill all that with love! There's so much of it!"

"I believe it's a matter of reinforcing others so that they too become part of our team. I'm going to take a little walk. Why don't you settle back and think about it? See if any ideas come to mind."

"Okay, I'll give it a try. I'd hate to think it's just you, Justin, and me." Joy walked off and disappeared behind a small hill. I took that as my signal to close my eyes again and see if any ideas came to me.

I tried with all my might to concentrate and see something. But there was just nothing at all. After quite a while of this abject failure, I relaxed and decided just to see if something would come to me. I must have fallen asleep because what I remember was kind of vague and indistinct, like a dream vision.

I felt as if I were gathering something. It was as if there were lots of threads, or maybe strands like yarn. There were many colors, and they formed a kind of web or matrix that seemed to go everywhere. There were areas in this web where the strands broke and others where they bound up together in bunches, no longer smooth and even. I was untangling the bunched-up areas, realigning the uneven sections. As the pattern smoothed out, I began to see thinner strands covering everything, millions, maybe even billions of these tiny fibers. Again, there were areas where the colors were dark, gray, and black in places where many were broken and disconnected.

I began gathering up many strands of different colors and weaving them together into a new pattern. I was pulling each strand very carefully. As they connected with the others in my weaving, they began to glow. It was imperative to draw in each strand carefully and deliberately and fit it precisely into the pattern. It was as if some unknown force was guiding me; I knew which color strand I needed to complete each part of the design.

As I gathered and worked, I could see places where the light was replacing some of the areas of darkness. I felt a huge relief with each shift. Eventually, most of what I saw was smooth, vibrantly colored, and light. There was enough light that even the darkness was only slightly gray, not wholly black.

I came back to myself and consciousness slowly. I lay for a time, wondering about what I'd seen. How could this fit into our quest to find an answer to keep love and magic alive, to stay ahead of the dead-eyed Unmakers? Perhaps there's even a small army at work to account for the many areas of darkness I'd seen.

"We need an army of our own," I thought aloud. I slapped my forehead, "Of course, that's what all the threads represent. If each thread connects to a specific person, then what are the larger strands?" Thinking about the broader bits, I began to see the vision of a woven strand changing to a wide river and the threads as capillaries.

What are the rivers? Could they be squadrons, gatherings of people with specific talents and skills needed to fight the enemy? I needed to talk to Joy.

But she wasn't there. Wildly I looked around, about to panic – well, panic more, when I remembered that she'd gone down a path. That's when she came strolling happily around a little hill.

"I was just checking on my garden. I didn't mean to worry you."

"Your garden?" I seemed to have lost the ability for coherent speech. Her comment was so far from what I'd been thinking about that I couldn't make sense of it.

"Well, yes. I keep many gardens throughout Creation. This garden is one of my favorites."

"What does your garden grow? Aren't we on a star?"

"Yes, we are on a star. This garden grows magic wands, of course. Where do you think fairy godmothers get those pretty little wands with tiny stars at the end? Well, they don't grow on trees. Someone has to plant them and tend them, and eventually, when they are exactly right, they are ready to be harvested."

I confess I was so excited to share my experience; I blew right past what she'd said as if magic wand garden harvests were the norm. "Joy, speaking of exactly right and ready to be harvested, I saw something! I'd love to hear about your garden and magic wands, but this can't wait!" We sat while I explained my vision to her.

Joy grasped my hands, smiling, "Zemma, I think you're on to something."

"Um, Joy, in case you haven't noticed, I don't see anything of these strands or rivers anywhere in the real world."

"That's because they're symbolic. I think your idea that each river is a needed skill, and the capillaries are people is a good place to start. Why don't we let that sit a bit? I'm sure that'll allow the answers to bubble to the surface as they always seem to do."

"Okay," I answered. "Around you, things do seem to come clear in time."

"It's not only around me. It's been happening all your life, but you're more aware, making it stand out more obviously."

Together, we walked the short distance to Joy's wand garden. I looked out over acres of artfully arranged wands of all shapes and sizes. Hundreds, maybe even thousands of sticks, topped with various ends sticking out of the ground. The caps of some were stars that emitted little sparks. Others were globes, glowing like small suns. There were wands with moons in varying phases and some that cycled through all the phases of the moon. There were even hearts that seemed to radiate love and peace.

"Is there a big market for fairy godmother wands?"

"Oh, yes. Fairy godmothers keep losing their wands; they can be ridiculously forgetful at times. Not all these wands are for fairy godmothers. Some are for wizards, warlocks, and witches. Let me tell you that crew is tough on wands. They break them, melt them, and destroy them in some imaginative ways. Sometimes their vanishing spells go completely wrong, and the wands disappear, instead of whatever they were aiming at."

She continued in her lovely singsong voice. "Then there are the wands that don't work quite right and explode. Unfortunately, we haven't figured out how to test them ahead of time. Using a wand for the first time is hazardous; there is a huge chance the wand will explode right in the user's face with their initial spell. And that isn't always a pretty sight!"

"Why, what happens besides the wand blowing up?"

"Well, my dear, it depends on the spell. If it's a simple spell like turning a prince into a toad or vice versa, it can have unexpected results. I've seen

49

fairy godmothers who turned into frogs themselves. Or sometimes the frog, instead of turning into a prince, just gets as big as one. I'll tell you; it's challenging to find enough flies for a frog that large until we can get a new wand sent in to reverse the spell."

"What are some of the spells gone wrong that you've seen?" I was fascinated!

"Beauty spells are the most unpredictable. We need to figure out the meaning of beauty for the person asking to be made beautiful. Even with a good wand, the results aren't always as desired. You'll find that people's ideas of beauty vary from culture to culture and place to place. When I was young and far less experienced, I accidentally turned an exceptionally large Hawaiian woman into a skinny one. She cried for days, and I don't think she ever forgave me."

"Why not? I thought all women wanted to be thin."

"Well, there you would be wrong. In Hawaiian culture, having an opulently large body is a sign of being wealthy and well cared for."

"Why did she want a beauty spell if she was already considered beautiful?"

"Clever girl! Now, there's the question I should have asked first. She wanted her nose to be wider and her hair to be thicker. She didn't want anything else changed. I learned to ask more questions, many more questions."

Joy continued, "Another time, one of my favorite fairy godmothers was casting a beauty spell on a hideous old crone. The wand malfunctioned at the abracadabra bit. I think she might have gotten a little carried away with the embellishments and showmanship, trying to put on a good show and all. But the wand blew up just as she was finishing."

"What happened?"

"The old crone became a complete ravishing beauty by anyone's standards."

"Okay, so why was that wrong?"

"She could only stay beautiful half the time. She would always be an ugly crone the other half of the time. She would turn into a crone whenever anyone saw her until her wedding night. She was only beautiful when she was alone or with her beloved. We tried to improve the situation later with a new wand, but we were never able to correct that spell."

"What did she do?"

"The story eventually became famous. Sit back and relax while I tell this tale. I'm afraid it's rather long, but it is entertaining and enlightening."

We settled on a comfortable-looking rock. I was glad to give my somewhat shaky legs a rest.

A long time ago, in the age of King Arthur and the Knights of the Round Table, Arthur was holding court, hearing his subjects' problems, when he heard a loud commotion outside.

A woman of great dignity was riding a magnificent steed. Her face was a mask of anguish as she cried out, "Gentlemen, I require your help. A villainous Knight, Sir Jiles, has stolen my lands and reduced my people to beggars. Please help set things right!"

Not one of the knights dared to take up her cause; they'd heard many horror stories about Sir Jiles. Of course, they couldn't admit to their fear and instead came up with a succession of lame excuses.

Arthur called for his horse and sword to go to the Lady's aid. He wasn't just about to be scared off by a bad reputation. Sir Gawain insisted on joining his king. The two brave men rode to the lady's lands, the forest becoming darker until it was like night. The animals and birds were silent. The entire forest had a feeling of death. On the rise, they saw a lake far below. The Lady's castle was built on a rocky island in the middle of the lake, with a bridge connecting the land's castle gates. The waters of the lake were murky, black, and forbidding. The castle, which the knights remembered as bright and shining, was dark and falling to ruin.

Sir Jiles stood in front of the castle, dressed in armor so dark it did not reflect the light; he was quite a fearsome sight. Arthur bid Sir Gawain stay back as he went into battle. Two on one isn't sporting. As soon as his feet touched the castle grounds, Arthur's strength left him, and he was weak as a babe.

"What trickery is this?" he cried.

The Dark Knight laughed, "You are on my grounds, and I have the power to do as I wish." Arthur fought as bravely as he could, as powerless as he was,

51

but finally fell to his knees. Sir Jiles wanted Arthur's complete and utter defeat, not just this quick death. Thus, he stopped before beheading him. He desired control over Arthur's lands and the Round Table.

"Arthur, I will spare your life for now and make a bargain with you. The bargain is one I think you cannot keep. Return to me in a year and a day, with the answer to a question I will put to you. If you answer correctly, you will keep your life, and I will return the Lady's lands and property to her. If you answer wrongly, your life and lands are forfeit."

"Done!" said Arthur. "Ask your question."

"Do not be hasty," replied the knight, in a mocking tone. "Think carefully before you answer. The question is, what is it that women want most in the world?" He snickered, sure Arthur would never learn the answer. He'd put this question to dozens of men, and not one had come remotely close. He relished the idea of Arthur and his men searching in vain, finally despairing, knowing they had lost.

Arthur opened his mouth to speak but quickly closed it. For he knew in his heart, mind, and soul that the answer he was about to give was not the correct one.

"That's good," said Sir Jiles, "Do not be so quick to speak. When you hear the right answer, you will know it. Now be gone!"

Sir Gawain, who had also heard Sir Jiles' taunting query, proposed, "Let us go about the land and ask all the ladies of all ages the question and write their answers down into books. Surely one of the answers will be the right one."

After Arthur and Sir Gawain's return, the other knights were anxious to atone for their failure to join their king. All the knights spent a year on horse-back and foot as they went from village to village, farm to farm, house to house, asking all the women the question, "What is it that women want most in the world?"

The women said many different things, "Riches!" "Beauty!" "A fine marriage." "Children," "Silks and Jewels," and some said with a sigh, "Time."

Arthur knew that not a single answer was the right response to the evil knight's riddle in his heart and soul.

Arthur and Gawain returned to the castle at the edge of the forest to meet the Dark Knight on the appointed day. When they entered the forest, they saw a richly dressed damsel with a loathsome face, in complete contrast to her beautiful clothing and stance. So ugly was she that they could not look upon her without feeling ill. They attempted passing by without a word and certainly without looking at her any more than necessary.

"Hold up, good sirs!" she called out. "Do not be so quick to pass by me. I know of your quest, and I can tell you the true answer you seek."

"If you know the answer, tell us!" cried Sir Gawain.

"Not so fast," said the lady; "It's not so easy to win the truth. You must pay my price to hear my answer."

"What is your price, my lady?" asked Arthur.

"The price I ask in return if my answer is true is that one of your fair knights willingly marries me."

Arthur could not command any of his knights to marry someone so ugly, even if it meant saving his life and kingdom. It was not his to command.

Sir Gawain spoke up, "Sire, I will marry the lady if you know her answer is true."

"Done," said the lady. She whispered the answer into Arthur's ear. His heart, mind, and soul lit up with the truthfulness of it.

Leaving Sir Gawain and the loathsome lady, Arthur rode to the castle where Sir Jiles was waiting for him with a sharpened ax.

"Well, do you have the answer?" the Dark Knight demanded with a sneer.

Arthur presented to him all the books containing the ladies' answers written down.

Sir Jiles looked through every book, laughing as he tossed them aside into the dark waters of the lake, saying, "The answer is not here. It is not in any

53

*of your books. You have searched far and wide in a fruitless search. You have
lost. Prepare to die, and forfeit your lands and the Round Table."*

*"Hold!" said Arthur. "There is one answer that I did not write down. Ask
your question again, and I will answer."*

*Sir Jiles confidently asked, "What is it that women want most in the world?"
Arthur gave his answer. The minute the Dark Knight heard it, he shouted,
stamped his feet, and shook his fists to the sky, yelling, "She told you! The
Witch has told you!!" He disappeared in a vile-smelling pillar of flame.*

*"As if by magic, for that was what it was., the dark lake became blue and
clear, and you could see the fish swimming in its depths. The castle returned to
its former glory. Light flooded the woods, and the animals returned in happy
droves. Bird songs and the scent of flowers filled the air.*

*Arthur and Gawain returned to Arthur's castle with the loathsome lady. A
squire went ahead to have the castle prepared for a wedding and feast. The
cheers that greeted them quickly turned to silence when they saw the revolting
face of Gawain's bride. The wedding was a somber affair. Not a single person
smiled except for the beastly lady. Many were in disbelief that Gawain would
marry someone so ugly, even to save his king and the kingdom.*

*The bride was the only one who had an appetite and appeared to be enjoying
herself as she entertained the onlookers and well-wishers with stories of great
wit and intelligence. Her stories and beautiful voice held all entranced as long as
they didn't look at her. One sight of her face could make all their admiration turn
to disgust in a moment, any fascination or enjoyment of her story forgotten. A
small number of people felt guilty for their contempt and chided themselves for
being judgmental and superficial, yet couldn't seem to get past her looks.*

*After a day that seemed to stretch on forever, Gawain and his bride retired to
their wedding chambers. The lady readied for their wedding night as Gawain
looked out at the stars.*

*He knew he had done the right thing by marrying her to save Arthur's life
and perpetuate the Round Table's good work. But a lifetime with her? No! He*

planned to see Arthur the next day and ask for a quest that would take him far away for many years. Surely Arthur would not refuse him.

"Husband?" said the lady, "What is wrong?" Shame crept into his heart when he heard her beautiful voice. How could he be so heartless as to leave her alone and friendless?

"Sweet Husband, give your wife a wedding kiss." Gawain turned towards her with pity, steeling himself to do his duty to king and country. He closed his eyes tightly and gently kissed her. When he opened his eyes, he was astounded to see a beautiful maiden in her place.

"Where is my wife?" Gawain gasped.

"I am she," said the beautiful woman, "I am your wife. I was placed under a curse many years ago. If a gentle knight kissed me, that would break part of the curse. But now we must make a choice."

"Choice?" asked a baffled Gawain. He was thrilled to discover his wife was beautiful and scarcely heard her until she repeated herself.

"We have to make a choice. Do you want me to be beautiful by day and ugly by night? Or do you want me to be ugly by day and beautiful by night?"

Gawain thought and thought. If she were beautiful by day, all the court would see how lovely she was, the men would envy him, and she would have friends flocking to her door. If she was ugly at night, could he even possibly face her night after night for the rest of their lives?

On the other hand, if she were beautiful by night and ugly by day, he would have the delight of enjoying her beauty, but she would be alone and shunned by the members of the court. Gawain thought and thought. Either answer, he knew, would be a painful rejection for her.

Finally, he said, "My Lady Wife, I cannot choose for you. Either way, it will be a painful path for you to walk. Only you in your own heart will know what is right for you, for I do not know what to choose for you. Only you and you alone can make this decision. I will honor your choice."

His wife cried with joy and danced around the room. She hugged him joyfully, "My Love, you've broken the curse, and I can be beautiful both day and night!!"

Gawain looked at her in baffled joy. "Gawain, do you know the answer to the question, 'What is it that women want most in the world'?"

"No, Arthur didn't divulge that secret to me."

"How, then, did you give me that which all women want?"

"I am delighted to have pleased you, but I don't understand what is it that you believe I have given you? I have done nothing more than to allow you to make your own choice, as it should be."

"Ah, good husband, you have given me sovereignty. It is a most unusual word, sometimes defined as ruling over someone or something, and then just the opposite, to be free of domination. In its most straightforward meaning, it is the expression of independence to make one's own choices. You have given me my sincerest desire.

"Sovereignty – the ability to rule over oneself – is something toward which every person and every country strives. Young boys wish it fervently to the point that they will battle with their fathers, not fully understanding that sovereignty comes with responsibility for one's actions and choices. Serfs under the thumb of a greedy tyrant pray for it so that they can enjoy the freedoms that many of us have taken for granted here in Arthur's kingdom. Thank you, husband, for being wise and seeing into my true heart."

"And they lived happily ever after," concluded Joy.

"Zemma, this is something I feel deeply in my soul," Joy said in a more somber voice. "No one, not a person or a country, should attempt to tell another person how they must live, what to eat or not eat, which movie to see or not see, what book they may read, what god to worship or even how to vote. A wise individual, group, organization, or country may only suggest, give guidelines, and provide truthful, unbiased information to make a choice. A free country will have rules to prevent chaos and bring about order, but a person can still have the freedom to choose within those rules. No one should deny another freedom. No organization or person should ever deny another person their right to sovereignty." I continued to listen to her wise words in silence.

"You give that to me, Joy." Zemma smiled.

"Yes. Those of us who care about the truth must recognize the sovereignty of each individual. While a person is growing and learning, we must take up the hard work needed to give them the wisdom to understand the responsibilities that come with this precious gift. We must guide them to a time when they have their answers of their own, then let them go to make their own choices."

Joy's words floated through the night air, "Not only is sovereignty something that all of womankind is seeking, so too is all of humanity. All should live in freedom and sovereignty. It should be our birthright, not something to be given or granted or taken away at will. To lose that right is heartbreaking."

I nodded. "The Unmaker wants to take that away. Maybe that's why he's so dangerous to people and the Universe."

Joy looked proud. "Yes, Zemma. Yes! In the story I just told, we were surprised when the miscast spell righted itself in a way we could never have imagined. The moral of the story is to 'trust in the ways of the Universe even when things don't make sense right away.' There's more to it, though, and I think there's a reason for this particular story to come up now."

I shook myself out of my reverie, even though I'd happily sit and listen to Joy's tales forever. "Joy, I'm still new to all this synchronicity stuff. Is it a tale about how important freedom is or reminding us that we have to step up and defend others' independence? I mean, I've seen over and over in history how even small infringements on liberties can become an unstoppable avalanche, and before you know it, you have no chance of getting free. It appears at times that the will to freedom is lost. Is that what the dead-eyed Unmakers do?"

"Yes. We're being called upon to spread the word and to help people fight back. When people lose connection to their passions, they lose any hope of freedom."

"I don't know if I could have been as unselfish as Sir Gawain under the same circumstances. I don't feel like anybody's heroine, and what you're saying sure sounds like you think that's what's needed."

"You might be surprised. It is when you must act that you're able to see if you're heroic or cowardly. If you've been living in truth and oneness and are faced with an honest challenge or test, the experience is likely to bring out the best you can give."

"Test? Who tests us?"

"Humans are constantly tested. It doesn't help to rant and scream at God or the Universe or fate. Many complain and bemoan the unfairness of all their tests. They act as if put upon by outside forces. Imagine their surprise if they were to know the real source of their ranting!"

"Well, don't keep me in suspense. Who sets up the tests?"

"Think about it, Zemma."

I stood up, stretched, and pondered about God, Allah, angels, fairy godmothers, the Universe, the Fates, and all nature of magical beings. As I thought of each one and brought in sovereignty and free will, I knew that none of these was the cause of our tests. Who, or what could it be?

"I've thought and thought. I cannot imagine the answer. Please tell me."

"Oh, where would be the fun in that? Let's go back to Earth. I think we've spent enough time in the stars. Eventually, you'll get used to intergalactic travel, but in the meantime, it can be moderately disorienting."

"MODERATELY?" I said at a pitch just under a yell.

"Well, perhaps a little more troublesome than that. Maybe you'll feel less anxious when you're back in surroundings you're more familiar with." She touched one of the stars in her hair, and whoosh, we were once again swirling through space. I was so upset over Joy's refusal to answer my question about the tests' source; I confess I didn't take the time to enjoy the trip.

We landed where we'd taken off from hours, minutes, days before. The waterfall still sparkled, the water in the pool was clear, and we took time to relax and enjoy a snack together.

Joy fumbled at her belt, passing over items with a thoughtful frown. I was nervous. I wasn't sure I was ready for another adventure or revelation; it had already been quite a day. She grinned mischievously as her hand rested on a daisy-rimmed mirror. My first impression was correct; those flowers were real! How did she keep the flowers fresh and in bloom? I bit back my question, determined to meet her next challenge with equanimity…or at least a semblance of poise.

CHAPTER 8:

Cheating, Tests & Magic Mirrors

"This is a unique mirror. Oh, don't look so worried! It's not as bad as all that! You are getting that Zelia Maria Magdalena look about you, so dark and doubtful and sure that something horrible is about to happen. Unexpected, surprising perhaps, but hardly horrific."

She handed me the mirror. "Think about some of the 'tests' you've had in your life, times when you've had choices to make that were difficult or stretched you to your limits. Where have they come from?"

I slowly shook my head as I searched my thoughts and came up with nothing.

"Zemma, look into my magic mirror and see what you see."

I didn't expect to see anything; at that moment, I felt like a kid. Up to now, my life seemed empty of the kind of heroism Sir Gawain had chosen. Indeed, I'd had no hard tests or challenges in my life. Entirely unbidden, a scene sprang into my memory.

I'd just finished taking a quiz in a fifth-grade math class during one of my brief stints in an actual school. As I was leaving the room, a classmate in the next class period stopped me asking what had been on the quiz. I shook my head and walked away, not willing to answer any questions. She grabbed my arm and refused to let me go, badgering me incessantly.

I needed to get to my next class and needed to get rid of her before we attracted attention. I finally answered with a vague, general response saying just that the quiz was about equations. That surely wasn't giving away anything of substance. Several days later, that classmate and I were called to the principal's office, loudly over the intercom in the middle of a full student-body assembly. I was at a loss as to why the principal called us to the office. I know my face was red with embarrassment.

When we got to the office, Sue was already there, with a tissue dabbing at both reddened eyes. The principal explained Sue had repented her cheating ways and confessed her sin.

"I know you're new here, but we simply don't allow cheating. Giving someone the answers is just as bad as getting them. Sue says you offered her the answers. What have you got to say for yourself?"

I was seething with angry disbelief. After all, I had not given out any actual answers, not even one. I don't know how anyone can construe a general response of 'gee, the math test is about numbers' as giving answers! I started to defend myself and expose her as a liar, but I couldn't manage to say a thing when I opened my mouth. I didn't want her to get in more trouble. Besides, I was sure he wouldn't believe me.

"I'm sorry, sir. I promise it won't happen again."

Since it was the first time I was ever in his office, the principal let me off with a stern warning. "See that it doesn't. The next time there will be consequences!"

I left the office confused and upset with myself for covering up for her. She stopped, thanking me profusely, saying that she'd been in trouble before. She was afraid of being suspended. My willingness to take some of the blame had let her stay in school. I was distressed that I'd been set up and used unfairly.

"You know, Sue, you shouldn't have said I gave you answers. You know I didn't. But more than that, cheating doesn't help you in any way. I hope you'll remember almost getting kicked out of school and never give in to the desire to cheat again."

She hung her head, not meeting my eyes, "I'm sorry. I completely panicked before the test because my Mum had been sick, and I'd been taking care of the little ones after school and hadn't been able to study. When I got accused of cheating, I was afraid I'd get expelled and upset my Mum, who is still sick." Before I could say another word, she turned and ran down the hall.

I thought about it and was proud that I hadn't made excuses and simply apologized.

Joy held up the mirror. "If you still wonder who it was who arranged that test, take a look in this mirror."

I looked in the mirror and saw my face frowning back at me. "Joy, that's not a magic mirror, it's a regular mirror, and it's showing me my very own face just like every other mirror I've ever seen."

"Let me see that." She took the mirror and held it so that it reflected both our faces, together, side by side. "Now, ask your question again."

I did so, and the image in the mirror wavered slightly and went black and smoky. When the smoke cleared, there was only my face in the mirror. We hadn't moved. The mirror should have shown us both. The image and answer were clear; I arranged my own tests.

"Why would I create hardship for myself?"

"Well, the conscious you doesn't, but the part of you that is watching and guiding your life from a higher perspective does. That part is committed to your growth and learning and will do whatever it takes to move you along continually, willing, or not."

"Okay, I kind of understand, but it all seems pretty far-fetched."

"I can see how it might be from your perspective. Let's take this one step further, shall we?"

"All right," I said cautiously. The events of the day were beginning to take their toll, and a prickle of anxiety passed through me as I tried to imagine what could possibly happen next.

"Have you ever had a time in your life when you felt like you might be dying? I know you're young, but even the young sometimes have close calls."

"Sure, I've had a couple of close calls, or at least they seemed to be at the time. I had the flu so bad I hoped I'd die, and my mother was worried. I had a bike accident when I was about nine and landed on my head. I woke up in the hospital ICU with all kinds of beeping equipment around me, my parents and doctor hovering over me. Later I was told my heart had stopped beating briefly, and they were afraid I was dead. But it started up again by itself, and I was okay."

"Let's explore that."

"How do we do that? That was years ago. Anyway, I was knocked out and don't remember a thing except starting to fall, then waking up in the hospital with my folks looking upset and crying beside me."

"Even when you are unconscious, your spirit remains aware of everything that happens. We can tap into your spirit to help you remember what went on while you were knocked out."

"Sure, why not? It sounds interesting and a bit creepy, too. But I'm game."

"Okay, I love how willing you are to experiment. You're a good sport, Zemma." Joy leaned forward and lightly touched my forehead. "Close your eyes and breathe. Just breathe."

I took a few deep breaths, feeling a moment of dizziness and confusion. I opened my eyes in a hospital room, looking down at my own, apparently, sleeping body. I was pulled into my still, quiet body on the bed. It was uncanny. I was unconscious, and yet this part of me could still think and feel. I was shocked out of my reverie when my mother started screaming for a doctor, alarms were going off, and doctors and nurses were running. My heart must have stopped beating. Doctors were pounding on my chest, although I didn't feel a thing.

I turned towards a beautiful golden light. Its force field drew me in until I was within its warmth and peace. It was the most glorious feeling I've ever experienced. I felt completely loved, safe, warm, and joyous. But it was more than that; I'm not sure I can even describe it. There was more than just light; there was a presence with me, a being of pure love, with no plan or agenda, no desire. It wasn't even unconditional. It was utterly pure love. I felt cherished, uplifted, and energetic; I wanted to remain that way forever.

I can hardly say this because it's such a cliché. I heard a voice saying, "No, you cannot stay. You still have a life to live, things to do. You must go back, but remember this feeling; it will guide you back when your time comes."

I fought to remain in the light, but it faded away, and I was back in my physical body. My body took a deep breath, and I was back among the living. I sobbed deep wracking cries. I was happy to be back with my parents but inconsolable over what I feared I'd lost forever.

Joy's compassionate gaze greeted me when I opened my eyes. "Joy, who was the being in the light with me? It felt so warm, so loving, so safe, and so wise. I wanted to stay there always. But it rejected me and told me I must go back. Who was it?"

"Does it matter?"

"Yes! I must know who or what that was. Was it Jesus? Was it you? Was it God?"

"No."

"Just 'no'? Why won't you answer me?" I screamed at her, stomped my feet, completely beside myself with emotion. I was sure if I knew the answer, somehow, that might let me recapture the experience. It was beyond anything I'd ever known, and I longed for that peace.

"Zemma, you will discover that some answers have more meaning when they come to you of their own free will instead of being given to you. If I give you the answer, it loses something important. The answer will come to you in time when you're ready for it."

"In time? IN TIME? I want to know now!"

"If you were calm, you'd probably already have the answer. Your anger and anxiety are pushing the answer away. Lie down in the grass. Rest. I'll sit with you."

"All right, Joy. I'll try. Maybe something will come clear," She nodded, and I lay on the grass with my backpack as a headrest. I was out almost before I got comfortable.

I dreamt I was back in that glorious warm golden light. I wanted to stay there this time. Yet again, I felt myself being firmly but gently repelled and told to return to my life. I recognized that voice; it seemed so familiar! I looked closely at the light. It was almost too bright to make out a form, but I persisted, determined to know the truth behind the mystery. With a gasp, I recognized the face within the light.

Cursing and sputtering, I sat up. "No freaking way, that can't be it!"

"What is it, Zemma? What cannot be?" said Joy as she softly touched my shoulder.

"I saw... I saw a face in the light and...."

"Go on."

"I must be making things up; it's not possible even in my wild imagination. That being was warm, wise, beautiful, strong, and simply incredible. So, it can't be..."

"You keep saying that. Who was it?"

"You already know the answer, don't you? I think you've known the answer all along and just refused to tell me. Didn't you?"

"Yes." She nodded at me to go on.

"Why wouldn't you tell me?"

"If you discover the answer on your own, it carries much more meaning for you. There's an immense difference between being told something and *knowing* for yourself."

"I saw her, but I'm afraid I'm just making this up. I don't believe it."

"You know you do believe it. If you didn't, you probably wouldn't be this upset. If it helps, I'll corroborate, but I won't make that a habit. I'd hate to ruin all the fun."

"Thank you." I shuddered and took a deep breath. It was hard to get the words out and reveal what I thought to be true to the outside world, even to Joy. It was too incredible. It was a lot to take in and was, even more, to live up to. I wasn't sure I was ready. My whole body was shaking as I pushed the words out from what felt like the depths of me. "It was me!?"

"Yes, so it was!"

"It was?!"

"Yes." She spoke gently. Her compassion and sweet voice calmed and soothed my fears.

"Why does that make me so afraid?"

"When you don't know how magnificent and wise you are, it's easy to go along being this little lowly human struggling through life. But once you've seen your truth, you can't pretend to be small and powerless any longer.

"I'd like to share something with you that Marianne Williamson wrote in her book, 'A Return to Love.' Just listen."

Joy took a breath and said in her beautiful, lilting voice:

Our deepest fear is not that we are inadequate.
Our deepest fear is that we are powerful beyond measure.
It is our light, not our darkness
That most frightens us.

We ask ourselves
Who am I to be brilliant, gorgeous, talented, and fabulous?
Actually, who are you not to be?
You are a child of God.

Your playing small
Does not serve the world
There is nothing enlightened about shrinking
So that other people will not feel insecure around you

We are all meant to shine
As children do
We were born to make manifest
The glory of God that is within us

It is not just in some of us
It is in everyone
And as we let our own light shine
We unconsciously give other people permission to do the same

As we are liberated from our own fear
Our presence automatically liberates others

I sat thoughtfully on my rumpled sleeping bag, at a loss for words. I wanted to talk, but I was suddenly so sleepy. "I don't think I can keep my eyes open…."

I felt but didn't see the mattress underneath me, the blanket over me, the tent around me. I fell into a dreamless sleep.

CHAPTER 9:

Birds Have Feelings & So Do Worms and Fish

I woke refreshed before the dawn. I couldn't remember the last time I'd seen the sunrise. I nearly sprung out of my sleeping bag, too alive and energetic to stay wrapped in my warm cocoon. As I stepped out of the tent, I wondered if my previous habit of wanting to sleep the day away had come more from boredom rather than from the need for sleep.

Stretching and yawning, I stepped into a misty morning. Joy, of course, was already up and outside. I heard her talking to someone. Curious, I moved closer, thinking that perhaps there was a small person hidden behind her voluminous skirts. No one was there! To whom or what was she talking? I tried to move silently and not disturb her, but, predictably, she turned to look at me with a smile. I swear she must have eyes and ears in the back of her head or maybe some type of radar.

"Good morning, Zemma. Did you sleep well?"

"Yes. I feel great! To whom are you talking? No, wait, let me guess, it was the invisible man!" I asked, only half-joking; at this point, I was willing to believe practically anything.

"No, I wasn't talking to myself, silly. My companion is still here."

I looked and still could see no one. "Uh, so your companion is invisible? I wasn't serious?"

"Open your eyes, and you'll see."

I looked closer and saw a small red bird perched on the bush in front of her. "Sure, you're talking to a bird. Right!" My voice dripped with sarcasm.

"Well, sure, I guess that's normal. We all either talk to ourselves or our poor, dumb animals. It's almost like we expect to hear an answer sometimes."

"Oh, but I am answered. I thought after talking to the tree; you would have given up your idea that humans are the only species capable of communication."

"Oh, no! Now you're telling me birds can talk. That red bird is a wild forest bird, not a magic tree or a parrot."

She sighed, shaking her head, "Zemma, Zemma. This bird can talk. But you must be willing to listen."

"Okay, okay, I'm willing already."

"Gee, with a tone like that, I don't think so. Apologize to Reddy, and maybe she'll talk to you."

Reluctantly, I went over to the bird. Strange, but I almost would swear the bird was laughing. "I'm sorry, Reddy, I didn't mean to doubt your ability to speak." I tried my best to be civil, but after all, it was early morning. I hadn't had my breakfast, and, for goodness sakes, the sun wasn't even up. It seemed a lot to ask so early in the day.

A tiny, lilting voice answered. "My, aren't you grumpy! Are you always like this in the morning? Perhaps you should take a clue from the early bird and go get a worm and then come back and try to carry on a mannerly conversation."

"I don't eat worms!"

"It's just a figure of speech. Don't take everything so literally. I meant that perhaps you were surly because you're hungry."

"I'm sorry. I *am* hungry, and I really and truly have never met a talking bird before!"

"Are you sure? Maybe you just weren't listening. Besides, just because you haven't met a talking bird before doesn't mean you shouldn't be polite."

"I said I'm sorry. A lot has happened recently, and I'm feeling a bit out of sorts having to face yet another strange thing before the sun or breakfast or *coffee*. I woke feeling great, looking forward to the day, but now I'm not so sure. I'll do my best, but I'm beginning to wonder how much I can take. Please accept my humblest apology." I bowed to the bird.

"You don't need to be snarky. Birds have feelings, too." She shook her wings and fluttered off, giggling a little. "People are funny!"

"Okay, that's it. Now I must think about the birds' feelings, the trees, and who knows what else. It's all a bit much!"

"You'll be surprised at *what else*!" said Joy with a smile and a knowing chuckle.

"Very funny! I'm sure you're getting a kick out of all this."

"Yes, you can be quite funny at times. Why don't you go have some breakfast?"

"You haven't seen a restaurant around, have you?" I growled.

"Well, no, I haven't. But there is a lovely stream just over that hill, and it's filled with trout."

"Hmmm, that does sound good. Oh, gee, I forgot my fishing pole and my frying pan." I slapped my forehead.

"Not to worry, Ms. Grumbles. Here are a needle and thread," She said as she pulled a large needle and threaded off the red scarf dangling from her waist and handed them to me.

"I fail to see how a straight needle is going to catch me a fish."

"Oh, silly girl, just bend it to make a hook. You've got the tools. But," she said, holding up her index finger as a signal for me to pay particular attention, "there's one crucial thing you have to know before you go catching any fish."

"Yes, I'm listening."

"Keep your mind open." A stern look came over her face as she emphasized what she was about to say with a wag of her finger. "Before you put the hook in the water, thank the fish for choosing to become our breakfast and ask only for those who wish to serve us in that way to come take the hook."

"What?! You're telling me I should ask the fish to come and let me catch it willingly so that we can cook them?"

"Yep, that's pretty much it."

"Now, why would they be willing to be caught, and whoever heard of asking a fish anyway?"

"Zemma, you're back to your doubting self. Don't forget all you've learned. Some animals have lived a good life and are ready and willing to go on to their next level of existence and are eager to serve others by becoming a good meal. They prefer that to dying and rotting away like so much garbage. In their world, it's a great honor to become the meal of someone who appreciates and honors their gift."

"Okay, I'll give it a try." I knew I was still ungracious. I stomped towards the stream, thinking about the whole concept, and decided in the grand scheme of things; it made a crazy kind of sense. I rather liked the idea of animals volunteering to be eaten rather than just murdered. I shuddered. That was ridiculous! If I had to fish for my breakfast, I would fish for my breakfast, but I would keep my feet on the ground when I did it.

I got to the stream, prepared my hook, and threw it into the water. I ignored Joy's advice about asking the trout to volunteer. I felt guilty, but I just wasn't in the mood for such nonsense. I sat on the grassy bank, hungrily wishing the darned fish would hurry up and bite. I realized I didn't even have any bait for my hook.

But then I remembered the early bird. The grass was long and dewy, just the kind of place to find nightcrawlers above ground early in the morning. I looked around until I spotted a giant, juicy worm. I grabbed it up and started to stick the hook in its head.

"Hold it, just a minute! Whattaya think you're doing? Did ya ask me if I wanted to be fish food this morning? No, I don't think ya did! Well, I don't! Put me down. I got children to feed."

"What the…." I gaped idiotically at the worm wriggling in my hand.

"Whatsamatta, ya never seen a talking worm before?"

"Uh, no."

"Oh, boy. These kids today, just no upbringin'!"

"Hey, I had upbringing."

"Where ya from, Mars?"

"No, I'm from right here. Well, not here-here, but I am from Earth, and I'm camping just over the hill."

"Chickie lemme tell ya, ya gotta listen. You're just too deaf and dumb to bother to listen."

"Well, excuse me!"

"If ya want me to forgive ya, ya gotta say it with a little less attitude, if ya know what I mean."

"Geesh!"

"That's still a lotta attitude!"

"Okay, gee, Mr. Worm, I'm so sorry to have disturbed you without your permission."

"You still sound kinda snarky. Given your overall level of unconsciousness, I'll let it go this time. Tell your mommy to teach ya better manners."

The worm wiggled out of my fingers, dropped to the moist grass, and was gone.

"Yikes, now I've been chewed out by a worm." Exasperated, I flopped back down on the bank.

"Well, I think he let you off lightly," said a deep, throaty voice.

"Okay, who said that?" I looked wildly, still not seeing anyone or anything on the bank.

"Not that way, dumbbell, I'm here. In the water."

Sure enough, there was a fish with his head out of the water. I knew it was a "he" because of the voice, like someone's cranky grandpa.

"You talking to me?" I asked.

"Well, do you see anyone else around?"

"Uh, no."

"Well, good, now that we've got that resolved, let's get on with it."

"On with what?"

"Correct me if I'm wrong, didn't you come here to catch a fish?'

"Yes."

"What am I, chopped liver?"

"No, you look like a fish to me."

"Am I too small?"

"No, you're just about the right size for breakfast for two."

"What's the hold-up?"

"Well, frankly, I'm having a little difficulty with this whole talking worm, talking fish thing. I know Joy said all I have to do is ask for a volunteer, but that sounds crazy to me."

"Why's that?"

"Are you telling me you're ready to die, and you want me to eat you?"

"Yep, that about sums it up."

"Why?"

"Why, why, why? Look, sweetie, you're young, so maybe you don't understand. But when you get to be as old as I am, you've done everything, been everywhere, and it's getting downright boring. I'm ready to die and be reincarnated. In my next life, I get to come back as a cat, and I can hardly wait!"

"You want me to believe there's reincarnation for animals?"

"Sure, why not? Once we get good at being whatever we're being, we get to come back as something else. I am looking forward to being on land, having fur and feet, and chasing mice around. It sounds like a great life to me. I'm asking you again, would you get on with it already?"

"On with what?"

"Were you born stupid?" The fish almost seemed to be shouting at me in exasperation. "Ask my permission to catch me! Then throw the danged hook in so I can eat it, and then you can eat me! Geez, do I have to tell you everything? Are you waiting for me to jump on the bank?"

"But, there isn't any bait on the hook."

"And your point is? Bait's there to trick fish that don't want to get caught into thinking they're getting a free lunch. You don't need to trick me, so you don't need any bait. Just throw the blooming hook in already! I can feel one of my cat's lives slipping away already!"

I decided to quit arguing and threw the bare, bait-less hook into the water. I didn't expect the fish to chomp down on my lame excuse for a hook anyway. Womp, he took the hook and ran with it. For a fish who said he wanted to get caught, he put up a fight. With some effort, I finally landed him. "Thanks," he gasped as I was taking the hook out of his mouth.

"Look, I don't get it. If you wanted me to catch you, why'd you put up such a fight?"

"I didn't want to make it too easy for you, and the show's half the fun! Have a good life…and be nice to pussy cats." His eyes glazed over, his gills stopped moving, and he died, practically in my arms.

I'd caught a lot of fish in my life, never giving it a second thought. I didn't feel the same about this one, a beautiful, shimmering trout who practically begged me to kill and eat him. I know he explained that he was willing and all that, but I couldn't shake the guilt. It's just flippin' strange to catch a fish with whom you've just had a conversation. Maybe I should have had coffee first!

I gently picked him up by the gills as I had been taught and walked dispiritedly back to camp. The tent was gone. Joy was sitting on the ground with her legs crossed and eyes closed, looking very much like a statue of Buddha. It was only her skirts billowing up behind her that absurdly spoiled the picture – Buddha wearing a circus tent! Ha!

I sat down quietly so as not to disturb her meditation. I held the fish in both hands as I attempted to make sense of the situation.

Her eyes popped open after no more than a minute. "Ah, breakfast! Great, I'm starving." She looked closely at me and smiled softly. "What's the matter, cat got your tongue?"

"Well, the fish did say he's going to come back as a cat."

"Oh good, you got to talk to him and find out all about him. Why do you look so down?"

"Well, I never killed anything that talked before."

"Sure, you have. Everything you ever killed talked."

"But they didn't talk to ME!" I wailed.

"Would you have liked them to talk to you?"

"Well, no. It's a little late for that, anyway. They're dead! I killed them! Murdered them!"

"Did you? Did you really?"

"YES!" I was feeling distraught. I was sure that I'd done the unforgivable many times over.

Joy pulled out her handy little daisy-ringed mirror again. It grew bigger and bigger until it was so large I couldn't see the edges. All I could see in front of me, beside me, even behind me, was a mirror. Fear roiled in the pit of my stomach. What was I going to see now?

The mirror did its smoky routine again, but this time, it was terrifying because it was all around me, and I felt like I was being sucked right into the mirror! When the smoke cleared, I saw hundreds, maybe thousands of animals and insects. There were cows, deer, turkeys, chickens, ants, lizards, a few snakes, flies, mosquitoes, fish flopping around on the ground, even some colossal fish which I figured must be tunas, pigs, sheep, lambs, and calves, and I don't know what all else. They seemed to stretch on into eternity.

"Hey, I didn't kill all of them. I shot one deer with an arrow once, and I've caught some fish, but that's it."

"Well, Zemma, you did step on a lot of insects and swatted a bunch of flies. The one little deer over there is the one you killed with your arrow, but the others, well, you just ate them. Someone else killed them, but you dined on them without giving thanks or even giving any thought of appreciation. Now's your chance."

"You want me to say 'thank you'?"

"Now's as good a time as any while you've got their attention, don't you think?"

"Yeah, I guess so. But why are those calves and lambs there? I don't eat babies."

"Remember veal? Leg of lamb? They are baby cows and sheep."

"Oh, no! I'm so sorry. It's one thing to eat an old trout who's ready to go on and become a cat…how can I justify eating a baby that never had a chance to live!?"

"Ask one of them."

"You want me to talk to the baby cow?"

"When are you going to get a better chance?"

I walked to the part of the mirror where an adorable little calf was standing. I looked the calf straight in the eyes. "I'm so sorry. I didn't know. Can you forgive me for eating you?"

"No problem," chirped his tiny baby voice. "I never wanted to be a grown-up. They're so boring just standing around chewing their cud all day. I only wanted to come and play for a little while. I got to do that, and then I got to be dinner." I kid you not; he said that like it was a good thing and did a little dance with his tiny little hooves.

"Excuse me. But you sound happy about being dinner," I said to the calf.

"I am. You see, when you eat us, a tiny bit of our consciousness goes into you, and we live on in you for a while. Your cells renew every seven years… during the seven years after you ate me, I got to be part of your life, and your mother's and your father's and part of some other people whose names I don't remember."

"Oh, boy. Now I have to think about a whole bunch of other consciousnesses sharing space with me in my body?"

"Well, technically, no," said the calf.

"Oh, thank you." I felt a bit relieved.

"Technically, they ARE your body."

"Oh, gee, that's so much better. I thought I was my body."

"Nope, it doesn't work that way. That's what's wrong with most of you humans. You think you are your body. In truth, you are much more than that and a lot less because it's a lot of other consciousnesses making up your body. Hey, you paying attention? Is this getting a bit overwhelming for you? Let's just get to the part where you say thanks, and we'll be on our way."

I took a deep breath, afraid I was about to pass out. The thought of every meal I had eaten in the last seven years, having a consciousness or soul or spirit that was living in my body with me, was just a little too creepy to take in. Then when I thought of them being my body, I felt even more freaked out. I looked around at all the animals in the mirror surrounding me. "Thanks."

The calf spoke again. "Not good enough. It sounds to me like you're just trying to get rid of us. Put some feeling into it, girl."

I closed my eyes and searched deeply for some gratitude. I was surprised when I found it. Somehow, despite myself, I discovered that I was thankful for the way they'd all nourished and sustained me. I bowed deeply to every one of them, touching my fingers to my lips and saying "thank you" as I blew them each a kiss. When I'd blown my last kiss, the mirror disappeared, and I was suddenly sitting on the grass near Joy with a dead trout still in my hands.

I felt utterly drained, which perhaps was a good thing as I set to the work of cleaning my old friend, the trout. I couldn't think about that anymore. I forced myself to think of him as food.

Somewhere, somehow Joy had found some vegetables which we cooked with the fish in a frying pan that she'd pulled out of a pocket under her skirts. How could she even walk with her collection of magical things bouncing against her legs? I didn't have the heart to ask if she'd given proper thanks to the wild carrots and greens. I was afraid of what the answer might be!

CHAPTER 10:

Push the River or Go with the Flow

Breakfast was among the most delicious meals I'd ever eaten. I was fuller and more satisfied than seemed possible for the small meal. Joy giggled when I mentioned it.

"Oh, yes. That's one of the surprising advantages of the giving thanks ritual. Food that has come to you willingly, blessed by your thanks, is, in fact, more filling and nurturing to your body than that which you haven't properly acknowledged."

"Well, it's good to know that all this has advantages other than just making every meal an up-close and personal friend."

"The funny thing is that if you fake the 'Thank you,' it doesn't work the same way. You'll end up with indigestion."

"Oh, of course." My tone was a tad bit peevish. It wasn't that I didn't believe her, but it seemed that my natural defense mechanisms were on high alert. I was staggered by all the new information and responsibilities I'd obtained over the past 24 hours. Was it only 24 hours, or were we living in a different time frame, I wondered, not for the first time? I apologized with my eyes and a shrug. Joy, being Joy, laughed and twirled around.

"So, Zemma, which way are we headed today?"

"Oh, no!" I groaned, "It's your turn to choose."

"Nope, this is your journey. I'm just along for the ride. You choose."

I sighed. For some reason, I knew this day wasn't going to be easy. It would be interesting surely, but there was already too much to process and absorb.

"Why do I have to choose? Can't we just start walking and see where we end up?"

"Oh, and I suppose wandering about with no direction at all, not being in contact with your surroundings and worrying all the time is easier than making a decision?"

"Joy, can't you just let me get away with feeling put upon, even for a little while?"

"Why, did you want to go through the day feeling like everything's soooo exceedingly difficult? It tires me just watching you. What would happen if you just went with the flow?"

"I could get swept away!" Oh, Zelia Maria Magdalena, why don't you just go away, I thought, mentally pushing her away.

"Hmmm, I wonder." She put a delicate finger on her chin, tilted her head to one side, and shot me what could only be called a mischievous look.

"Oh, no. We're not getting into one of your crazy philosophical discussions again. I say we go that away!" I pointed toward the river hoping to stave off something…no idea what the something was or would be, but I could sense it coming for me.

"All right, let's go that way!" Joy trounced off across the meadow in the direction I had indicated, paraphernalia bouncing merrily from her belts. I wondered if she intended to cross the sparkling waterway on foot, find a bridge, or get a boat, or maybe she had a bridge scarf.

The answer, unsurprisingly, considering that this was Joy, was none of the above. When she got to the water's edge, she didn't even pause before jumping in clothes and all.

I yelled to her as she paddled, splashing merrily, to the middle of the wide river. "Do you think we can get across here?"

"No."

"Then, what are you doing?"

"Oh well, I thought you pointed to the river because you wanted to float down it."

"I hadn't thought of that option. But why not? I guess it could be fun." I immediately jumped in and began paddling downstream for all I was worth. The water was cold and refreshing. I've always been a decent swimmer and was making good time. When I turned my head, expecting to see Joy way behind me. I was surprised to find her at my side. She wasn't even paddling, merely laying back in the water floating along; her skirts gathered up around her ankles created a canoe-like silhouette that parted the waters as she gracefully drifted downstream.

I paddled harder. Joy stayed even with me, still just lying back and letting the river take her along. We kept this up for a good hour, and despite all my efforts, we remained even. Seeing my frustration, she laughed.

"What's so funny?"

"You are. You are working so hard, and here I am, just going with the flow. It's no effort at all. You're exhausted while I'm still fresh as a daisy. You are working ridiculously hard to go the same distance. Is it worth it?"

Chest heaving, breathing heavily from my exertions, I stopped swimming and turned over, feeling the river move under me, supporting me, taking me along with it at a slightly faster speed than I'd been able to paddle. Sheepishly, I grinned back, "Gee, I guess not. I always thought you had to work hard to get anywhere."

"Most people do think that. Don't feel bad. You just weren't brought up with right thinking."

"Hey, my folks brought me up just fine." Where on Earth did the defensiveness come from, again?

"I didn't mean there's anything wrong with their intentions. They can only teach what they know, and they don't know any better. Your mother is my sister; we grew up together. I'd expect her to teach you the same way we were. Now you have a chance to learn a new way of facing challenges."

"If you both had the same upbringing, why are you so different?"

"When our mother died, our lives took different paths. We handled our grief completely differently and just drifted apart. We just quit talking to each other."

"Is that why you don't talk much now?"

"Yes, sadly, it is. We still love each other. We aren't the same people any longer and, until recently, hadn't managed to find a way to reconnect."

"So, how did I end up here with you?"

"It's funny how that worked out. A few months ago, I was looking through some old photo albums feeling nostalgic. Before I could stop myself, I picked up the phone and called. Your family is usually off in some exotic place on the other side of the world when I've called. I hadn't expected her to answer, but she did. We got to talking over old times. Despite our differences, we found love once again. It had always been there; we had merely lost touch with it and each other's hearts. We started talking regularly again, trying to understand or at least accept each other. For the most part, we weren't that far apart. When the chance to go to the Amazon came up, your mom called me."

"Yeah, to be my babysitter."

"No, not as a babysitter. She called hoping you and I could have some fun together and make up for the lost time."

"Oh," I wasn't sure how to respond but was somewhat relieved to know Joy wasn't my babysitter.

"Are we going to spend all day 'going with the flow'?"

"Well, I sure hope so."

"I didn't mean literally staying in the river, floating along. I'm starting to get rather shriveled and prune-like. I'm about ready for some dry land."

"All right." With those words, she stood up in the river like a bobber and began wading to shore.

"Wow, you take everything literally, don't you?"

"No, but in this case, I didn't see any particular reason to continue floating downriver. Don't you feel that maybe something interesting is waiting for us just around the corner?"

"I thought I was directing things today."

"Oh, you are. You said, 'Gee, let's get out of the water.' So, I did. Now you're about to start walking down that path around the corner, and I'm going to follow you."

"How did you know I wanted to go that way?"

"Well, it makes sense, doesn't it? If we go the other way, we'll just be going back the way we came." She turned and looked away from the river, shaking her head. "And that direction looks all prickly and could be rough going. It makes sense to be going that way," pointing in the opposite direction.

"Ah, right," I said churlishly, trying to hide how silly I felt. I was trying hard to rein in my sarcasm, but when I'm out of my element and have no idea what to expect, I tend to get a little sullen. Judging by my attitude, I felt very much out of my element and more than a little apprehensive. All this 'going with the flow' stuff was great, but it seemed more than a little crazy to be wandering around willy-nilly without a plan, a map, or any idea whatsoever of where we were going or what lay ahead. Although I guess it wasn't totally without a plan, since we did stop to make choices at every crossroads. I did have to admit, though, I was feeling just a little curious about what was around the bend. I shifted my backpack, which miraculously was dry, as was I, and pushed on.

We headed off, trudging along a graveled, shrub-lined country road. We rounded the bend and saw nothing, just another curve, snaking in the other direction. The path followed the river's slow meanders, curving this way and that through the undulating landscape. "I thought you said something was waiting around the corner."

"Well, yes, but I didn't say which corner. Sometimes you need to turn more than one corner to find your future. If you stop and give up every time there's nothing there, you'll never get anyplace."

I don't know how far we walked; I counted ten bends before I gave up and quit counting. I stomped. I shuffled. I lagged. I hurried. I vacillated between being anxious to 'get there' wherever 'there' might be and being reluctant to do so. Joy seemed unconcerned about where we were going. She stopped to look at flowers along the way, singing, dancing, twittering with the birds. She even carried on a conversation with a butterfly. Inwardly I marveled at her ability to enjoy even the smallest things.

I shuffled along in rather a daze. I managed not to tread on any tree roots as I walked. I saw a couple of fairies dancing on the daisies we passed, but I was in too much of a hurry to stop and look. The fact that I had no destination and no idea where I was going didn't seem to affect my usual way of traveling: hurrying to get there, even if it meant being oblivious to what I was passing. I know, I know, I can hear you. After the events of the previous day, you'd think I'd have learned to slow down and pay attention. But, hey, I've been going along like this for twelve years. I couldn't change overnight. Could I?

81

CHAPTER 11:

Skinnyville & Hippos that Aren't

I kept walking, head down, intent on the path. When I finally looked up, I stopped so suddenly; Joy nearly bumped into me.

There was a hippo in the river! I looked around to see if perhaps I was missing a real circus menagerie pitched nearby. The hippo didn't notice me, just turned over and floated on her back. Goin' with the flow.

Flabbergasted, I sat down on one of the logs that lined the bank. She was graceful, for a hippo. She swam in circles in the middle of the river, where the gently flowing waters were deep. She radiated complete happiness and peace. Then, when she turned towards me, I saw that she wore large gold hoops in her ears! And blue eyeshadow and false eyelashes! I looked around again, expecting to see circus tents or her trainer, at least nearby. There was nobody. She was not your ordinary wallow-in-the-mud kind of hippo. Why was she in the middle of nowhere in this unlikely place?

"Gosh, can't a gal bathe in peace?" The hippo's voice was low and kind of sexy. She reminded me of some actress I'd seen in an old black-and-white movie who was known for her voice and her big…well, never mind that. That hippo reminded me of that actress in more ways than one.

"What's the matter, don't you talk to strangers?" I swear she batted her false eyelashes at me.

"Uh, sorry. I wasn't expecting to see a hippo. I didn't mean to be rude."

"Don't they have hippos where you come from?"

"Well, no, not really."

"Hmmm, where are you from then, Skinnyville?"

"No. Where's Skinnyville?"

"Oh, it's just about everywhere these days," she said with a kind of drawl. "That's what I call all those places that only welcome creatures who are thin and fit some perfect ideal. No one actively excludes them; they just are invisible or insulted if they don't fit the Skinnyville stereotype. Everyone outside that scrawny normal is considered a hippo."

"But you ARE a hippo."

"No, not really."

"Uhm, gee. I'm looking at you, and you look just like a hippo."

"Yeah, I know. That happens occasionally. When enough people call me a hippo or treat me like I'm a hippo, I start to believe it too. I briefly turn into an honest-to-goodness hippo. But that's not who I am. Not really."

"I still don't get it. What are you?"

"I'm a woman, human and all that. I'm just larger than most. You know, of course, words have meaning, and thoughts can create reality."

"Yes, I'm following you so far."

"Well, usually, I have a great feeling about who I am. I know I don't fit the norm, and some people think I'm ugly or unintelligent just because I'm big. Let's face it; I'm fat. But, mostly, that doesn't bother me. I dress well. Truth be told, I take more care of my clothing and appearance than a good many skinny chicks. I make sure I wear great clothes. I even manage to turn heads from time to time. Well, most of the time. Many men won't even admit it to themselves, but they love to see my womanly curves. I can even feel some women and feel them wishing they could be bodacious like me. But alas, they usually don't let themselves acknowledge that and instead push it away by being offended by me.

Disgusted looks and nasty comments typically just roll off my back. I ignore them. But sometimes, those comments hit me with such force that they get past my guard. If I'm feeling tired or disappointed or just run down, it all gets to me. Dining out, I feel like I should apologize for eating anything more substantial than ice cubes. And then it happens...I become what I've been seeing in everyone's eyes. I become a hippo."

She took a big breath, splashed some water by shaking her massive head, and continued, "So what do I do then?? I come to the river where hippos can live free and be happy. Normally I'm all alone here, and I don't have to apologize for my true nature." Quite a mouthful for a hippo!

"So how do you get back to being a woman again? At least I'm assuming that you don't stay a hippo."

"After a day at the river, I get so happy being here, in nature playing in the water, I stop worrying about what people think of me. I feel reconnected to myself and this whole wonderful Creation. Poof, I'm myself again, literally. I get up, dry myself off, go home, and promise to stay connected to my real self, not to let narrow-minded, prejudiced people get to me. I can resist for longer and longer periods. But eventually, the sheer force of the thoughts and feelings coming my way drag me down, and I'm back here, playing in the river."

"That's terrible!"

"It could be far worse. Some people even get seriously ill when bullied. I'd much rather be a hippo playing in the water than let it affect me physically."

"I don't get it. If you don't like being made fun of for being big, why don't you lose weight?"

"I've tried. I get discouraged when I've eaten a tiny bowl of cereal for breakfast and then salads for lunch and dinner, and instead of losing, I gain weight. I'll be truthful here… I do like to eat. But believe it or not, I have a pretty healthy diet. It gets frustrating. I've decided to simply live my life, dress well, and enjoy myself."

I've often overheard beautiful girls talking to each other, complaining and moaning about how much they hate their bodies, their thighs, their stomachs, themselves. I'd look at them, wholly baffled because they always looked beautiful to me. And I've traveled enough to know there didn't seem to be a common ideal of feminine beauty. It seemed to me there's too much emphasis put on one idea of perfection, but it keeps changing. It's a little crazy, really. I'd never been able to talk with anyone about it.

I was also starting to feel somewhat guilty for the times I'd joined in with the other kids in teasing some nerdy fat kid. I had a hard time meeting her eyes.

She rolled flirtatiously. "I have a naturally expansive personality. Of course, that expansiveness seems to want to express itself in my body as well as my life. I do things in a big way. I live large, exceptionally large, enormous, colossal, huge, great! If I tried to live large in a tiny body, I'd probably just burn up."

She gestured to her body. "When I start losing weight, I sometimes feel like I'll just float away like a giant soap bubble. All this body," she gestured with her enormous head again, flinging droplets of water every which way, "helps me stay grounded and in touch with who I am. If turning into an honest-to-goodness hippo on occasion is part of the picture, then so be it."

It never occurred to me that there could be any comfort or compensation for being overweight. Her insight and self-acceptance surprised me. Feeling suddenly gawky and awkward, I wondered how she managed to maintain her composure.

I dangled my feet in the water. "Wow, you've got a great attitude. I don't ever feel satisfied with myself. Boys don't have to live up to the same ideals. But we girls are always comparing ourselves to the celebrity of the moment, trying to look like the most popular pop star or actress and, of course, always falling short. I don't know how you do it. Don't you ever get mad at the people who put you down?"

"Sometimes. But mostly, I feel sorry for thin people. They live narrow, tight, little lives."

"Who's being judgmental now? I doubt all thin people live narrow little lives."

"Ouch. Sorry, maybe I mean bullies. Otherwise, it's just a difference in body chemistry."

"Maybe they don't relate to their physical bodies the same way you do… so their bodies don't expand with their thoughts."

"Hmmm…." She looked thoughtful, flicking her grayish, leathery ears at some unseen fly. "I don't know. I've quit making myself wrong for it. I'm just doing my best to be myself."

"What's your name?"

"Sonya."

"Nice to meet you, Sonya."

"You thought I was going to say 'Hilda,' didn't you?" She laughed, shaking her head and spraying water all over me again.

"No, of course not," I fibbed.

"Come on, you can admit it."

"Well, maybe," I said with a shy grin, not wanting to make her feel bad.

"And you are?" The question was evident in her eyes.

"Zemma."

"That's an interesting name. I don't think I've ever heard it before."

"I made it up out of parts of my name, Zelia Maria Magdalena. But to me, it's integrating who I was, who I am, and who I'm becoming."

"Well, you aren't bad-looking. Yeah, I'd call you becoming."

"Not *that* kind of becoming. What I meant was 'beginning to be.'"

"So, becoming Zemma, how will you know when you've succeeded?"

"I don't know. I guess I'll feel wiser. I'll just know," I murmured.

"Well, don't count on it. There's always so much more to learn. It seems the older I get, the more I realize how much I don't know."

"This morning, I talked to a trout in the process of becoming a cat. Well, he was going to be a cat after I killed and ate him. Wow, that didn't sound good, did it?"

"Not really. I know what you mean, though. He was becoming something too. It's nice to know you've learned about talking to your dinner before you eat it."

"Breakfast."

"Pardon?"

"He was breakfast, not dinner."

"Oh." She paused for a minute before a large hippo grin spread across her face.

I watched as her form shimmered and began to shift. Fascinated, I watched as she morphed from a hippo to a large, curvy, decidedly beautiful woman. Her beauty so transfixed me that I forgot to notice that she was fat...or naked.

"Hey, give a girl some privacy, please."

"Oh, sorry." I turned away and could feel my face turning deeply red. "I didn't mean to stare, but you are…."

"I know, I know. I'm fat."

"No, that wasn't what I was going to say. You're beautiful. You're magnificent."

"Thanks." Her voice turned bashful. Even with my back to her, I could feel her blush. "You can turn around. I'm decent."

I turned back, and she indeed was beautiful. A figure-skimming red dress caressed her ample curves and flowed as she walked. She moved toward me with assurance and poise.

"I meant that in the nicest way. You are dazzling. I don't know how anyone could look at you and not see how gorgeous you are."

"It's funny about people. We look at them all the time and don't see who they truly are. I admit to being just as blind as the next person. I'm becoming, too." She put her lovely hand through my elbow, and we walked companionably further on up the bank to a shady grove of oak trees.

"The funniest thing has been happening to me lately," she continued as we settled ourselves on a log. "I call it instant karma. The minute I look at someone I don't know and have an immediate negative judgment about them, circumstances arrange themselves so that I'm having a conversation with that person within five minutes. I kid you not, Zemma; almost every time I have one of those conversations, I feel sheepish and small because my assessment was utterly unfair, and I didn't see the person hiding behind the stereotype. I, of all people, should know better. Perhaps that's why the Universe takes care to change and enlarge my viewpoint immediately."

"I think I know what you mean. But it's never happened to me."

She took a deep breath, settled that gorgeous body down in the shade of a large oak like a cat, and began. "Let me give you an example. I've had dozens in the past month." The other day, I saw a homeless man begging for change. In my ultimate wisdom, I decided he was probably a good-for-nothing bum. I brushed past him, pretending to be all business, in a hurry to get where I was going, so I wouldn't have to acknowledge him.

The crossing light turned red, and, of course, as fate would have it, I ended up standing at the corner with him. I tried to ignore him, but as I turned to check for traffic, he caught my eye and smiled one of the most beautiful smiles I've ever seen. I knew he wasn't asking me for anything or expecting anything from me at this point. We were just two people crossing the street. We ended up talking on the corner, for I don't know how long." A wistful look crossed her face.

"He told me about losing his job a few years back. He didn't complain about how unfair it all was, or how it was all the boss' fault, or the economy or the state of the world. Instead, he smiled sheepishly and said, *Heck, if I'd been my boss, I would have fired my lazy self years earlier. I was so busy drinking and playing the big man I wasn't doing my job very well. I didn't figure out until after I was out on the street that my drinking had gone beyond the party stage, and I'd become an alcoholic. I've tried to kick it, but, well, here I am. The best thing I can say about myself is that I don't hurt anyone else, and I've found peace with myself and my god.* He patted my shoulder, grinned, and walked off, whistling happily."

She held up a finger and went on before I could open my mouth to say something about him. "That same evening, I was driving home on the freeway, and a woman in an SUV cut me off. I nearly hit her. I honked, and she didn't even seem to notice. I swore, 'Inconsiderate witch' and continued to be grumpy about the incident. When I stopped at the grocery store, I saw the SUV in the parking lot; the woman stood beside her car, crying, looking pretty much at wit's end. I asked if I could help."

"The woman, a stylish-looking 30-year-old, looked up at me. She was younger and thinner, and if she weren't crying, she would fit right into Skinnyville. I asked if I could help. She said, *No, but thanks for asking. I was just leaving work when I got a call from the babysitter that my daughter is sick again. I need to pick up some cough syrup and realized halfway to the store that I left my purse under my desk. I must have rushed out too quickly. I can't drive back to the office and get back to the babysitter on time. I can't afford the $20 late fee. If I take the time to go back to the office, I won't have any time to spend with my kids before bedtime, and that's something I promise them every night. Their dad isn't in the picture, and they need me to be there. Sometimes it gets to be too much. It sure wasn't how I thought my life was going to look. I got no picket fence, no partnership, just three kids and an ex-husband with a little sports car, and a new Barbie-doll*

89

secretary wife. The tears continued to run down her face. *It's even more awful because it's such a cliché!*

I hugged her and pulled a $10 bill out of my purse. *"Will this be enough to cover what you need?"* I asked.

"I can't take your money!" She said, obviously shocked that anyone would give her anything.

"Look, take it. Someday, if I have kids, maybe somebody will help me out when I need it."

"Give me your address; I'll send you a check." She insisted.

"Why don't you just pass it on to someone else who needs it and ask them to do the same. Maybe we'll start something."

"She hurried into the store. I got my groceries, smiling at every person in the aisles, and sang as I drove. It's incredible how listening leads to kindness leads to joy."

Sonya took a deep breath and peered into my face with those fantastic eyes. "We see people's actions and then make judgments based on that little bit of evidence. We don't see the person inside who's in pain or struggling."

"But isn't that human nature? We make decisions based on appearances."

"That doesn't mean it's right," she said with conviction.

"But what about being so gullible that we get taken or cheated?" I asked, recalling a time that I'd helped a friend by loaning him the money he said he needed to get out of a jam. I never saw a dime in return. I was being patient and hadn't even mentioned the loan months later. You can imagine how stunned I was when he accused me of being angry with him for not paying and cut off all contact."

"That's a tough one. I'd like to think there's a difference between discernment and judgment. In discernment, we don't decide that people are bad or wrong; we just decide that maybe we don't want to do business with them or have them in our personal lives. I think it's possible to draw healthy boundaries for ourselves without necessarily making judgments about the other person."

"I'll try to keep a more open mind in the future when I see people who push my judgment buttons."

"If you don't do it on your own, the Universe has a way of helping you along!" She laughed. "Zemma, can I ask you a question? It's completely off the subject, and I hope you won't take offense."

Cautiously I replied, "Sure, you've been honest with me, so ask away."

"I know you said you were twelve, but you don't talk like any tween girl I've ever met. Why is that? I hope you don't think I'm making fun of you. I'm simply curious because you talk more like an adult than a kid."

I laughed, "Mostly, that's a compliment. The answer is simple. I spend most of my time with adults. My parents are archaeologists, and we travel all over the world. They are free-lance or contract rather than attached to any particular university. They're good at their jobs and are in high demand for their organizational skills and how they sometimes just seem to intuit where to dig. Rather than working the same dig for years, even decades, they get called in worldwide to work on tricky digs or when particular expertise is needed. This also means they don't have to teach or deal with university politics, which can be soul-crushing from all I've heard from their colleagues.

"Most of the time, I'm home-schooled and surrounded by my parents and their colleagues. I've probably spent less than two years all told in traditional schools. Because of my education and the fact that I'm not going to be anywhere long, I don't fit in. I don't 'hang out' with other girls my age much at all. They bore me."

She reached out and touched my arm, nodding. "That makes sense. Most of my life, I've been more comfortable with older people as well."

I realized I had been so intent on her story that I'd completely forgotten Joy. Where was she? I looked around wildly and spotted her sitting happily under a tree watching us. "Sonya, come on, I want you to meet someone."

Sonya smiled. I could tell by her bemused expression that she was wondering just how she'd not noticed Joy earlier. Joy wasn't usually at all inconspicuous. "What's her name?"

"Well, that's a good question. You can tell her what name fits her."

"What, she doesn't know her name?" said Sonya.

"She knows it, but she prefers to let each person she encounters call her the name that fits her."

"I've got to ask. Is your aunt crazy, a head case or something?"

"She seems less crazy than anyone I've ever met, but she goes by her own set of rules."

"Sounds confusing."

"More freeing. I'd never realized how stifling rules can be. If it makes you more comfortable, you can call her the 'Story Lady' until you know her better. I named her Joy." I felt a spurt of pride run through me because Joy was my aunt.

"Isn't that a defining term?"

"She likes it. It defines us together."

Joy smiled, welcoming us as we approached. "Zemma, you are so right. Join me under this tree. He's a quite lovely chestnut and has agreed to shade us for as long as we wish to stay."

"Um, the tree has agreed?" When would I stop questioning and start accepting?

"Yes, it's always polite to ask permission before disturbing anyone's peace and quiet. Please, sit down. I'm afraid I'm getting a kink in my neck from looking up at you." She patted the ground next to her.

Sonya sat beside Joy, and I plopped in front of them to watch both their faces more easily as they talked.

"Forgive me, my dear, I have to admit to eavesdropping while you and Zemma were chatting," Joy said to Sonya. "It's unusual to experience the instant karma you were describing. Do you have any idea what triggered it?"

"Triggered it. Hmmm, I hadn't thought about it. I don't know what started it. You think something did?"

"That's usually the case. The Universe only gives us lessons of this magnitude if we've made a specific request for knowledge or understanding."

Sonya looked thoughtful. "A few months ago, I was walking down the street and heard a little girl ask her mommy why that lady was so fat (meaning me). The woman answered, *Well, honey, she's fat because she's just a pig and eats and eats and just stuffs her face all day with pastries and candy. If you don't want to grow up like her, you've got to eat your veggies.* The little girl just accepted what her mother said. And I felt fat and ugly. It didn't matter that I'd carefully done my makeup and hair and that I was wearing an expensive and tasteful dress. I looked at the woman insulting me. Her hair carelessly pulled back into a ponytail; she wore baggy, colorless, slightly wrinkled clothing with a small rip in the hem of her T-shirt and untied shoelaces. She was the one who was calling me a pig! I made a statement that was more like a prayer at that moment. Please, don't ever let me make unfair judgments about people I don't even know. I believe that was the beginning of my instant karma."

"The world would be a kinder place if more people had your experiences," Joy smiled, patting Sonya's arm.

"When you see the error of your thoughts, it's nearly impossible to remain judgmental and closed-minded. But I must admit that I haven't been looking at this instant karma as a gift; it seemed more of a curse. It makes me feel guilty. I, of all people, should know better."

"Judgments are learned. We hear them from an early age. They come at us from all directions: our parents, television, books, movies, our peers, even social media. It's normal to absorb attitudes without being aware of it. Your request woke you up so that you almost instantly see the errors in your thinking and realign your viewpoint. You even take a little extra time to hear their story. You see a whole person and not just a stereotype. People are never one-dimensional. When we pay attention, we begin to see how much more they are than we initially thought." Joy took Sonya's hand.

"I sometimes wish that I could find a way to share this with other people," Sonya mused. "It's been mighty lonely for me. I see so much bigotry; it seems my heart will break. I don't share because I don't want to become what I've always resisted, an unwelcome preacher."

"You're assuming that what you have to say will be unwelcome."

"How would it be otherwise? I can't just start walking up to people and saying, 'Oh, by the way, do you know you're narrow-minded?' That could get me lynched!"

"Good point. There are ways that you can make a difference without making people wrong."

"I'm listening," Sonya leaned forward eagerly.

"I want to be extremely clear, Sonya. I can't tell you how to do this."

93

Deflated, Sonya sighed. "Oh. I was hoping you could help."

"I can help. I simply cannot tell you what you need to do. If you'd like, I can assist you in finding the answer for yourself."

I laughed. "Perpetually the woman of mystery. Do you ever give a straight answer?"

"Perhaps." Joy answered, provoking another round of laughter.

"Is this where you pull a magical charm off your belt?"

"Now, Zemma, not all situations call for magic. Most don't. Normally all that is needed is a sincere wish to know and a quiet, open mind." Smiling fondly at me, she turned to Sonya. "I feel confident that the answer you seek is not only close but one you've discarded many times. Don't take the time to think about your answer. I'm going to ask you a question in just a moment. Answer it by saying the first thing that comes to mind."

"Doesn't it make more sense to think about it before I open my big mouth?" Sonya blurted out.

"Nope. When you overthink, your critical, doubting self gets involved, filtering out your heart's answer. Close your eyes and clear your mind. Breathe and focus your senses on your heart."

Sonya closed her eyes. It was clear by her intense expression that she was trying extremely hard to follow directions.

"Don't try so hard. Just relax and breathe. It's not a test. You can't get it wrong. Yes, that's better. Just a little deeper. Nice. Feel how relaxed you are? Good. I'm going to ask a question, and I want you immediately to say the first thing that comes to mind. If money, training, and talent were no object, what would you most love to do?"

"Write!" Sonya's eyes popped open with surprise. "Write? Yes! No!" Everything in her seemed to puff with excitement and then entirely deflate.

"Where does the 'no' come from?" Joy asked.

"Well, writers have to be creative. They must have something to say. They need to have talent, perseverance, and money to support themselves while writing and then getting published. There are tens of thousands of flops for every successful writer; it's hard."

"So, you've given this some thought, have you?"

"Yes! Being a writer has been my dream for as long as I can remember. From the time I started reading books in grade school. I love being transported by the words and worlds of others. I wanted to write something meaningful."

"Why don't you?"

Sonya paused, deep in thought. "I had a teacher in high school who laughed when I shared my ambitions. I remember one day after class, Mr. Roberts opened his desk and showed me a stack of his manuscripts with an equally high stack of rejection letters. He explained how difficult the field was and how many failures there were; he took every chance he could all that year to discourage me. He counseled me to pay more attention to my bookkeeping and managerial classes and forget my silly dream."

"That's a sorrowful story, Sonya. All too often, disappointed people in life pass their discouragement on to others. I'm sure he meant well, but he has no idea the amount of damage he may have done to potentially talented writers. Did you do as he suggested?"

"Yes. I'm good at bookkeeping and organization. Those things always came easy for me, and they're relatively challenging. I've had a fairly good career and been lucky enough to work with some interesting people."

"But?"

"Something is missing. I used to be passionate about things. Not anymore. But you know, Joy, almost everyone I talk to feels that lack of passion. They may feel the drive to succeed, but that's not the same thing. They don't have any inner excitement and heartfelt intensity that comes when you know you're doing what you're here to do. It seems to be the human condition. I tell myself to be content and count my blessings. For the most part, I'm pretty happy with my life," said Sonya unconvincingly.

Joy looked intently at Sonya before speaking. "Sonya, Zemma and I have a story to tell you. I am sure that when we tell you our story, you'll have a better understanding of who and what your teacher was."

Joy explained our meeting with Justin. I shared my vision and our idea about the spread of the dead-eyed Unmakers and what they are doing to kill people's dreams and desires.

Sonya said, "I'd love to sluff this off as just a fanciful story. But I can't. I've felt the truth of this without a way to explain it. But how do we know it's the

Unmakers and not just normal?"

"What if I were to tell you that this lack of passion does seem to be the 'human condition,' but I don't think it's the norm, or that these blank-eyed Unmakers have existed throughout history. I am positive it isn't the way it has to be. Passion is our birthright! We deserve to do what we love! If more people were living out their dreams and fulfilling their deepest desires, there would be much more joy in the world."

"People can't just go around doing whatever they want!"

"Why not, Sonya?"

"There would be chaos."

"I'm not talking about anarchy. I am merely talking about a world where it's a priority to discover our deepest desires and talents, then find a way to put them into practice. With a little thought, creativity, and ability, you can fulfill almost any aspiration. If you don't find a way to turn it into a career, turn it into a hobby or even volunteer and share it with others. The important thing is to find a way to live your dream in some way. Sometimes it helps to start small and then work into doing it more. Zemma and I have concluded that it's important to all of humanity, not just your personal sense of fulfillment." Joy folded her hands in her lap.

I piped in. "Sonya, in my vision, I saw a way of pulling light into a web to connect people into a matrix. I believe the message is that we need to find and reawaken others like you. Then you spread the word and help others find their way back to themselves, and it continues."

"Zemma, that sounds a bit fanciful to me. How can my becoming a writer make a difference?"

I spoke passionately, "Sonya, each one of us makes a difference. We each touch the lives of many people, who inspire many others, and the cycle continues. I'm not talking about giant acts of heroism, but just living your life, staying connected, and living your passions and dreams. When you do that, you inspire others to do the same."

Joy jumped in. "Sonya, picture this. You're this little spark in the darkness, and as you write or do whatever you feel called to do, your spark grows brighter and brighter. You begin to light the way for others, and their souls catch fire, and the light spreads until large numbers of people have awakened and reconnected with themselves, the Universe, and All That Is. All because you nurtured your spark."

"Joy, I'm sorry, but that all sounds a little New Agey to me. I'm a practical woman; I don't go in for all that do-gooder, love, and light stuff. It sounds delusional."

Joy laughed, "I can see why you might think that. It's nearly impossible for me to find the words to explain the vision I see without using this kind of terminology. After all, I am talking about reawakening love and magic and keeping it alive. Think back to times in your life when you were down, and someone came along and shared something with you that got you excited again."

"Okay, Joy, I can see quite a few times when a teacher or even someone I just happened to meet did that for me. Even more often, though, it was something I read, a turn of phrase, or a concept that reached deep inside me. It's as if great books reached inside and awakened my sleeping heart. Sometimes the words did more than that; they inspired me to action or to search for even more," said Sonya with a tiny laugh of recognition.

Joy smiled and clapped her hands, "Exactly. Wouldn't you love to be an author that does that for another person?"

"Absolutely. But that's a long, difficult process. I've saved up some money, but it can take years to write a book. I wouldn't be able to support myself without working."

"Sonya, you don't have to wait until you have a book. Start with short stories. Hasn't some of your inspiration come from blogs or other things you've read that touched your soul?"

"Yes. I guess that could be a good way to get started. But even that takes a lot of time and effort! What about having a personal life, getting errands done. I can't fit it all in!"

"If your desire is strong, you'll find a way. Streamline your life, cut out all the busy little errands that seem so necessary. You'll be surprised by how many details can be changed to give you more time. Take the laundry as an example."

"I live in an apartment and go to the laundromat every week; it takes two hours out of my weekend, and it's so boring!"

"You have a couple of options here. Do laundry once a month. Move to an apartment with a washer and dryer in the unit. Keep doing laundry on your regular schedule like you always have but buy a laptop and take it with you where you can sit outside and write while the clothes spin."

"Once a month! I'd run out of towels and underwear!"

"Sonya, isn't it amazing how quickly the excuses pop in? Buy more undies and towels! Decide your priorities. Sometimes an extra investment that frees you from chores is well worth the cost. What about grocery shopping?"

"That's another thing on the list of tasks I dislike. It's not only the shopping but the lugging all that stuff up two flights of stairs. It takes a lot of time that I'd rather spend doing other things."

"I seem to have heard that you can order groceries over the Internet, and they deliver right to your door."

"Well, yes, but they charge for it."

"Again, it's about priorities and deciding if a simpler life is worth the extra cost. I am assuming you work a normal forty-hour, five-day workweek?"

"Yep, just like everyone else."

"Does the work you do require you to be there from 9 to 5 every single day? Could you do some of the work from your computer at home? Could you work four ten-hour days instead?"

Thoughtfully, Sonya responded. "I could work from home part of the time. I wonder if they'd go for a four-forty schedule. You know, I bet it would work. We have 'flex time' as it is, with everyone choosing his or her hours. Wow, three-day weekends, always! That would be amazing. I could have a day to devote to friends and errands if needed and still have a day or two for writing. If I got a laptop, I could even take it to the beach and not miss out on sunshine and fresh air." Sonya jumped up and twirled around. "Joy, I just know this will work!" Sonya plopped back down in front of Joy. Taking both of Joy's hands in hers, Sonya looked Joy straight in the eyes. "How can I ever thank you? You've given me my dream back!"

"You never lost it. You just buried it under someone else's disappointment. It's been there, nagging at you, poking, prodding, and striving to get your attention for years. I think you'll be surprised how much more satisfying you find all areas of your life once you start feeling more fulfilled in this one."

But delight left Sonya's eyes as quickly as it had arrived. "Oh no! I can't do it." A colossal sob split the air. Sonya covered her eyes with her hands.

"Why ever not?" said Joy as she reached over, pulling Sonya's hands down.

"I don't have any talent," Sonya mumbled. "I simply don't have any creative thoughts. When I try to make up a story, it always sounds so lame. Being a writer is for someone a lot more ingenious than I am!"

"Nonsense. In the past, it was always 'you' trying to do the writing. That 'you' is plagued with doubt and gets stuck in the worries of day-to-day life."

"Well, if 'I' am not doing it, then how else can 'I' do it? That doesn't make sense."

"It does when the 'you' is your mind. Your mind tends to doubt and worry. Try connecting with the 'you' that lives in your heart and leads through your heart to the Universe. That 'you' is broader and more expansive and isn't plagued by doubts, rules, and worries. That universal, heart-centered you can tap into a creativity that knows no bounds. I guarantee that if you can quiet your mind and write from the deeper place within you, you will have plenty to share and will be amazed at your creativity."

"How will I know if I'm writing from my head or my heart?"

"Oh, my dear, you'll know immediately. That which comes from your head will feel trite, stale, and forced. When you're writing from your heart, the words will flow, and you'll hardly be able to wait to see what happens next. You'll be *in* the adventure and find delight in the words you write. Your characters take on lives of their own and tell you what they are doing. If you read biographies of many great writers, you'll find that they describe their best works this way."

"I have always thought they were being modest."

"No, they are truthful. Real creative genius comes from that deeper space. Do you remember the writing assignments you had back at school? Weren't there some that seemed to flow effortlessly?"

"Yes! How can I ever thank you?" Sonya said softly, her voice choked and happy tears in her eyes.

"You already have! My passion in life is to be part of the awakening of passion in others. I have a feeling that as you write and share, you'll understand what I'm talking about. Keep in touch with us. We are beginning to build a team, a family, and as we grow, it'll be helpful to connect with the entire group. It's hard to stay strong alone when faced with the Unmakers, but we are exponentially stronger and more influential as a group. I don't know yet how this networked group is going to work; it'll have to evolve as we go."

"Joy and Zemma, I love that idea. It gives me more confidence to know that I won't be floating around alone, trying to hold onto these enormous ideas on my own. Reconnecting with you and meeting others would be such a blessing. I've always wanted a big family; maybe we can create a family of choice and purpose."

Joy was grinning widely. "Sonya, the idea of creating a family makes my whole body and soul smile. Maybe someday we'll even figure out what to call ourselves."

"Joy, do me a favor and don't make it sound too flakey. I don't want to be embarrassed or cringe when I say the name."

"No worries. Even though we have a huge purpose, I want to keep us grounded in reality…even if that reality is a bit farfetched and unusual for most to grasp at first," laughed Joy. "Let's all give it some thought and see what 'pops' into our heads!"

"That's a great idea. Knowing me, it'll be one of the 2 AM inspirations that tend to wake me out of a sound sleep with an 'ah-ha'!" She laughed ruefully.

Joy got a thoughtful look on her face and reached into her pocket. I watched with anticipation to see which of the hearts she was going to give to Sonya.

Joy held up a beautiful dark blue stone flecked with gold that caught the light. "Sonya, this Lapis Lazuli is an extraordinary stone for several reasons. Do I have permission to put it on you?"

"Joy, I'd be honored," said Sonya with tears glistening.

Joy put it over Sonya's head, then touched it to her third eye and throat before letting it hang just over her heart. It seemed to my eyes that Sonya straightened, got taller, and become somewhat regal.

"Let me explain the purposes for this heart pendant. Lapis Lazuli will help in your writing. It is a stone of truth that promotes honesty when speaking or writing. You may even find the right words as if by magic. It also opens your third eye allowing you greater ability to tap into your inspiration and creativity. The other beauty of this particular gem is that it helps you connect with the core of your self-confidence and brings forth the strength of remembrance of past lives in which you've been regal, a queen, empress, or the like. Did you feel how you straightened and grew taller, more in your body?"

"Yes, but I thought I imagined it."

"No, it's not giving you qualities that aren't already yours, but merely strengthening your ability to connect with the wise, strong, inspired woman within you. That's not the only purpose, however. I will give a gemstone to each who joins us. They are energetically connected and will help us to communicate through time and space. We'll be a 'Crystalline Heart Family.' It's a fitting name for our budding family to weave light into the world."

"Here's my card; I can save your contact information in my phone. I'll keep in touch and look forward to seeing you both again." Sonya stood slowly, hugged us both tightly, then started to sit down again, obviously undecided. Seeming to decide, she remained standing. "I don't want to seem ungrateful. I would love to stay here and talk to you longer. Zemma, I envy your journey with this woman. It would be great to have it be part of my destiny to join you, but I know it's not. My destiny involves a new laptop computer and a lot of writing."

Turning to Joy, she said, "I hope it's okay that I called you Joy as well. Zemma explained about each person choosing his or her name for you and calling you Joy. The moment I saw you, I couldn't imagine that any other name would be more fitting. You are, indeed, a bestower of joy. Thank you. If you'll excuse me, I must get to the computer store before it closes!"

Laughing and crying, she hugged us both more fiercely than before. Her resolve and excitement were apparent. Her eyes had a faraway look as if she knew what her future would be, and she saw the path distinctly.

CHAPTER 12:

Communication from the Other Side

Sunlight shone in through a window in the tent, waking me out of my restless sleep. I stretched, willing the blood to start flowing in my body once again. It was as if I'd spent the entire night thinking and worrying, running in endless circles. My mind was foggy and in pressing need of coffee. Wishing that I had preplanned the contents of my backpack to include at the very least some instant coffee, I resigned myself to a sleepy morning. Sighing, I opened the tent flap and stepped out into the bright sunshine.

Joy sat against the tree with a large steaming mug and a look of extreme satisfaction on her face.

"What's that you're drinking?" I asked, with a bit of hope creeping into my tone.

"Latté. Do you want one?"

"Latté? Correct me if I'm wrong, but I don't remember seeing a Starbucks anywhere nearby?"

"Silly girl, once again, you are asking the wrong questions."

"Uh-huh, then where did the coffee come from?" I asked, anticipating a fantastical answer that only Joy could give.

"Well, the beans came from Colombia."

"You know that's not what I meant!"

"Dear girl, you're going to have to learn to be more specific."

Exasperated, I decided it was too early in the morning to play games. "Okay, I'll bite. Where did you get your coffee? No, don't tell me! I know the answer to that question, the store. Right? Let me rephrase once again. There's only one answer I genuinely care about this morning. Do you have any coffee you'd be willing to share with me?"

"Would you like a cup?"

I am afraid I was unsuccessful in keeping the snarkiness out of my voice. "Yes, please. That would be lovely."

Joy laughed as she reached into one overly puffed sleeve and brought out a coffee pot. Then, reaching into the other puff, she pulled out a mug. I watched in amazement as she poured me a steaming latté.

I sat holding the cup, savoring its warmth, muttering a brief prayer of thanks to the beans, those who gathered, roasted, ground, brought them to the store, and all the other efforts to get this cup into my hands. I took a sip and looked up with a smile. "It's fabulous! How did you make it?"

"The old-fashioned way. I boiled water, poured it over coffee grounds in my French press, added steamed milk, which I heated over the fire, and voilà, morning coffee." Looking around wildly, I expected to see some kind of magical fire. I was chagrinned to discover a very average-looking campfire.

"I don't do everything by magic. Most things are just as easily accomplished the usual way. All it takes is a little planning. It's all about priorities once again. Good coffee is important to me; therefore, I provide for myself wherever I go. I'm never disappointed with campfire coffee."

"What else have you got up your sleeve?"

"I do like my surprises," she smiled as she sipped her coffee.

"And I wouldn't want to ruin your fun."

"And yours."

"Mine?"

Joy took a deep sip of coffee. "Don't you find yourself enjoying something unexpected now and then?"

"Yes, a predictable life would become boring. I don't expect that will be an issue if I continue traveling with you."

"If? Are you having second thoughts?"

"Not really.... But ..." I trailed off.

"But?"

"It was exciting seeing Sonya discover what seems to be her true-life purpose and how it fits in with our vision and mission. Gosh, just thinking of having a mission is pretty unbelievable. But how do I keep going after summer ends? Mom and Dad will come back from the Amazon jungle, and I'll go to school somewhere, or we'll go on another dig, and I'll learn from them. Shouldn't I figure out what I want to do with myself once I go out on my own? Sure, we have this overall purpose, but I still don't fully know how I fit into this and what my piece of the pattern will be." Suddenly I missed my parents and wondered what they were doing. Our more predictable adventures felt pretty good suddenly.

"Zemma, I don't know that a 'final' purpose exists. I like to think that our mission keeps unfolding and evolving as we go through life. A lucky few may have a complete vision of what they're to do, be, and have even from an early age. All of us are born with a soul's purpose we've chosen before birth, but not everyone has a path that is 'set.' There are options as we come into this life, and we get to improvise our way through."

"We choose?" I asked, feeling stupid.

"We choose. Before we're born, prior to incarnation, each soul sets distinct goals. Usually, these goals involve a specific task or purpose. Sometimes, however, the end goal may be decided, but there aren't any specific details about how to reach it. The soul may decide to be free to find its way during a lifetime, kind of 'winging it' as they go along."

"So, everything is not decided for us when we're born?"

"No. You have free will. You choose the goals which you feel to be important to your evolution. A few examples of such goals would be learning unconditional love, finding forgiveness, or clearing karma. One of the most challenging 'purposes' is choosing simply to 'be.' Individuals who take that path have all options open to them and sometimes sorely feel that lack of direction."

"Do you know what my goal or purpose is?"

"Don't yell at me when I say..." she said with a mock cringe.

"Oh, no! I know; you can't give me that answer! You honestly can't give me a hint? Please!"

"Nope. If you discover it on your own, you will then know it with your heart. What you experience with your heart is inordinately more powerful than the things you merely think," Joy explained. "Imagine that instead of having a vision of weaving patterns in the darkness, I just told you about it. Would it be the same? Would you even believe me?" Asked Joy softly.

"I get your point. But does everyone have to get that on their own, even though we have to overcome the darkness as soon as possible? Do we have to help each of them to have a vision? Weaving the light felt natural. All this feels complicated."

"It is complicated. But it'll unfold as we go, and you'll learn as you go. When you finally get it, I believe you'll be surprised at how much of a 'clue' you've always had about your purpose and how to help others learn. Ordinarily, your life purpose ends up fitting very closely with what's important to you. Some things are better when they've percolated a bit. Along the way, just ask for clarity."

"Clarity? From whom?"

"From yourself and the Universe," she said gently. "Don't look so sad. It's not that hard. You'll figure it out. You could even make a game out of it, like your own personal scavenger hunt. One clue leads you to the next until you've gathered all you need, and the picture becomes clear."

"Okay, I'll give it a try," I said.

"Zemma, not to change the subject, but I'll just bet you're ready for some breakfast. Want some scrambled eggs?"

"Wonderful! Do I need to negotiate with some hens?"

"No. I had a chat with some ducks who offered us some of their eggs. They've got all the ducklings they can handle and are more than willing to give us enough eggs for breakfast."

"Aunt Joy, that still seems weird to me."

"I struggled at first, too."

"You haven't always talked to animals?"

"Oh, heavens, no. I remember talking to them when I was a child and being made fun of, rather like you and your fairies. It wasn't long before I didn't hear them any longer."

"You hear them now. So, what changed?"

"I will tell you everything over eggs!" She went off to visit the ducks while I busied myself, adding more wood to the fire. I thanked the chestnut tree for his gracious contribution to our cause. He gifted me with a handful of chestnuts to roast and save for a snack later in the day. Breakfast with the large fresh eggs was ready in short order. We happily settled down over another cup of coffee and took a moment of gratitude for the food and all those who made it possible before digging in hungrily. There did seem to be something to this idea of asking permission and giving thanks, or perhaps it was just the fresh air and the incredibly fresh eggs. I swear those were the best eggs I've ever eaten.

Joy watched me eat. It was apparent she was getting a kick out of my visible appreciation. "So.... Talking with animals. It's funny; I had to think back for a bit because I don't often remember those dark years when I didn't hear the animals. I must have been about six years old when I lost fairies and couldn't see auras anymore. My world had become pretty colorless. Some children in especially restrictive environments lose theirs when they're even younger. Only a rare few manage to hold on past their first year in school."

"What's school got to do with it?"

"Well, most school these days is all about learning to think with your brain. That narrows the world and eliminates all the other ways we have of gathering information."

"What ways?" I wanted to know. Even though my parents wanted me to get a good education, I always felt more drawn to the three "Rs. It seems that archeologists dealing with artifacts and myths would have more of a mystical side. But to them, it was more about the science, history, and psychology of it.

Joy continued, "We gather information through all our senses. I always include the sixth sense because that's one of the most important yet much misunderstood and ignored. Regretfully, most have come to believe that only a select few have extrasensory abilities. Some don't give any credence to the possibility of a sixth sense.

She set her plate down. "We all have it to one degree or another. Some are simply more in touch with this sense, which frequently manifests as a gut feeling or an intuition about something. School is set up to work with definitive information gathered and processed by the left brain, like our civilization. We've moved away from giving credence to that which isn't verifiable. It seems only those things that are proven without a doubt are valued. The intuitive information processed by the right side of the brain has become suspect. School children quickly learn to fit in and survive and soon shut down a good deal of their intuitive abilities.

"I shut down too. The difference for me seemed to be that I had previously relied very strongly on my sixth sense, and now I felt cut off from who I was. Oh, mind you, I wouldn't have described it that way. I would have just told you I was sad. I was never noticeably, dangerously depressed, or suicidal, nothing like that. I was just a serious, studious, somewhat melancholy kid.

"Other than that, you'd say my school life was pretty average. My grades were good. I had friends and activities I enjoyed. Your mother was my older sister and best friend. I had a decent life.

"But then, our mother was diagnosed with cancer and went through six months of chemo and radiation when I was sixteen, and your mother was nineteen. And then she was gone. I ranted, raved, and screamed at the Universe but kept all that grief inside around my family. I didn't know how I could go on without her. And I refused to go to church. I'd dropped out years earlier after I heard one of the pastors stating that the way to God was through fear. That feels so wrong to me; I know it's through love. Because of this, I didn't have my pastor or other congregation members to call on, and there was no one able to help me understand my mother's death. I was furious and withdrawn.

"Your mother went off to college and never called or wrote. It didn't occur to me that she was dealing with her grief by shutting it out. Now I'd lost my best friend and my mom. Inconsolable, I was doing poorly in school, and my friends were avoiding me. I knew I was acting beastly, but I couldn't seem to pull myself out of it.

"One night, I took a long walk on the beach. Under the light of a full moon, I screamed, cried, and pounded the sand. I ranted and railed at the

Universe, God, Goddess, everyone who had ever lived, hating them all. I was pure emotion erupting without cessation until nothing remained. I collapsed onto the cold, damp sand and cried for my mother.

"Zemma, she answered me. At first, I thought I was hearing things, but I heard her voice, and then I could see her beside me. She calmly assured me that she was real and had never left my side. We had a long discussion about death and suffering. She told me that, yes, her illness and treatment had been painful, but they'd brought her many gifts. That made no sense to me! But she said:

Darling, I didn't understand at the time either. It's only now, from this higher perspective, that I see what I gained. I was always enormously proud. I was determined to do everything for myself, to need no one, to prove I was strong and capable. During my illness, I was forced to ask for and accept help from many people. I needed help from practically everyone. I'd always thought that asking for help was a sign of weakness. Instead, I learned it allows others to feel strong, needed, to be loving and compassionate. I was so bent on being the strong one; I had robbed my loved ones of the opportunity to be there for me.

I learned to accept love. It wasn't that I hadn't felt loved; I had not been able to let go and receive unconditional love. I discovered there are times it's more loving to receive than to give. Funny, we've heard that saying about it being more blessed to give than receive, and I'd believed it wholeheartedly. I don't know who thought that up, but they are so very wrong. Hold on, don't get the wrong idea. It's NOT okay to stop giving and become a taker. That's not what I mean. If you never allow yourself to receive, you deprive others of the joy of giving and being accepted. Sadly, it took dying to bring me to a place where I could finally let down my guard and welcome the love. It was worth it!

Forget all the stuff I taught you about being strong and independent. Well, not all of it. Find a balance between that and a more receptive place. Let people into your heart. It's safe. You'll be doing yourself and the others a favor.

There is one more thing I want to say before I leave. Death is not the end. It is a new beginning of an existence that is vastly more beautiful than the heaven described in the Bible. It is a merging with all the love that is. The biggest surprise is what I want to share with you. You don't have to wait until you die to perceive that beautiful state of being. You can feel this incredible love while you are still in your human body.

"Well, Zemma, I was as confused as you feel sometimes. I couldn't believe I was choosing to suffer. Or that I could choose to shift my ideas, or that I could tap into universal consciousness and understand while I was alive! She told me I could open to love as she had, but without dying. Well, the world seemed like such a hard place that all I could think of was that she wanted me to see everything through rose-colored glasses! She said the lenses weren't lies but cleared the way to see the truth, the whole picture, and all my angst would no longer be necessary. She taught me all I needed to do was:

Ask for help. Each time you find yourself feeling pain or negativity, ask the Universe to help you see more clearly. Be open to how that awareness may show up. The Universe has myriad ways of helping you if you are open and pay attention. You may find yourself struggling with something. After requesting assistance, you'll turn on the television, and there will be a program that directly or often indirectly addresses the issue. The book you read, the conversation you overhear, the joke you get in your email, all these things can shed new light on a subject. If you want additional confirmation that you're getting the message right, pay attention to the patterns. You'll frequently find that the same message comes from three or more varied sources in a short time. The ways of the Universe are many and can be extremely creative. If you acknowledge the insights and give thanks and keep asking for more, you'll discover your life starts transforming in multitudinous ways.

"And she was right! It is simple, but it's certainly not always easy. You're finding that out, Zemma. You must be willing to see your shadows, release them, and forgive yourself. The process can become excruciating, and you'll wish you could go back to being less aware. But there is no going back; you'd be miserable if you tried. She told me she had found such joy! That she'd found a new form of life that far transcends the limited experience she knew while in her body. She said passionately: *Darling, don't wait until you are dead to know this space. Do what it takes. Be here now! Allow the love in now!* And then she was gone."

Joy paused, gathering herself from those memories, and then continued.

"I sat for a long time watching the place where she had been. I felt at peace; no more anger and grief overwhelming me. I was no longer drowning. I sensed there were still many demons to be faced. But I had been given a glimpse into possibilities I'd never imagined. I felt that life was good again." Joy's powerful voice floated toward me.

We sat silent for a few moments. Then I said, "It's nice to know that once upon a time, you were a screwed-up, angry kid, too. It gives me more hope for myself. How did you get to where you are now?"

"I kept asking the Universe for help and clarity, Zemma. Soon, the veils fell away. I was perceiving many layers of existence and seeing fairies again. My world expanded because I was ready. I won't pretend it was all easy sailing or that I figured things out right away. Sometimes I had to be almost literally hit over the head with a two-by-four before I'd pay attention. If I still weren't aware, there'd be the huge Mack truck of a big life lesson barreling down on me. For a little while, life moved between extreme highs and dismal lows. When those down times came, I'd remember my mother's advice and start asking for help and clarity again. At times I even heard her voice. If I kept my perceptions open and remained willing to do the work, the help and insights I needed to move up out of the swamps always seemed there."

"What work?" I asked.

"The shadows I mentioned are where the work comes in. I needed to be willing to face my faults, make changes in myself, my attitudes, and drop my unconscious knee-jerk reactions. I had to make amends for hurts I'd caused in the past. I'd approach each one of these tasks shaking in my boots. Desperation and determination kept me going. Sometimes it was me I needed to forgive. With each completed task or transformation, I was lighter, happier, and more peaceful."

"I don't know if I'm ready for all that. Isn't there like a halfway path that one can walk, one where you'll eventually get there, but the process is easier?"

"Of course. Each one of us chooses our level of commitment."

"Phew, I was getting worried there for a minute!" Joy lightly put her arms around me. I felt the love, and deep in my heart, I desperately desired to be just as light, loving, and joyful. My spine straightened in resolve; I hugged Joy tightly and stood up, my body tingling. I felt about ready to burst.

Spreading my arms wide, I closed my eyes and turned round and round. As I twirled, it felt as though all my cares and worries streamed out the ends of my fingers. I opened my eyes, amazed to see rainbows of colors flying out of my fingers. I waved my hands overhead and all around. I pretended I was playing with Fourth of July sparklers, writing things in the air. I marveled at the designs that hung in the air before dissolving.

Joy joined in the fun. Initially, we took turns creating our designs. We spontaneously began doing mirror images of the same patterns, hearts, stars, arches, spirals, loops, and whirls. The combinations were breathtakingly beautiful, and each seemed to linger in the air longer than the last.

We progressed from random images to creating a vast landscape, including mountains, valleys, sunny skies, talking trees, quaint houses, smiling people, singing birds, various animals, jumping trout, and a vast rainbow spanning all. When I moved back to look at our handiwork, the light that seemed to glow and pulse within the scene struck me. Watching for a few moments, I began to perceive movement. I laughed inwardly, assuring myself it was probably a light breeze dispersing our artwork.

My skepticism died when I realized that the birds, people, and other animals were heading in the same direction. They were going down a pathway and up over the hill. The glowing light where the path led called me. I had the feeling that light was inexorably drawing us forward. I wanted to go with these rainbow creatures.

I'd never felt as strong a pull in my life. But I couldn't move and stopped twirling. Soon, every iota of the scene had dispersed in the breeze.

"Zemma, you look like you've seen a ghost. Are you okay?" Joy asked.

I nodded, squaring my shoulders and standing just a bit more upright. "I have no idea where that place was or what was creating the light at the end of the path. I know that reaching it is my destiny. Joy, what does that mean?"

"Ah, so you've seen it?"

"It?" Zemma said

"Yes. I call it the Land of Dawn. I don't know if it has another name or if it exists as a real physical place. It may be a symbol, an inspiration, or a reminder of the energy of love and peace within. But I don't know."

"How can we find out if it's real? Who can we ask?"

"Just Trust for now. Whether this is a real place that can eventually be reached or merely a way of inner being, I, too, long to go there. I believe ultimately, in whatever form, it is my destiny as well. I've met others who have envisioned it; we all have similar reactions. When we finally arrive, we'll be in some particularly marvelous company."

"If you are there, the company will be exceptional." Even though I still had no answers, I sat back against a tree for the moment, content and dreamy.

Joy suggested that it might be helpful to stay put and not pack up and move on. I heartily agreed. So much had been happening; it would be a relief to go to bed knowing I'd wake up in familiar surroundings.

CHAPTER 13:

Donkey Games, Hoopla & Being Manly

Morning dawned bright and crisp. I bounded out of the tent, ready for whatever was to come. It was going to be another incredible day.

Joy was calmly sipping coffee beneath our friendly chestnut tree. We shared a cup in silence while coordinating our efforts to make breakfast of scrambled eggs sprinkled with jerky from the depths of my backpack. We cleaned up the dishes, and Joy carefully stowed everything in her sleeves, pockets, and under her skirts. The tent reverted to its former life as an overskirt. Our blankets and mattresses wound around her waist, looking once again like silk scarves. Our campsite disappeared, and the meadow looked as if we'd never been there. Satisfied that we'd returned the land to its original state, we turned with anticipation to the trail ahead.

We walked quickly, our strides long and swinging. Never one to go slowly, I relished the freedom of movement. We easily kept pace with each other. I didn't feel hurried or rushed, but something was propelling me on.

We topped a high hill and met with mystifying sounds. Screaming? Crying? Laughing? Fighting? I was baffled. I knew for sure that it was loud and seemed to involve several men and one or more donkeys. We ran to get a better look at the commotion.

As we got closer, we were able to make a little sense of things. There was a donkey with wooden pack-boxes affixed to either side of a colorful blanket standing in the middle of great confusion. The donkey's mane and tail were braided and embellished with colorful beads. He wore a wildly colored fringed sombrero. I'm sure it would have flown off if not tied under his chin. He was twisting and turning in all directions, like a spinning top.

Men were circling him with ropes, taking turns struggling, unsuccessfully, to get a lasso over his head. How did they expect the line to go over the sombrero? One of them appeared to realize the problem and started throwing the lasso at the donkey's feet instead, again without success. The whole process looked like a scene out of a cartoon. I completely cracked up.

That probably wasn't the smartest response. The men appeared to think I was laughing at them. Well, now that you mention it, I guess I was. A couple of them started menacingly towards me, turning away from the donkey and the turbulence.

"So, you think this is funny, do you? Well, you've got another think coming." He said, brandishing his lasso like a weapon.

My heart was in my throat. Should I start running? Unfortunately, prudence has never been one of my strong suits. Nerves, combined with the absurdly funny scene, got the better of my judgment, and I started laughing even louder. I admit there was a touch of hysteria mixed in, but try as I might, I could not stop myself,

The man got closer. I was gasping for air. I couldn't seem to stop, despite my attempts to get myself under control. The man stomped up to me until we were nose to nose. "Universe, help me!" I thought as I laughed helplessly in his face. He looked dangerously angry and unbelievably mean, never a good combination, especially when he was twice my size and armed.

I knew I should stop laughing, just stop. I was positive that he was going to beat the heck out of me. He turned around and looked behind at the commotion, and he broke down in laughter. We were laughing, slapping each other on the back, hee-hawing like crazy people. Hearing us, the other men turned our way angrily. One by one, they cracked up. Joy, seven strange men, and I all stood on the side of the road laughing our heads off, hiccupping and slapping our knees.

The donkey kept jumping and twisting around for a while longer. Then it seemed to dawn on him that there was nothing to fight. I swear that when he stopped, his expression was bemused and perhaps even a little disappointed.

Without meaning to, I spoke my thoughts aloud. "I'll be darned if that crazy donkey doesn't look disappointed that there's no fight."

The first man spoke up. "He is! He loves to fight! I think he lives to give us a good struggle."

"Is this a common occurrence?"

"Oh, sure. We make several trips a day, and each time when we get about here, he gets fed up with carrying everything and starts throwing a tantrum."

"If this happens a lot, it seems like you'd figure out a way to deal with him."

"We have! Finally, someone gets a rope on the donkey, and he quiets down and stops resisting. We go back to walking along peacefully until we get back to the stable and unload."

"It would seem there might be some more creative ways to calm him down." I looked around for Joy, hoping that she would back me up and even provide some new thoughts to the situation. She was standing on a rise, just staring at us, appearing to be thoroughly enjoying herself. Deducing that I was on my own, I plunged ahead. "Have you tried throwing cold water on him?"

"Yep, and that stops him right away."

"Then…why don't you do it every time?" I paused mid-sentence to reign in my sarcasm. I figured there was no sense in generating animosity when severely outnumbered.

"Well, where would be the fun in that? All this excitement breaks up the monotony."

"Ah, I see, I think." Still puzzled. "You enjoy running around, throwing lassos, getting knocked around, and making a scene?"

"Yeah, that's about it. See, we're not really crazy. We put in a full day of work, and mostly it's decidedly boring and routine. As we see it, a little excitement is a good thing."

"You do this several times a day? Aren't you exhausted by the last trip?"

"Nah. We're tired, but all the hoopla gets our blood going again. When we walk in the door at home, we're glowing from all the exercise, and we look manly to our women. If you know what I mean." He winked.

I couldn't believe it; he winked at me. I turned to see the others nodding their heads, grinning foolishly. I howled with laughter as they gathered around, slapping me on the back.

I watched in wonder as they strolled down the road with a now-well-behaved docile donkey.

"Zemma, aren't you glad you talked to those men and heard their stories? You could have watched the entire operation and deduced they were just ignorant and inept. You may have even decided that perhaps they mistreated the donkey or that his pack boxes were hurting him. In that case, you may have even gone running in to 'save' him."

"I was close to doing just that. The rescuer in me was sure the men were cruel to that poor donkey and that he was simply fighting back. I could never have imagined that it was a game if I hadn't talked to the men. What an inventive way to work off a little frustration; and have some fun in the process. I'm impressed."

I paused to think for a moment. "I'm dumbfounded that the men admitted it was a game to a stranger. Most guys I know would never own up to it... not only that, but they most likely wouldn't even recognize it as a game or why they were playing it. They would have continued pretending, even to themselves, that they were fighting a bad-tempered stubborn donkey."

"I know what you mean. Many people fight the same battle continually, with little change from day to day, even year to year. Sometimes the people or circumstances change, but the essence remains the same. You'd think they'd wise up and admit that they like it or change their tactics so that they aren't constantly fighting the same battle ad nauseam, but they don't. If you sit back and watch the process long enough, you can only conclude that somehow they get some satisfaction or confirmation out of the process."

"If I ever do that, I hope someone will do me a favor and put me out of my misery."

"That sounds a little extreme for the circumstances. Instead, why not ask them to give you a swift kick."

"Yeah, thanks. I'm sure I'd end up with a sore backside fairly often." We walked, tittering softly to ourselves as scenes of the play we'd just witnessed reran in our minds.

Joy turned to me, "Zemma, what else does this story make you think of?"

I kept walking and thinking for several minutes. "There doesn't seem to be a purpose behind it, but I think it's their way of not getting dragged down by the monotony of a job that probably doesn't hold many challenges for them. They've found a unique way to keep the passion and spirit alive in their lives."

"That's my thought exactly. The world needs people who are willing to do some of the less glamorous or seemingly unsatisfying jobs, but too often, they can get mired in resentment and despair. These men have learned to find enjoyment and camaraderie. And you know, they also add a little excitement for those they meet along the way! I think it's their unique way of fighting off the Unmaker and spreading pleasure as they go."

"Joy, while that's all true, a good lunch would bring me a lot of pleasure. I'm starving, and I think we're almost to the town."

CHAPTER 14:

Doubt Kills Dragons

Although I hadn't been going hungry by any means, and Joy's a good cook, something is gratifying about sitting down and ordering a meal at leisure. I admit it's nice to have someone clean up afterward, too.

A man came to take our orders. He was so shy he could barely look at us. I was curious about how he managed to do his job and remain so bashful and withdrawn. His mousy brown hair hung limply almost to his shoulders, jaggedly cut, giving the impression he'd done it himself. He was thin, too thin, shoulder blades pushing against his sagging uniform. Was he ill? I wondered. Looking closely, I didn't see any signs of actual illness, but instead, he appeared scared. I wondered what that was about.

He still hadn't made eye contact when we finished giving him our orders. Joy stopped him, placing her hand on his arm as he turned away from us to take our order to the kitchen.

"Yes, Ma'am, was there something else?" he asked very softly, still not looking at us.

"Yes, there is. We are new in town and would like to make some friends and explore the area. You seem like a nice person. Could we prevail upon you to show us around after your shift?"

"Me?"

"Yes, you're the first person we've met. I would be delighted to see this town through your eyes. That's normally much more interesting than being a tourist and seeing nothing but what's in the Chamber of Commerce's brochure. If you're too busy or have other plans, we'll understand."

"Other plans? Hardly, unless you count going home, staring at four walls."

"Well, good then. What time do you get off?"

"I'm done at three."

"Lovely. We'll have our lunch and wander around a bit and come back and meet you here at three."

"Okay," he said a little reluctantly, as he practically ran back to the kitchen with our orders.

I leaned over, whispering, "Joy, are you sure this is a good idea? He can't even bear to look at us! He can't be much of a companion."

"Zemma, it's not about him being a companion to us. It's about us being one to him. I believe he is a man with a story and some deeply buried dreams."

"Oh, great, now I'm a rescuer?" I watched our soon-to-be new friend as he went about his work. He seemed younger than me in many ways, and yet his hair was graying at the temples. I took a closer look, realizing he had to be older than either of my parents, and they were in their mid-forties!

Lunch arrived, steaming and fragrant. We'd both ordered chicken stew and dug in after thanking all those who'd helped it come to our bowls! Nonetheless, I fumed through our meal and refused to talk to Joy. What could she possibly be thinking? Our server didn't look like he could be interesting at all. Besides, if he couldn't even look at us, what kind of a guide could he be, anyway? I bet he doesn't know his way around town at all. He's probably one of those loners who sit at home with a cat, reading books, watching television, or playing online role-playing games, only going out to work before he hurries back home. Boy, this was going to be a lively afternoon.

While I ranted and raved to myself, I heard a small voice in the back of my head reminding me about making judgments based on appearances. I ignored it, unable to snap out of my gloomy thoughts.

We had just under two hours before our newfound 'friend's' shift would be over. We wandered into a music store. To pass the time, I asked if we could listen to some of the CDs. I decided to play the synchronicity game, close my eyes, pick something, and play it without looking first. I'd been doing this for years with music and books. I'd select something at random and either play a song or open to a page and read. I still found myself pleasantly surprised at the frequency of the relevance of these chance choices. More often than not, I'd get an answer or response to a question I'd been mulling over. Sometimes, much to my chagrin, I'd see my patterns showing prominently before me. I shook my head as I realized how closely this fit with Joy's theories of how the world works.

Looking for a diversion from my dark thoughts, I popped in my first random choice. I couldn't get that song out of the CD player and back into its jewel case quickly enough. It had been about green-eyed jealousy. I felt like something had hit me between my eyes. I wasn't jealous, was I? I took a deep breath and forcefully let it out, willing myself to release my negative feelings with it.

Joy came up and put her arm around me. "It's okay, Zemma. You'll learn to play nice and share."

"You knew?"

"You don't honestly think you were being circumspect, keeping your feelings to yourself, do you? My goodness, you were broadcasting your distress to anyone who was around."

"But what right do I have to be jealous? That's uncharitable. I know better."

"Yes, but the little kid in all of us jumps up from time to time. You've met yours, and she can be a bit of a green-eyed monster."

Embarrassed at my bad attitude and transparency, I moved on down the row. Once again, I popped open a disk at random and hit the play button. Entranced, I listened to a favorite song from my childhood, *Jeff the Magic Dragon* [Appendix B]. My mother used to play that on the stereo when I was little. Peter, Paul, and Mary sang in cheerful, familiar harmony. Tapping my toes, I hummed along to the music. I played the song over twice as I watched a mini-movie in my head of the little boy, Jackie Pepper, and his magic dragon. I used to cry with the dragon when Jackie left him for older boy's games. I wondered if the boy ever missed Jeff or regretted having forsaken his childhood friend.

I randomly played several other CDs. All the songs seemed to be about re-finding lost love, second chances, or forgiveness. Unlike jealousy, nothing seemed to fit my life. I quickly deduced that I must be off my game, wasting time.

In disgust, I turned away and motioned to Joy that I was going outside. I half expected her to follow me out directly and point out what a brat I was being. Instead, I had to cool my heels for a good ten minutes. My thoughts were seething and mostly turned in on myself.

"Zelia Maria Magdalena, get a grip on yourself! Knock off this childish behavior!" Oh gee, I seemed to have regressed even more. I could hear my mother's voice inside my head telling me to quit pouting and to come out and play nice. Well, I didn't want to play nice. I didn't want to share! Why am I acting like such a brat? Am I afraid that Joy will like him better and won't be friends with me anymore? Yeah, and I sound like a two-year-old. Come to think of it, I feel like a two-year-old gripping a toy! I found her first!! The idiocy of it hit me like a ton of bricks, and I started to laugh inwardly at myself. Eventually, I started laughing out loud.

I wound down to a chuckle when I realized Joy was sitting on the bench with me. My mother would never have missed this golden opportunity to point out my shortcomings. I braced myself for Joy to say something about my conduct; she just smiled.

"It's almost time to go to meet our new friend. Shall we?"

"Yeah, that would be fine." As I said the words, I knew I was ready to play nice.

Our waiter stepped out onto the sidewalk as we returned to the restaurant. He looked down at the ground, shyly looking up through eyelashes to greet us.

"I'm so pleased you can join us this afternoon. You may call me Joy for now, and this young lady is Zemma," she said, pointing at me.

He looked up sharply. "Joy, for now? Will I call you something else later?"

"Perhaps. I go by many names. We've only been to the music store and the restaurant. That's all we've seen of your town so far. However, we did meet a group of men and a donkey on the way in. They were making quite a ruckus. Do you know them?"

Laughing, he looked up. "Oh, dear, I hope you don't think the entire town is as ridiculous as those men. It seems that after all these years, they'd figure out a better way of calming that crazy donkey down or replace him with a donkey that is better behaved."

I jumped in quickly, explaining our discussion with the men. Our companion shook his head bemusedly. "Well, that's one of the silliest stories

I've ever heard. Huh, who would have thought?"

"What's your name?" I prodded.

"Jackie. Jackie Pepper."

"Jackie Pepper as in *Jeff the Magic Dragon*?" I laughed despite my resolve to be on good behavior. "I'm sorry. That was rude of me. I shouldn't laugh. I'm sure you've heard that lots of times. You can't help it if you had the misfortune to be given the same name as a boy in a song."

"To be honest, if you hadn't laughed, I'd have thought you were phony."

I was beginning to like this guy. I glanced at Joy, and she raised her eyebrows at me in an I-told-you-so way. "Can you tell us what's fun or interesting around here?"

Scratching his chin, he mused, "Fun or interesting? Gosh, I haven't thought it was either of those things for many years. It's a boring town these days. You've got your basic few restaurants, gas stations, grocery stores, a bar or two, a library, schools. Heck, even the red-light district only has one light. There's not much happening in Honah Lee."

"Honah Lee?" I yelped.

"That's not the official name, but that's what we've always called ourselves. It's more of a nickname."

"Honah Lee? Unbelievable! We're in Honah Lee, talking to a guy named Jackie Pepper?"

"Yep, that pretty much sums it up."

"Alright, Jackie, my friend. You've got to level with me. What's going on here? Coincidence? Do you have nutso parents? A town with a strange sense of humor?" I was laughing. The whole thing was absurd. Jackie was turning red.

Joy watched him thoughtfully. "Jackie, why don't we go sit under that tree and talk." She pointed across the street to a welcoming shade tree that I swear was stretching its branches to us.

"It's been a long time since I had to explain all this to outsiders." By the time we got settled, Jackie had turned shy again. He looked down and picked at his cuticles. Judging from the state of his manicure, he was an extremely nervous man.

I couldn't stand the tense silence any longer. "So, what's the story?!"

"Hey, when I finish telling you this, if you don't want to hang out with me any longer, I'll completely understand. Not many people do. They kind of think I'm crazy around here. And if they don't think I'm nuts, they think I'm slow-witted."

Joy leaned in closer and asked, gently, "So do you think you're crazy?"

"No! But I can see how people might get that idea. Most people don't believe in anything they haven't seen with their own eyes."

"And you do?"

"Well, I don't know if I do or not. That would be hard to say. Because the truth is, I DID SEE Jeff."

"What?" I croaked. "You're telling me that song is a real story…about you?"

"Yep, it's pretty much the way it was."

"So how did Peter, Paul, and Mary find out about it?"

"Oh, Peter lived here and was in a class a couple of years ahead of me. I mean, it wasn't like I was friends with him or anything. He heard the story because some kids were making fun of me. He asked me about it, and a couple of years later, he wrote a song and made us famous."

"Okay, I'm following you so far."

"I was kind of a dork when I was younger and didn't have a lot of friends. Gee, not much has changed, I suppose. I spent a lot of time by the ocean, pretending I was a pirate. I got bored with pirate games after a while and decided that what I needed was a playmate. Now you'd think I'd invent another boy, but see, I didn't have much luck with other kids and wasn't sure even an imaginary child would be my friend.

"I was feeling down. The other kids had been teasing me. Four-eyes! Pencil legs! And a bunch of other stuff. I went to the beach, wishing I had a big brother who would protect me. That got me thinking about how cool it would be to have a fire-breathing dragon who could scare off the mean kids, but who would be my best friend, like in the stories I'd been reading. No one would give me any crap! Oops, sorry."

Joy patted his hand, and he kept going. "I began pretending that there was a real dragon, and his name was Jeff. I'd run around on the beach, making believe Jeff and I were playing tag. I even conjured up a country of my own, Honah Lee. Jeff and I were the only ones who lived there. We had no school, no chores, nothing to do but have fun. We fought pirates and entertained kings and their whole families and courts when they sailed by."

"After a few weeks of pretending, a strange thing began to happen. I began seeing him. He was kind of misty and ghostlike to start with, but after a week or so, he was as real as you and me! I could touch him and even climb on his back. Honestly, I'm not making this up. I could talk to him, and he also spoke to me. He was real, and I was in heaven; Jeff was the best friend I ever had. I was at the beach with my friend, Jeff, every spare moment I had. We did things just like in the song. At least Peter got that part of the story right when he decided to turn it into a song."

Joy looked kindly at Jackie. "Did he get the whole story right?"

"Maybe. I honestly don't know what happened to Jeff."

"What happened to you?"

"Jeff and I were the best of buddies for years. I've never had such a good friend. When I was eleven, going out for sports was mandatory. In gym class, we were supposed to sign up for one of the teams. I didn't. In front of the entire room, the teacher called on me to explain. I told him I had something imperative I had to do after school every day. When he pushed, I told him I had to feed my dragon. Well, as you can guess, that created quite an uproar. I was laughed right out of class. Everywhere I went for the rest of the day, kids teased me, telling me what a loser I was. That wasn't anything new. I could handle it. I knew I had Jeff, and he didn't think I was a loser.

"They got ruthless, yelling that dragons don't exist and making the 'crazy' gesture rolling their eyes and twirling their fingers on the side of their heads. I was in tears and hid in one of the restroom stalls until I could calm down.

"The school counselor called me to her office and started talking in a very calm, condescending voice. *Jackie, you are a bright boy. Surely you don't think you have a real dragon.*

"I tried to argue, but she said, *We don't tolerate lying in this school! I'm sending you to the principal's office.*

"Both the principal and the vice-principal told me I was either crazy or a liar. They threatened to send a note to my parents if I persisted in telling this fanciful story. So, I pretended I agreed with them, but I went to the library, frantic to find proof that dragons existed. I asked the librarian for help finding some books. To my horror, every single book I opened described dragons as mythological creatures. I ran out of school and didn't stop running until I got to the beach. I had to see if everyone else was right. What if I'd been just making him up all this time?

"I called and called. Jeff didn't come; I went back to our beach every day for weeks. No, Jeff. Maybe he *was* just my imagination. But I miss him."

"What a sad story!" I said. "But in the song, they say it was you who abandoned Jeff."

"That's the only part Peter got wrong. I guess it made for a better story. Jeff will forever remain the greatest mystery of my life."

"Not necessarily," said Joy with a special twinkle in her eye. "Let's go down to the beach so you can show us where the land of Honah Lee used to be and where you and Jeff played."

"Really? Do you honestly want to go? There won't be anything to see except an empty beach."

"We'll see," said Joy as she practically bounced toward the beach.

As we walked, Joy and I took turns telling Jackie about some of our adventures. He laughed as we told him about talking trees and fish, fairies, the woman who becomes a hippo, magic wand gardens, and several other tales of our adventures. Joy took great pains to let him know that we both see and hear things that most people would say don't exist. She made it clear that she believed there was much more to this world than most are aware of or ready to admit even to themselves.

Jackie was more relaxed by the time we arrived at the beach. Joy got him talking, sharing the places where he and Jeff had their adventures. With only a little prodding, Jackie began to regale us with some of their stories. His eyes shone as he talked, and he looked happy, no longer the bashful man we'd met.

I enjoyed the afternoon, but in all honesty, after a while, I began to get a little bit bored with fantasies of a magical dragon who probably never existed. There was a difference between the talking trees and fairies we had seen and Jackie Pepper's lonely childhood memories. Joy, on the other hand, couldn't seem to get enough of Jackie's stories. I suspected her attention and 'what ifs' may have even prompted him to make up a few new stories.

The sun was getting low, not quite to the horizon, but hovering in that place that creates long shadows and turns everything a warm, golden color. I've always thought that to be the most magical time of the day, especially at the beach when nearly anything is possible.

Seagulls flew around a bend in the beach, squawking as if something were chasing them. And then it happened….

There was a mighty roar! Around the bend came Jeff! He was magnificent, about twenty feet tall with green scales on his body, iridescent rainbow-colored wings, and huge golden eyes. He breathed out a puff of fire.

Jackie stared with his mouth hanging open. Jeff looked at him and roared again. His entire colossal body shook, causing the ground to vibrate. The shaking seemed to jar Jackie out of his stupor. He ran to Jeff and threw his arms around the leg of this huge dragon! Jeff reached out a front paw and patted a sobbing Jackie on the back.

Jackie collected himself about five minutes later and stepped back, grabbing Jeff's paw. Turning to Joy and me, "I'd like to introduce you to Jeff."

We went up and shook Jeff's scaly paw. Jeff said, "Nice to meet you both. Would you like to come for tea?"

"Certainly," replied Joy, as though talking to dragons was an everyday occurrence. Knowing Joy, perhaps it was. I felt a little embarrassed that I'd doubted her. We followed Jeff around the bend to a cave set back under the cliff. Jackie was a gracious host, pouring tea out of a china tea set he'd saved from his earlier days with Jackie.

The hot tea revived Jackie somewhat. He looked at Jeff and asked the question I'd been dying to ask. "Where did you go? Why didn't you come when I called you?"

Jeff sighed. "Jackie, I came. I was right here all the time. But you couldn't see or hear me, no matter how hard I tried. I don't know why. You'd stand day after day calling and calling brokenheartedly. I would run and jump and romp in the waves. I'd even roar right in your face, and you didn't hear or see me. I've missed you so much; you're the only friend I've ever had. It's been so lonely without you."

"No, Jeff, you weren't here! I don't understand!" Tears of frustration and confusion sprang into Jackie's eyes.

Joy spoke softly. "Perhaps I can explain. Jeff does exist. But, and here's the critical part. He doesn't usually live on this plane of existence. All planets have various dimensions, or parallel realities, in which life has evolved differently. Jackie, all those years ago, when you 'invented' Jeff, you were using your imagination to open your senses. You didn't make Jeff up; you tapped into an alternate reality where Jeff was real. By continuing to 'pretend' he was present, he was eventually able to manifest here and become real in this reality, but only to your eyes."

"Why did he leave?"

"He didn't leave. You did."

"No, I was here, calling and calling!"

"Yes, that's true. But you didn't believe anymore after having so much 'proof' that he wasn't real. To see Jeff here through the veils that separate the worlds, you had to know in your heart that he existed. Once your knowing was in doubt, you were no longer able to see your friend. It must have been terrible to have felt that he abandoned you."

"Yes, it was the worst!" Jeff and Jackie both cried.

"I don't think you'll ever leave each other again."

"NO!" They yelled together.

We were all laughing and crying. Joy and I excused ourselves and left Jeff and Jackie alone to reminisce.

The following morning, Joy and I stopped by the restaurant for breakfast before going on our way.

A new Jackie met us, calm, confident, and easily looked me in the eye. While we waited for our breakfast, I watched him greeting other customers. He appeared equally assured with everyone. Gone was the shy, shuffling middle-aged man of the previous day. What a transformation!

When I looked over to comment to Joy, she was smiling broadly. "I see you, too, have noticed the changes in our Jackie."

"He's a completely different man. How could there be such a huge change in just one day?"

"When Jackie lost Jeff, he lost his confidence. He stopped trusting anything, particularly himself. He has spent years unsure of everything around him. Not only did he re-discover Jeff, but himself as well.

Once Jackie got all his customers seated and orders either taken or delivered, he had a bit of a break to chat. "I can't thank you enough for helping me find Jeff. I'm still amazed that he was right here all along. Jeff and I stayed up all night talking! He reminded me of all the things I wanted when I was young. They seemed quite important back then, but they faded away just like Jeff."

"After Jeff was gone," he continued, "nothing seemed important or real. It was as if I couldn't do anything that mattered without Jeff, or was it that nothing I did mattered? Do you understand what I mean? My boyhood dream was to go to college and become a marine biologist. I love the ocean and want to learn all I could about it and help preserve everything that lives there. I've decided to follow through on that plan. I am finally going to go back to school and spend the rest of my life working with the ocean and its inhabitants." His eyes sparkled with excitement as he spoke.

I couldn't help myself. I burst out with, "But aren't you a little old to go back to school?"

"Perhaps, but as I see it, either way, I'll only get older. I can spend years making do, or I can fulfill my dream. The choice seems clear. If I go back to school, in five years, I'll be a marine biologist. Imagine that, me a marine biologist!" He said with a bemused grin.

He pulled a scrawled graph out of his pocket. "Did you know that the health of the ocean affects the ecosystem for the entire Earth? I've been doing some research. Things have changed a lot since I was a kid. People are eating more fish than ever now that the old meat-and-potatoes diet has mostly died out. But the actual fish population has been depleted, and it's only 5% of what it once was. I won't even get into mercury poisoning and other contaminants. I realized I also have kind of an advantage to finding a solution."

"Advantage?" Joy and I said at the same time.

"Yes, Jeff may not be visible to people, but the sea creatures do see and talk to Jeff. So, he can tell me their struggles and concerns and find out what they need. We humans can study and think we know the answer, but I think the fish know better than anyone else about the ocean."

"Congratulations! I believe you've made an outstanding choice. Your care and insight will be a blessing to the oceans and the Earth. I am pleased that Zemma and I were able to help you," Joy beamed at him.

"Not only that, but I've got half a mind to call Peter and tell him the ending to our story. I wonder if he would write a new song with a happy ending."

"Jackie, what a wonderful idea. Many have cried over your loss and would be thrilled to learn the truth and discover the real ending."

"I'll do it! I'm going to call Peter. I hope he'll talk to me. What if I can't get through to his publicist or whoever takes his calls?"

"Jackie, I guarantee if you introduce yourself as Jackie Pepper, you'll get put through immediately."

Joy touched Jackie's shoulder. "Zemma and I have another story to tell you." He leaned forward eagerly as Joy told him about the Unmaker and the dead-eyed people in his wake. I couldn't help it, but I broke in a few times, talking about my vision of all the strands coming together.

When we stopped talking, he smiled sadly. "I understand completely. Looking back, I'm sure those who convinced me that Jeff was all in my imagination were either Unmakers or under their influence. I do hope you're telling me all this because you want me to join your new family?"

Joy smiled brightly, "Absolutely. As a symbol of our Crystalline Heart Family and a connector to help us all stay in touch, I give you this blue Apatite heart to wear. This stone helps to clear any confusion or negativity. It also enables you to expand your knowledge, perfect for your upcoming studies. Blue Apatite is also a manifestation stone that promotes service to others and a humanitarian outlook with a sense of hope in the future."

As Joy put the leather cord over Jackie's head, I believe he stopped breathing for a few moments. Maybe that was his attempt to keep back the tears I could see welling in his eyes. Then he took a deep, shuddering breath and hugged us both.

"Can Jeff be part of the Family as well?" Jackie asked, almost shyly.

"Of course. Hmmm, let me think, which stone wants to work with Jeff?" She got a huge 'Aha' smile on her face and came out with a larger heart pendant than the others. The stone was translucent reddish-brown with intense orange, green, gold, and red flashes, almost like living flames. "This is a fire agate; it's believed to contain the essence of fire. It will help Jeff tap into his interdimensional creativity!"

Jackie took it reverently. "It is perfect for Jeff. It's about twice my pendant's size, and I don't know if you noticed, but the cord is about five times longer. I'll bet it'll be perfect around Jeff's neck."

Joy laughed, "Funny, I didn't even notice that the cord was so ridiculously long. But I agree, it should fit exactly right. I love how things come together!"

We finished breakfast wishing Jackie all the best in his new future. Closing the restaurant's door, I looked back, noticing not one but two women watching Jackie's every move, appearing more than a little interested in him. What a difference a day can make.

CHAPTER 15:

Horses that Aren't

We practically skipped down the road. We were so pleased with the outcome of that story! The words of "Jeff the Magic Dragon" kept playing in my head. I resisted the impulse to sing aloud as long as possible, but when I couldn't hold them back any longer, the words just burst forth from my mouth. Joy joined in, and we sang delightfully in unison as we walked. We tried to rewrite the end but only ended up humming and grinning. That was Peter's job – and, of course, Jackie and Jeff's adventure.

Have you ever noticed that when you are already happy and joyous, even more, incredible things happen? Perhaps it's that like-attracts-like idea. I'm not sure exactly what causes it, but I do know that it's true. When I am happy, everything seems magical, and anything seems possible. That's how it was even before I met Joy. I was thinking about this as we walked. I wondered if it would work the same now that I honestly believed the possibilities to be endless.

It was in this state of mental musing that I walked along, nodding happily to every creature we passed, carefully making sure I didn't stumble over tree trunks. Fairies and bumblebees flitted from flower to flower companionably.

We crested a hill overlooking a small, well-kept ranch, the fields green with crops of hay and clover. Cows and sheep grazed on opposite sides of the road; bright white fences encircled various pastures and a small riding arena. Two beautiful white horses grazing in the nearest fenced field completed this idyllic picture.

I ran forward to see if I could get the horses to come close to pet them through the fence. I've always had an exceptionally soft spot for horses; they're so strong and majestic. I could hardly contain my delight when one of the horses looked up immediately at my call and started towards me. I fished in my backpack and brought out an apple I'd been saving for an afternoon snack. Holding it out, I awaited the horse.

As he neared me, I blinked and blinked again. I was sure what I saw was an optical illusion. The horse had a horn, just one, long and straight in the middle of his head!

Unicorns are merely a myth; this is impossible, I thought. But then again, I reminded myself, I used to believe there are no dragons, talking fish, rainbow villages, fairies, hippo/women bathing in rivers, or overly sensitive trees. Gosh, maybe this confirmed it. Anything IS possible. I thought I was ready for anything, but this…this genuinely…it was… astounding!

I didn't have a coherent thought in my head. Unable to speak, I held out the apple for the horse…no, the unicorn. He came right up to me and immediately took the apple from my outstretched hand. He nuzzled my hand and whinnied when he'd finished making the apple disappear.

"Wow, he whinnies just like a horse. I would have expected something different from a unicorn," I murmured under my breath.

"Oh, I expect you thought perhaps I'd talk instead?"

"But you do talk!"

"Yep, it appears that I do. I don't talk to just anyone, though, mind you. Most people look at me and see a white horse and pass by. Even though I'm purposefully in disguise, I still find it rather disappointing."

"Why are you in disguise?"

"Well, you know unicorns don't exist. Right? Everyone knows we're just a myth. If someone were to discover a real, live unicorn, can you imagine all the commotion? I'm sure they'd lock me up in a cage and parade me for circus entertainment. Hey, I admit I'm a little vain and being admired is great, but being put in a freak show isn't the same at all."

"If most people can't see you, why can I?"

"Don't you know yet? You see me because you believe in possibilities beyond your wildest dreams."

"I have had some eye-opening experiences. I'm finding it extremely difficult to believe what I see is real. Even when I clearly see your horn."

"You're right. You don't have to be walking along, hoping for unicorns. But you saw me because you were open to the possibilities."

"When did we decide you didn't exist? Have you always been in disguise?"

"You're a curious one, aren't you? Since you've asked, I'll tell you a little story. Back when the world was much younger than today, unicorns ran freely over much of this planet. We could appear and disappear at will. We were likewise able to think ourselves to other places we'd been. In the blink of an eye, we could go many miles down the road. We communicated through our minds to others of our kind, never separate from each other.

"We lived companionably with humankind for many, many generations. Then, because of our magical abilities, someone started a tale that they would have good luck if they touched a unicorn's horn. We made a game out of it, enjoying a good chase now and then. Occasionally we would allow ourselves to be 'captured' by an especially worthy pursuer. It was all in good fun and 'a good time was had by all,' as they say.

"As often happens with humanity, greed took over, and things changed dramatically. A king who already had everything a man could want deciding he wanted more. He wanted our magical abilities for himself. He posted a reward to any knight who could capture a unicorn, kill it, and bring him just the horn. If he ground the horn and consumed some of the powder every morning, he thought he would have our powers."

"That was the end of the good times. Although we were able to disappear and transport ourselves, men can be tricky. Several of my brethren were caught and killed by men pretending to be friendly and harmless. If they caught us in a net, we couldn't become invisible or relocate.

"Of course, the powder from a unicorn horn does absolutely nothing magical, and the legend refused to die. Hunters tracked and killed us ruthlessly. We feared for our very existence. One of my ancestors befriended a noble wizard and asked for his help. The wizard pondered the situation many months before returning with a proposal. He offered to cast a spell that would make us appear to be horses. We would be visible only to those with good hearts who believed wholeheartedly in the possibility of our existence. In exchange for his help, we would give him our abilities to disappear and to transport ourselves. At the time, the bargain seemed a fair one. This wizard had long been revered and honored for his integrity and kindness to all beings. Fearing that we would rapidly become extinct, we agreed to his proposal."

"Was it a good deal?" Zemma asked. "I mean, you're here. That's good, right?"

"You've heard stories of good men corrupted by power. Had they always just hidden their dark side? Does power have a seed within it of darkness that can corrupt? I have yet to determine the answer to this question."

"I only know that in this case, the once wise and noble wizard became one of the evilest wizards of all time. He committed crimes and would avoid detection and punishment. We were horrified at what we had brought about. A council of elders met to discuss the situation. Three volunteers left to find and stop the wizard. He was cornered and killed by the volunteers after a lot of effort. As he died, our powers returned to us. However, just before his last breath, he cursed us, so we would forever appear as horses except to people like you.

"He was wrong in thinking that his curse would be bad for us. Quite the contrary, our safety was assured. Only those who believed and were pure of heart could see us. Those who meant to do us harm would never see us. We were safe within this world of men."

I broke in, "I thought I'd read the only ones who can see unicorns are maidens, untouched and virtuous. Would I still see you if I was a boy?"

He whinnied; I could swear he smiled. "That's just a story. I don't know where these foolish ideas come from, but once started, they just continue forever! Yes, boys can see us too if they are open-minded and have no evil in their hearts."

He touched me with his horn, and a shiver went through me. I was cold and hot all at once. I felt something change deep within my heart. I must have looked startled. The unicorn laughed and nuzzled my hand.

"Well met, my pure-hearted friend. The horn of a unicorn is magical, but not in the way that the greedy king believed. We must give of our magic freely and willingly for it to work."

I gulped, "You're telling me that I now have magical powers?"

"Yes, although they won't be apparent at first. As you open your heart and mind, so too will your powers open themselves to you."

138

"What are these powers? How do I use them?"

"That I cannot say. What one needs to achieve one's destiny shapes the power needed for each recipient. The Power is a sacred trust and a huge responsibility, not to be taken lightly. With vast power comes enormous responsibility, as the saying goes, and was true even before Peter Parker's Uncle Ben said those words in the Spiderman movie. Do not forget this. I repeat. With vast power comes enormous responsibility."

"With vast power comes enormous responsibility. I will remember." I felt honored beyond my ability to comprehend. I was also sorely tempted to start waving my arms around, shouting magical incantations to see what would happen. Knowing I'd only look silly, I was able to restrain myself.

"How do you know about Spiderman? I don't see a movie theater, comic book store, or television anywhere nearby."

"You're not the only one who's come by to talk. Many years ago, when Stan Lee was a boy, he stopped by here. I gave him a gift, as well. He used it to entertain, but there was more to his storytelling, of course."

"Is that why, even though the tales and heroes were fantastical, I always believed in them?" I asked.

"Yes. Always listen to your gut; the truth feels right and somehow solid. Lies feel wrong or leave you unsettled and unsure."

"Thank you; I feel honored that you allowed me to see and talk with you."

I bowed deeply to the unicorn. The unicorn returned the bow and touched my forehead with his horn again, and another shiver went through me, pulsing from head to toe. He winked as he returned to an erect posture.

"Happy journeys, my young friend." He turned and walked away. When he turned back towards me, he appeared to my eyes as an average horse once again.

I rejoined Joy on the road. I knew she'd seen and heard everything, and yet I couldn't resist excitedly filling her in all over again.

Midway through, I stopped talking, "Joy, I think the unicorn is one of our family! Do we have a heart to give to him?"

"I believe I have the perfect one. Let's go back."

We went back to the horse that was so much more and held out a mostly dark green heart with flecks of red. Joy and I took turns explaining the story and our mission and why we were asking him to join us. Joy braided the pendant into his mane calling the gemstone Bloodstone. "It's a shape-shifting stone, allowing the wearer to travel invisibly between the worlds. I know you can already shapeshift, but there may be a time when that isn't enough. This will allow you to further protect yourself from all who may hunt you."

He briefly showed his unicorn form, bowing to both of us.

Joy and I started on our path again. As we walked, I asked, "What abilities do you think I got from the unicorn?"

"Zemma, I've been wondering when you'd get around to asking that question. You do, of course, already know the answer I'm about to give you." She laughed gaily, slightly shaking her finger at me.

"NO! You're not going to tell me you can't tell me again, are you? Joy, I'm dying here! I need to know. What if I inadvertently use this new power and screw something up?" I tried to sound angry or worried but was smiling despite myself. After all, I'd already known she wouldn't tell me a thing. But I still had to try.

"Good try. Do you honestly believe the unicorn would give you a power that could be dangerous to either yourself or others and not warn you? Nope, you're not getting it out of me that easily."

"Then, you DO know the answer?"

She smiled knowingly in her infuriating way and kept walking. Try as I might to just accept her response with patience, I admit I resent secrets kept from me and dragged my feet and pouted a bit as I walked. Mind you, my pout wasn't as long as it might have been once, and most of it was just out of habit. It was partly in fun. But I kept wondering how I could get her to tell me.

After about ten minutes, she turned on me. "Zemma, quit acting like a two-year-old. The gift you have received requires that you remain mindful of your responsibility. Do you believe you are showing the responsibility necessary for someone who wields power in any form?"

I stammered, "No! I'm sorry. I was playing –"

Joy nodded, "Like a spoiled child."

"Do you think that will make me lose this new ability?"

"Not yet, but I do believe you were getting close. You know better, and you can be better. You've talked about finding your destiny. Important answers only come when you remain centered and focused and strive to connect with the best self you can be. If you want to understand your purpose in life, you need to do your part. Not every mystery has an immediate answer."

I started to break in, and she quickly cut me off. "I said immediate…I didn't say never answered. If you remain aware and focused and continue to ask for clarity, all will eventually become clear for you. There is nothing to be gained by rushing. I know you believe you're ready to hear every explanation. I'll tell you this right now. You're not. If I were to tell you what you want to know right this moment, your fear and resistance would ensure that you might never arrive at your gift. "

"Why would that happen?"

"How did you feel when he said, 'With vast power, comes enormous responsibility'? Think back and remember your thoughts and how your body felt."

"I felt as if someone or something had kicked me in the stomach. I was scared."

"When you uncover the answers, it will be because you have progressed and grown to a place in which you will no longer feel that fear. You'll be able to accept the truth and use it to propel you forward to fulfill your destiny."

She paused a moment. I didn't break in for a change because I knew I didn't have anything intelligent to add and probably would have just asked more questions that wouldn't be answered, at least not now and not by Joy.

Then, with a sudden change of tone, Joy blurted out, "Speaking of destinies, there is lunch in our near future. I'm ready for a rest and something to eat. There should be another town just around the corner. Let's go!" She took off walking quickly, with me right on her heels.

CHAPTER 16:

Opening & Being Truly Seen

The town wasn't just around the corner. It was more like five miles down the road. I'd come to realize that Joy's sense of time and distance were different than mine. The time it took to arrive was probably a good thing because I was still worrying about gifts and responsibilities. I chewed my lip as I tried to figure out what powers the unicorn had given me. I knew she'd told me to let it go, but I just couldn't.

After four miles or more of walking, I knew I needed some time to reflect independently. I stopped and told Joy I would sit under the giant redwood tree I had spotted about fifty feet off the road.

"Good idea, Zemma. I was wondering when you were going to realize what you need."

"Sorry, Joy. I need a time out! I'm reacting out of fear, and trying too hard and pushing to get answers isn't going to work. Perhaps in my fear, I regressed to childhood. It was easier when I didn't have to do or be anything but a child. But what do you mean about centering myself?"

"Your energy typically runs smoothly through your body in a balanced way. When you are stressed, upset, or ill, that energy is out of balance. It isn't focused in your body or spirit and is scattered all over the place. Bringing your center into balance is essential for both mental and physical well-being. When you find your emotions and thoughts running out of control, as yours currently are, you know you're not centered or grounded.

Let me explain one last bit before I leave you. You know that scientists claim that we use only about 7-10% of our brain. The same is true for our spirits. Most humans on this planet go through life with only the tiniest little bit of their energy actually in their bodies. They appear to have nearly no energy or vitality, with only enough of their spirit in their bodies to maintain life. Some people manifest more significant portions of their souls in their bodies. They vibrate and pulse with life and energy. I want you to get back to that and live the world, Zemma."

"How do I get centered again?"

"Close your eyes and take a deep breath. Fill the center of your being with energy. The balance point is in the center of your navel. Breathing slowly and deeply, visualize your spirit as a tiny spark of light in that center. Fill yourself with light as you slowly increase your boundaries and brightness until your energy is vibrant within you. Keeping an anchor deep within allow your awareness to reach out to the edges of your energy self. Draw that energy body into your physical body. By this time, you should be experiencing a powerful sense of joy and love. Open to it. Sit for a time, allowing that awareness to strengthen within you. When you're ready, breathe deeply three times and stretch. You should be feeling more stable and more your positive self at that point."

I plopped down under the tree. Even with the exercise Joy described, it wasn't all that easy to let go of my unease. Somehow fear had taken hold; I sat for several minutes breathing and concentrating but couldn't seem to get past my unsettled feelings. I wondered if maybe, instead of overcoming my feelings, I should relax and try to focus on their origins. Instead of exploring outside, I could go deeper into my inside realm. This method had worked well to discover I was jealous of Jackie, and I hoped it would work now.

My entire body was tense; I seemed poised for a fight. Why was I reacting in so much fear that it triggered my fight or flight response into full-on fighting mode? I allowed my mind to go deeper, deeper still.

Suddenly, I could hardly breathe and felt pain in my chest. I had a vision of myself standing alone on a rock wall. There was a massive crowd of people in front of me, staring. Although I was clothed, I had the feeling that they could see me, truly see me. They saw everything about me – my innermost thoughts and secrets, and I felt utterly exposed. I was terrified they would reject me, or even worse, turn on me and throw stones. I tried to get off the wall and couldn't. I took a deep breath, steadying myself, centering. I reached with my senses and pulled even more of my spiritual self into my body, the way Joy had suggested.

I tingled as my spirit merged with my physical self. My fear left. I was aware of the crowd staring at me, but I was confident I could survive even this. Although

I'd thought the watchers were seeing all of me, they'd seen only a small portion. I wondered what would happen if I allowed them to see me…all of me.

The idea excited and scared me to the core of my being. I knew that if I was feeling this much fear, something important was happening. I hear you wondering if perhaps this wasn't foolhardy. After all, isn't fear meant to keep us safe, to keep us from doing things that will cause us harm? Yes, and no. I've discovered there are two kinds of fear. There is a fear that comes to protect our bodies. And we should listen to that fear. Then there is a more deeply rooted fear that our ego throws up to preserve the status quo. This part of us is terrified of growing, changing, and evolving. It feels safe only when our world stays constant. I was beginning to see the difference and realize that the first should be honored and listened to; however, the second fear should be faced and mastered.

Resolved, I relaxed my body and visualized opening my heart, and finally, all of me, showing who I was in all my expansive self. A strange thing happened; in my imagination, I was on the wall feeling more "in" my body than I'd ever been, alive and powerful. I was also in the crowd watching as I opened myself. I don't know how this happened. I was everywhere.

I watched myself on the wall, taking several deep breaths. The me who stood there looked ordinary initially, then with each breath, I/she/we began to become luminous. Within a few minutes, all that was visible was a brilliant light, shining nearly as brightly as the sun, although not painful to my eyes. I glanced at others in the crowd, and most looked either peaceful or joyous. I noticed a couple of dark figures at the edge of the group who were shielding their eyes and turning away. One man took off, running away from the scene. I brought my attention back into the self that stood on the wall. I took a deep breath, felt myself growing lighter, and was momentarily disoriented. When I regained my wits, I was standing on the wall. My energy felt as if it spread out for miles; it was brilliant, peaceful, loving, and whole.

How long could I maintain this level of power? I worried that I was feeding the electricity meant for a 220 circuit into a 110 wire. Maybe my physical body would disintegrate. I willed myself to close down the energy pouring into my body, not as closed as I'd been before, but to about halfway between the two extremes. I felt stretched. I was still struggling to make the adjustments needed to maintain this level, but I felt good. Heck, I felt amazing!

I opened my eyes and remained sitting for several minutes, stunned, unable to move. I could sense in every fiber of my being that what I had just experienced was real. I felt changed. Gathering myself together, I stood and concentrated for several minutes, feeling my energy move through my body, into the Earth, and back again. That helped me feel a little less spacy and more grounded. I shook myself and walked back to the road, where Joy was waiting with a smile on her face.

"Did you have a good nap?"

"Nap? You call that a nap?"

"Why, Zemma, whatever is the matter. I looked over, and you were sitting there so peacefully with your eyes closed. Are you telling me you weren't sleeping?"

"No, it was much more than…." I felt frustrated that she couldn't see what had happened. I wasn't sure I'd be able to find words to explain. When I saw her smile, I realized that she was teasing me. "You saw?"

"Yes, Zemma. You did well. Whenever you are afraid or uncertain, remember this experience and open to that larger part of you. Each time you do, you will bring increasing strength and energy to yourself. As humans, we have forgotten our true nature, and we've brought less of our essence to this Earth. With work and conscious effort, we can regain much of what we've lost."

"Why?"

"Why did we lose it? Or why do we want to regain it?"

"Yes."

"Zemma, you are always so curious. We lost it because we began to forget that we were more than our bodies. As we did so, we neglected the care and feeding of our spirits. Just as your body needs food and water, so too your spirit needs nurturing."

"How do you nurture what you cannot see?"

"Find what brings you joy, love, and peace. It's different for everyone. Do good deeds, be in nature, allow your creativity to flow, love, dance, or pray. The other side of this is finding out what drains your vitality and taking steps to staunch the outflow."

"Drains it?"

"I know you've been around a person who is angry or especially negative. What happens to you, then?"

"I get tired, irritable, sometimes even depressed."

"Yes, these people can be difficult to be around. Their negativity takes on a force that can deplete your system. Think carefully about people whom you've been around, and for no apparent reason, you find yourself exhausted or yawning continually."

"You're right; there are some people who, no matter what we're doing or talking about, leave me completely worn out. I've wondered about that. They aren't bad people or even really negative for the most part. An hour with them leaves me depleted, physically, mentally, and emotionally. So, what's that about?"

"Some people, unfortunately, have forgotten how to draw nourishment from the Universe to fuel their own spirits. Instead, they take it from the people who are around them."

"That's terrible. It's like those people who've lost their capacity to draw on the forces of the Universe become vampires!"

"Exactly. Most are good people who've lost connection with themselves and the Universe. They've forgotten their true natures and all the incredible resources available to them. They normally don't even know they are doing this. There are some, however, who are aware and draw a certain pleasure from their actions."

"How do I know the difference?"

"I can show you how to shield yourself from these energy drains."

"That still won't show me how to know who's who."

"Once you can shield yourself, you'll begin to see the reactions of those around you. Those who were unconsciously draining you will sometimes react in confusion, but the conscious vampires react with anger, possibly even doing things against you in an attempt to break down your shield."

"Like what?"

"There are many ways. Some will say things to bring up your doubts and insecurities. As you already know, doubt can have disastrous effects. Others

147

will challenge or bombard you with negativity. Some will play victim, acting on your desire to help, rescue, or heal. It's the last group that's the most difficult. You're kind, and you want to be of assistance and help others. You naturally open yourself, pouring out your energy to help."

"But, Joy, I don't want to go around closing myself off from everyone! I can't live like that!" I felt panicked when I thought about the idea of cutting myself off energetically from everyone around me now that I'd begun to understand and appreciate how interconnected everything and everyone is."

"Don't worry, Zemma; it's not about closing off. It's learning discernment. There are times it's appropriate to give energy to others. You'll learn over time when to give and when to withhold. Giving can be a loving and powerful act, and when it is, it doesn't drain you but nourishes you instead."

"Hmmm, so if I'm giving and it's suitable to do so, I'll feel more energized instead of drained?"

"Yes, but we've strayed away from what I was originally going to show you. Close your eyes and visualize a ray of golden white light coming in through the top of your head and out your solar plexus."

"My what?"

"Solar plexus. It's in the center of your belly, between your belly button and your heart."

"Okay, I'll give it a try." I closed my eyes and went into the visualization. It felt good, but I couldn't see how that would keep anyone from draining me.

"Outstanding, Zemma. The way this works is that you bring additional light and energy in through your crown, and as it goes to your solar plexus, it creates an outflow. The energy vampire normally goes energetically into your solar plexus to connect to the center of your energy and power, drawing it back into itself. When you have this particular type of outflow, they can't break through it to tap into your energy source."

"I still don't understand yet, but I'll take your word for it."

"Remember what I've told you. There will be times when you'll be glad of this knowledge, and it will make sense. Enough talk, let's get on into town. I'm hungry."

"Me, too!" We took off at a brisk pace. I had visions of hamburgers and French fries; I should have known better.

CHAPTER 17:

Lunch with a Vampire

The next town was a sleepy little place, with not a single fast-food joint in sight. I sighed and hoped they at least had an old-fashioned hamburger stand. I was to be disappointed yet again. The best we could do was a run-down café. Sitting down with the menu in hand, I attempted to ignore the fact that the table wasn't particularly clean, the menu felt sticky, and the surly waitress seemed to have better places to be.

I joked, "Joy, if the cook is as worn down as this café, I don't even want to eat here."

Joy nodded. "That's good common sense! The energy and mood of the cook can have a noticeable after-effect. That premise holds true in most activities; the feelings and intent of the creators infuse or contaminate the final product."

I admit to praying that even if the food wasn't delicious, please let it be free from negativity. Then I had a thought, "Joy, if we always bless our food and give thanks, wouldn't that get rid of any negative vibes?"

"In most cases, it does. But not always. Any combination of disgruntled farmers, truckers, kitchen workers, cooks, and waitresses can push that energy deep into the food so that it becomes one with its very molecules. In extreme cases, your body isn't able to absorb any healthy nutrients from what should have been nourishing fuel for your body, and the negative feelings can even affect your mood."

When I heard laughter from the kitchen, relief swept through me, and I turned my attention to the menu and my surroundings.

The two-sided, plastic-coated menu was your basic diner-in-the-sticks fare, complete with jam, fingerprints, and other substances I wasn't going to even consider. But at least they had hamburgers, French fries, and even a Patty Melt and onion rings. Happy to have a choice, I went for the latter. Waiting patiently for our orders to arrive, I engaged in people-watching. I was surprised to see the café was full; no empty tables remained despite its run-down appearance. A boy came in who was probably around sixteen. He couldn't find a place to sit and looked around, getting a broad grin on his face when he saw us. He came boldly over and asked if he could join us. We agreed, and Joy slid over to make room for him.

His name was John, and he lived just down the road. He explained that he was on his lunch hour and glad of a break. There was something about John that made it hard for me to look at him. Puzzled, I looked again and realized it was his eyes. There was a lack of light and energy in them, a kind of deadness that was uncomfortable and unsettling.

John started talking the minute he sat down, not pausing to ask if we were interested in his stories. He barely took time between words to breathe. It seems that everything was wrong in his life, his boss, customers, heat, and the dull town.

The first few stories he told were rather amusing, I was sympathetic towards him, and I found myself commiserating with him on his bad luck. However, after a while, I began to think that he seemed to drag his troubles with him wherever he went.

He was so intent on spilling all the frustrations of his life out on the table; he didn't seem to notice that I was paying less and less attention to his tale of woe. I found myself looking over my shoulder, hoping to see our waitress coming with food. As far as I was concerned, it couldn't come too quickly. I was hungry, but I also wasn't enjoying hearing John blame everything in his life on someone else, bad luck or circumstances. I was glancing around, not paying attention, when something he said made me take notice. I don't know the whole monologue because, frankly, I wasn't listening, but here's where I came in.

"…..I mean, wow, did you believe he dared to tell me I was negative? Me? I'm one of the most positive people I know. Can I help it if I keep running into creeps who screw me over and stuff like that? This guy, like, he told me that I was responsible for drawing these negative people to me like it's my fault or something. Hey, I'm doing the best I can. I'm there every day, and each time it's the same old stuff. I tell you, I've got to get out of this town and go someplace new. Things will be different then."

I was relieved when our orders arrived. I was intent on eating and managed to tune John out for the most part. I ate quickly, partly because I was hungry, mainly because I wanted to go someplace else. I couldn't wait to get away from this guy and his mouth and his constant negativity. His ability to blame everything on someone else, completely denying any participation or responsibility, was mind-boggling. Even before I'd met Joy, I'd been aware that when I was having recurring problems with people or having accidents, there was usually some answerability on my part.

He talked and talked and talked. I'm happy to say he didn't speak with his mouth full, but he never seemed to shut up. How the food kept disappearing from his plate was a mystery.

"…and that dude, well, he claimed that I screwed up his oil change. My boss threatened to fire me. He wouldn't take my word that I'd done everything right. He kept bringing up old mistakes, and everyone knows that's bogus. It's not fair to bring up the past all the time and try to say that just because something happened in the past, that's proof that it's happening now. I mean, that's not cool. Well, I blew my top and told my boss that if he couldn't take my word for it, then I couldn't work for him. And he said, 'Fine, then get out. You're fired!' I couldn't believe my ears. I mean, how could he fire me after all I'd done for him? Then I got a job down the street making deliveries for the drug store. Well, that didn't last long either because old man Baker's a slave driver. They started blaming me for orders getting mixed up. Hey, I can't help it if some of the names are almost the same or that the pharmacist's handwriting is terrible. Geesh. They expect a lot for their stupid low pay. Well, I took it for a couple of weeks, but I just had it with getting blamed for things, and so I said……."

Blah, blah, blah. I couldn't listen to any more of this and tuned him out again. I started yawning. It was nap time. I took a huge sip of my soda, hoping the caffeine would give me a boost. I was slumped over in my seat, pretending to pay the barest amount of attention to John's stories. I'd nod, and once in a while, I'd say, 'Uh, huh. Gee, that's too bad.' That seemed to keep him happy at first. The more he talked, the more animated he became. When he first sat down, he'd looked tired and almost gray-faced. He was a great deal perkier than when he'd sat down. I must have imagined his pallor because now he appeared to be practically glowing with health. I swear his eyes had changed, no longer the lifeless bottomless gray pools they'd been, but blue now with a spark of life. I thought I must have imagined the deadness before.

Joy hadn't uttered a word for quite some time. She sat in the booth's corner, smiling at both of us. Something suspicious in her smile made me take notice. What was she thinking?

I briefly tuned back into what John was saying, hoping to catch a clue to Joy's attitude in his words. "Hey, man, I mean, I was pretty tired earlier. This food must be good, 'cuz now I'm raring to go. I haven't felt this good in ages."

Like a bolt, I understood. John was a vampire. I had let my guard down; my initial sympathy towards him had given him an opening. No wonder he felt good; he had my energy to boost him! I sat up straighter in my seat and visualized the golden white light entering the top of my head, exiting through my solar plexus, just like Joy had taught me. It took only seconds until I started feeling better. John was frowning when I looked across the table at him.

I hadn't said a word or moved a muscle when he started in on me. "Well, hey, you don't have to get all huffy. I'm planning on paying for my lunch. It's not like I asked for a hand-out or anything."

"What?" I said, genuinely puzzled.

"Well, you didn't say anything, but I could hear you loud and clear, wondering if I was going to stick you with the bill. Now I don't know what I did that would give you that idea, but I resent it. And here I thought we were starting to be friends. I guess that's just beyond you, huh, city girl. Well, you can just keep on traveling back out of town. Don't worry about old John here; I can pay for myself."

"What?" I tried to be more coherent, but this blatant attack was a complete shock.

"Yeah, I know your kind. You're always worrying that some poor guy will take your money or expect something from you. Well, I never asked, and I wouldn't have, you know. I don't know where you get off being so high and mighty and thinking just because I don't have much that I'm a freeloader. I mean, I resent that kind of attitude." He jumped up and threw a couple of dollars on the table by his plate and stomped out.

I stared at the money. John strode past the window as he dashed down the street. I was utterly taken aback and shocked at what had happened. Joy was laughing. Her polite little laugh became an all-out, roaring, rollicking belly laugh. I was too shocked and drained to figure out what she thought was so funny. I didn't like being the butt of a joke, especially one I didn't get. My face was rapidly getting red. I was about to say something rude, and it was right there on the tip of my tongue. Thankfully, Joy spoke and saved me from myself.

"Oh, Zemma, that was priceless. You walked right into every one of his tricks. Talk about getting an instant lesson in dealing with vampires! Wow, you pulled in a doozy. This guy used all the tricks. He played on your sympathies, then, when that ran down, he just wore you down with talking. The best of all was that when you got wise to him and shut off the flow, he attacked you full-on. You didn't see the attack coming, and it caused you to let down your guard once again, and he zapped you good!"

"Yeah, and after all that crap about paying his own way, he didn't even leave half of what he owed!"

"True, but his theft of your energy is a much bigger loss for you than a few dollars for lunch."

Chagrinned at how easily I'd played into John's hands, I asked, "What else could I have done?"

"Zemma, one of the things I love about you is that you have a kind heart. You want to help people. Earlier, when we were talking, you proclaimed you didn't want to go through life, cutting yourself off from people. Well, here's an instance where you could have paid more attention to the clues and signals he was giving out right away and protected yourself."

"Clues? What clues?"

"First was his appearance. Didn't he immediately make you kind of feel sorry for him? Didn't you feel almost protective? Many 'vampires' have learned to give off that kind of helpless air to attract the 'assistance' of people like you. The second clue was when he sat down, so he was directly across from you. That way, he could more easily line up his energy field with yours…all the better to eat you, my dear! Just kidding! But it's not unlike grandma and the big bad wolf! Even if he hadn't been a vampire, the sheer volume of negativity coming out of his mouth would have been enough to leave you depleted. It's hard to be bombarded with that much negative energy and maintain your joy."

"Is that all?"

"Nope. Even if you'd missed all the others, as soon as you started getting sleepy, you should have checked in with yourself to see what was going on. You would have known there was no good reason for you to be so tired. Especially so quickly."

"What should I have done?"

"Stay alert. When you have even the slightest inkling of any of the above conditions, you should shield your energy."

"But I didn't, and I'm exhausted. What do I do now?"

"Go hug a tree. Go, look at the sky. Skip. Laugh."

"All of the above? Or can I do just one thing?"

"One or all of them will do fine. Let's pay our bill, and the rest of John's, and go."

We walked into the sunshine, and my spirits lifted.

"Joy, John didn't exactly have dead-eyes, but could he be one of the Unmakers?"

"Good question. I don't think John is an Unmaker, but I'd say the Unmakers have influenced him. Most likely, he feels the lack but doesn't know why or what to do about it."

"I did try to connect with his heart and spirit while you two were talking. I had hoped at first that I'd find something in him that was still open. I am incredibly sorry that I wasn't able to find even the tiniest spark in him. If I had, together, over time, we might have awakened his heart enough to give him at least the possibility of opening to love and magic. Sometimes all it takes is the smallest spark. But he was too entrenched in his belief of himself as a victim with all of Creation against him."

I heard a bird chirping loudly and looked up to see where it was as it flew over and took a dump. I had bird stuff running down my shirt. "Oh, crap!"

"You said it," Joy chortled, laughing so hard she nearly choked.

"Very funny."

"Yes, it is. Are you finished with being dumped on? Good, let's go find a tree for you to hug."

I laughed despite myself. I had to admit, however, that laughing made me feel good again. I had most of my energy back and could tell I'd nearly recovered from my experience. Maybe laughter and shared confidences could be as good as hugging a tree. But just to be sure, I'd still hug that tree.

I knew this encounter was a direct consequence of my desire to know and learn more. But I was starting to get annoyed with the Universe for continually playing these little games. I didn't enjoy being the brunt of someone's bad joke. I walked purposefully out of town and down the road, setting a steady pace, even though I had no idea where we were going.

My annoyance slowly dissipated as we walked. After all, it was a nice day. And I'd asked to learn, so I shouldn't have been upset that help came so quickly.

I began to feel excited about the adventure ahead. Perhaps something even more wonderful waited or (I hoped not!) lurked just around the next bend.

CHAPTER 18:

Zemma's Eagle Flight

Before we went on, I wanted to figure out how to protect myself.
Joy kept quiet, seeming to know when I needed time to think. I
rerun scenes in my mind, alternately scolding and being upset with John
and Joy for our parts in recent events. Mostly, I worried that protecting
myself would mean I would be cut off from other people. However, John
had taught me that there were circumstances that called on me to defend
myself. I wouldn't be much use if I allowed myself to get drained so quickly.

I realized I'd gone through most of my twelve short years of life completely
open to everyone and everything they threw at me. I was very connected to
whoever entered my energy, and I wondered how much that accounted for my
mood swings. I could remember many days when I'd been on top of the world;
then, after an encounter with someone who was having a bad day, or just a bad
attitude, I was down in the dumps, or even worse, angry at the world.

I was beginning to understand Joy's explanations of why some of
these ways of connecting weren't always entirely healthy. The alternative
seemed much worse, though. All my life, I'd felt things very deeply. I
didn't want to protect myself if it meant feeling things less intensely, but
then again, maybe I'd be able to keep the positive intensity and shield
out the bad.

I walked searching through my brain and feelings to find ways to express
my misgivings to Joy. I'd start to talk, then stop. I couldn't find a way to
explain myself that made sense. As always, Joy seemed unaffected by my
inner turmoil.

The road was sparsely traveled, which suited me fine. I wasn't in the
mood for people and was relieved to have a break from being friendly

or charming. The road became steep, and the countryside changed from rolling, grassy hills to the sandy desert with scrubby, thin pines, sagebrush, and even small cactus. The high desert scene fit my mood perfectly.

After an hour or so of hiking, thinking, and stewing in the hot, dry air, we came to a cliff overlooking a valley. I plopped down, legs dangling over the edge, and heaved a huge sigh. Maybe I could figure it out here. Still thoughtful, I rummaged in my backpack for some water. Predictably, Joy laughed.

"Oh, Zemma, you do give yourself fits! Rest and relax; quit worrying about everything. Put everything out of your mind."

"I'll try. I know, I'm a pill. I feel foolish, but I want to figure it out."

"What do you feel besides foolish, Zemma?"

"I feel afraid. Afraid that I'll be alone and cut off from the world of people and feelings. I know that sounds strange for a girl to say. Most girls I know don't think of much beyond what boy they like or shopping. I don't know if this makes me less than normal or just more in touch with what I'm feeling and thinking because I'm with you. I'm frustrated. I don't want to be obsessing over this stuff. Yet, I can't seem to help myself. I can't figure out why, but this idea of protecting myself scares the holy jeepers out of me."

"I thought so." She looked out over the valley, pointing to the sky, "Zemma, do you see that eagle flying?"

"Yes," I said cautiously.

"Watch him for a few minutes. Get a feel for him. When you've tuned in to him, close your eyes and let yourself go with him."

"Yeah, right. An eagle won't give me any answers about vampires."

"Zemma, I thought you would have learned by now that almost anything is possible if you allow for the possibility."

"Um, right. But there's a big difference between seeing and talking to mythical creatures and letting go. Maybe flying with them. Or letting them…. I don't know. It's different."

"That's true, it is different, but it's not so different than when you feel someone else's thoughts, emotions, or even pain and can't distinguish it from your own. In this case, you do it consciously."

"I'll give it a try." I directed my attention to the eagle. I watched as he swooped and soared, graceful and free. I closed my eyes, imagining being him. The wind brushed my face. I opened my eyes; I was flying, seeing through the eyes of an eagle! What a powerful feeling! Lifted easily on the warm air currents near the cliff, I was flying!

I, he, we flew steadily, gaining height. I was free. I was powerful. I looked down joyously at the cliffs and ravines below; what a sight! I was getting into this. I loved being an eagle! Maybe I should become a pilot or try hang gliding....or?

Without warning, I felt extreme, unreasoning fear. I breathed deeply, willing myself to continue flying as I explored the reason for my anxiety. I suddenly feared that I'd be cut off from all of humanity if I flew higher. I could become so high above everyone that I could no longer connect with others or relate in any way. I didn't want this! I wanted to be down there with everyone else. I started to tuck my wings and go lower.

A voice in my head urged me on. "Go higher. Trust me. It's all right. Keep going." I'd seen enough to know I could trust what I was hearing. I untucked my wings and caught the upward currents. Quickly I began soaring higher and higher. I struggled to trust and keep going. It wasn't easy. Waves of panic moved over me. I knew without a doubt that I was flying beyond my capacity to return and would forever be alone and lonely. I winged on, spiraling ever higher.

I couldn't see the ground clearly or distinguish details; I was at such a height. Was Joy that little speck over there, or was that a rock? I longed to return to Earth, to safety, and connection with others. Something called me upward. I flew higher still.

I soared above and through the clouds. My flight leveled out, and I took a moment to feel how high I'd come. I'd gone too far; I'd be alone forever. I breathed through the pain and felt a new upsurge. Well, if that's the way it is, I'd go as high as I possibly could.

I flew higher yet again. Waves of warmth spontaneously enveloped all my senses. I was one with all! The feeling was more spectacular than the greatest joy I'd ever known. I felt like I would burst, and yet within me, there was deep peace. How could it be that by flying so high, I not only didn't end up alone but became part of everything, humanity, Earth, the Universe, more than I could comprehend or even begin to explain?

I began to hear Bette Midler singing "From a Distance," [Appendix C] a song my parents love to play. I'd always found it moving but confusing. She sang of how from a distance, things are not always what they appear to be. Amid war and strife, there is harmony, the voices of hope, love, and peace singing in the heart of every man. God is watching us. I began singing out loud with new meaning and zest.

I looked down from my flight, feeling that I completely understood the song for the first time. I felt my oneness with everything and everyone and knew for that brief moment there was nothing but love, the Universe, and all of Creation was love, only love, and everything was perfect. It was possible to see without judgment, to experience everything as perfection.

Then, again, doubt came into my mind. How could it all be perfect? How can war, famine, disease, and death be part of the divine order? I plummeted towards the Earth. I caught myself and leveled out just before I hit the ground. When I next opened my eyes, I was back in my body. I was Zemma once again, standing on a solid foundation, surrounded by a golden desert.

"Joy, how can this be? How can everything be perfect? I'm still afraid!"

She smiled and gestured to me to sit down. "Zemma, we've discussed karma and the fact that many of us are here to grow and learn lessons. Each of us goes through the experiences that will make us stronger or more compassionate or more loving or…whatever our purpose is. Sometimes to learn, we must go through painful experiences that down here on Earth look horrific. However, when seen from a distance, it's possible to grasp the overall pattern of perfection." She put her finger to my lips as I began to protest. "Don't talk. You've been through a powerful experience, and some-times talking about it gets in the way of understanding. I think this is an excellent place to make camp for the night. I'll set up the tent."

I don't remember Joy putting up a tent or setting up the beds. I only remember waking up in my sleeping bag as the sun rose the next morning. I can't say that I completely comprehended all that had transpired the previous day, but I was at peace and ready for a good cup of coffee. For now, that was good enough reason to keep going!

CHAPTER 19:

Purple People Eaters Do Exist!

I was walking happily down the road when a commotion broke into my peace. It seemed to be coming straight toward us. I stopped, cocking my head to one side as I tried to figure out what all the commotion was.

I didn't have long to wait. I'm sure you've already figured out that I probably should have moved out of the middle of the road instead of standing still, listening. That thought finally came to me, and I'd taken only one step towards the side when something came careening around the corner and ran straight into me. Perhaps I should have stayed in the middle of the road after all. Then it might have missed me. But, oh no, not me, I moved directly into its path.

What was it? I wasn't sure of that answer at all. I was lying flat on my back, and it was mostly right on top of me. I saw purple fur, a silvery horn, and iridescent wings. Try as I might, I couldn't see its face. After a lot of grunting and groaning, we finally got ourselves untangled and upright. Neither of us was hurt, just a bit dusty. Of course, Joy was standing off to one side, trying to decide whether to laugh out loud or to keep her opinions to herself.

The creature had one huge green crazily turning eye right in the middle of its forehead. I couldn't decide if it was injured or was like this all the time. It appeared to think I was funny and made a sound that had to be laughter, but like none, I'd heard before or since. The noise was almost music, a cross between a donkey braying and a horn blowing. The sound came straight out of the horn smack in the middle of its forehead, just above the eye! As it made all this racket, it hovered slightly above the ground, silver wings beating rapidly.

I decided that it was nervous. I reached and patted its shoulder reassuringly. "It's okay. We won't hurt you."

"No, kidding. You don't exactly look dangerous, little girl," it squeaked.

"You don't know me!"

"Well, duh. Are you simple or something? Are you just going to stand there?"

"Well, yeah, I am," I said, starting to get huffy.

"Why?" Asked the purple guy.

"Why not?"

"Mainly because it's boring. Just standing around gets old quickly."

"What do you want me to do?" I asked.

"Well, first off, you could have some manners and introduce yourself. I'm PP," said the purple guy.

"PP? What kind of a name is that?"

"It's a nickname. Who are you?"

"Um, I'm Zemma, and this is the Story Lady," I gestured toward Joy.

"Great, nice to meet you, Zemma and Ms. Story."

"No, just Story Lady."

"Well, that's just not a proper name at all. Ms. Story, don't you have a real name?"

Joy laughed. "Yes, but it's up to you to figure it out."

"Oh, goody. I love riddles."

"Speaking of riddles, what's PP stand for?" I piped in.

"Guess. If I told you, it wouldn't be a proper riddle."

I stood studying him and started spouting names. With each name I said, he laughed harder. "Purple Parrot. Perry Plush. Purple Polly. Purple Pansy. Patty Perfect. Peter Pumpkin. Purple Panda. You do look a little like a whacked-out panda." He kept right on honking, giving me no clue as to whether or not I was even getting close.

A thought flashed through my mind. I remembered hearing a song when I was little about a Purple People Eater. In the song, he was a one-eyed, one-horned, flying purple people eater. But then he would be PPE, not PP. So, I dismissed that thought.

"Perry Penguin? Perfect Parable?"

"Nope, nope and nope. You get two more guesses, and then you're in for it!"

"In for it?" I felt my eyebrows go up to my hairline.

"Yeah, if you guess wrong, I sing. Trust me, you don't want that."

"Peter, Peter? Paul Prefect? Peter Perfect?"

He started to sing. I immediately wished I'd guessed his secret; the noise was horrendous. I imagined that he sounded like a cross between a brass band, an off-key tenor, and a soprano. Dreadful. I kept shouting names hoping I'd hit on something and make him stop. Joy doubled over. I'm positive it was years before he finally stopped singing. I never did figure out if it was a song at all. There were words and a tune but more noise and energy than melody. I didn't want to ask for fear there would be another penalty for guessing wrong, and he'd keep singing forever.

"PP, I give. You win. What's your name?"

"Do you honestly want to know?" He asked between verses.

"Yes!"

"Really?" How he worked this in with the ghastly singing, I have no idea.

"Yes, darn it all. Please stop." I was feeling desperate by this time. My eardrums hurt, and my head was starting to ache with the noise.

"Well, alright. It's Purple People Eater." (Appendix D)

"Purple People Eater? But that's PPE, not PP!" I shouted.

"Yeah, but that's awkward. You must admit that "PP" sounds better. PPE sounds like we're going to gym class or something."

"Right. Hey, PP, I've always wondered how you got your name."

"Well, isn't it obvious? I'm purple."

"But do you eat people?"

"Well, no. But don't let that get out. Some fool wrote a song saying that I eat people. The truth can't get out, or you'll blow my whole image."

"Your image. What image? What do you think your image is?" I asked.

"I'm the big, scary monster that kids are afraid of," said PP, puffing up his chest.

"Really? Hmmm, you haven't paid proper attention to your publicity."

"Publicity? I have publicity?" He looked taken aback.

"Well, yeah, kind of. I mean, what else would you call your theme song?"

"Oh, no, it's that witless, idiotic song again!"

"What, you don't like it? I think it's great publicity and a lot of fun."

"NO! I hate that song. It was all a big mistake. I thought nobody was around, so I was playing my horn and getting down with some rockin' music. Then out from behind a tree pops this geek. He starts saying childish things like 'Purple People Eater, don't eat me.' I laughed and said, 'I wouldn't eat you cuz you're so tough.' Until I met that guy, my name was Fluffy. He's the one who decided to call me Purple People Eater. I kind of liked it. I thought it was a lot more macho sounding than Fluffy! Since then, I've been flying around the world, scaring little kids, and pretending I'm going to eat them."

"Do they get scared?"

"Well, sometimes, but not often. I did scare a kid once," he said brightly. "Mostly they start singin' that dang song, and I can't get out of there fast enough. I don't know why they don't take me seriously."

"Well, maybe they have an idea that you only eat purple people."

"What! Where would they get that idea? What morons."

"Well, I thought that, too. Not that they're morons, but that you might eat purple people; after all, that's what the song says."

"But there aren't any purple people, silly! I'm purple! There are no purple people."

"Yeah, but if there could be a purple people eater, isn't it just as likely there are purple people?" I said, shrugging.

"Okay, if you insist. Have you ever seen a purple person?"

"No, but until today, I'd never seen a purple people eater either. Who's to say?" I shrugged my shoulders. "I keep running into things I didn't think existed."

"Really? Like what?"

"Unicorns, magic wand gardens, talking trees, worms that sound like they're from Jersey, Jeff the Magic Dragon…."

"Jeff! How is that rascal, Jeff?"

"Jeff, oh, he's good. He and Jackie Pepper got back together." Somehow it didn't surprise me that Jeff and PP knew each other.

"That's good. Jeff missed Jackie."

"They were pretty happy to see each other again." I laughed.

PP turned and looked at Joy, "So, Story Lady, what's your story?"

"I'm just a lady from the country, traveling around seeing what I can see."

"So why are you the 'Story Lady'?"

"Well, what I usually see are people's real stories."

"Their real stories? Do some people have fake stories?"

"In a manner of speaking, yes. Some people are living the stories that someone else laid out for them, never figuring out who or what they want to be."

"Give me an example," said PP.

"Well, you, for instance." Joy said, gesturing towards him.

"Me? What do you mean me? I'm not living someone else's story."

"Sure, you are. You're trying incredibly hard to be a big scary monster. But in no way are you a big scary monster. Besides, in case you haven't looked lately, you're not even big. You could be a scary little monster, but there isn't much call for that. I'm sure it's been difficult for you. People don't take you seriously. They don't run away in fear as they should. Don't you feel like a failure?" Joy was trying to get PP's goat, I could tell.

"I just feel kind of misunderstood. I keep thinking that someday I'll get it right, and I'll roar, and the kids will run screaming."

"Have you ever thought that maybe you just don't have it in you to be scary?"

"Sometimes." PP hung his head a bit sheepishly.

"If you weren't busy trying to be scary, what would you do?"

"I'd start a rock 'n' roll band, of course. That's why I came to Earth in the first place; that is something the dumb songwriter got right."

"You were pretty quick to answer. I'll bet you've been thinking about this a lot."

"It's always been my dream. Who would take me seriously, though?"

"Have you seen some of the stars out there? If they can make it, surely you can.

You're at least memorable. You won't have to work to come up with a gimmick or anything. You're unique, one-of-a-kind. No one else plays music out of a horn on their head."

"Wow, cool. But what if I can't do it?" Emotions flitted across his fuzzy, purple face.

"If you've always dreamed of something, you owe to yourself to give it a try. If you don't, you'll always wonder what could have been. If you don't do well at it, what's lost? You can go back to being your old self, trying to scare kids. At least you'll know you gave it a try."

"So, either way, I can't lose?"

"Exactly. I also have something to help you. But first, Zemma and I have a story to tell you." We told him about our Crystalline Heart Family and our purpose; then, Joy pulled another pendant out of her pocket. This time it was deep opaque purple that seemed to pulse with energy.

"I didn't choose this sugilite heart simply because it's purple. It will remind you of your reasons for being here on this planet. But for you, most of all, it empowers you to walk in strength and grace on the Earth, living your truth. If you ever doubt what is right for your path, just hold the heart and wait for inspiration."

He flapped his wings and flew around us in circles, clapping his hands gleefully. He slowed down and started playing his horn. In case he repeated his previous performance, I was ready to put my hands over my ears. This time, though, the music was great; the sounds he blew were clear and pure. I started to dance along. His music was the happiest music I'd ever heard.

He waved goodbye as he flew off, playing his horn. "Thanks. I'll write when I get work."

His horn faded into the distance. I said, "I bet we need all the happy music we can get to help stave off the dead-eyed Unmakers."

"You are so right, Zemma."

Joy and I were smiling as we sang the *One-Eyed, One-Horned, Flying Purple People Eater* song as we danced down the road.

CHAPTER 20:

Sally's a Klutz, or is She?

I halted abruptly in the middle of the road, cupping my ears. At the same time, I thought that perhaps I should quit stopping dead in the middle of roads. But then I heard the shouts again. Was that someone yelling for help? I grabbed Joy's arm to get her attention. We listened intently, hands behind our ears. Does putting your hands to your ears help? I wondered, again getting sidetracked. Our encounter with the Purple People Eater had left me loopy.

"Help! Someone, please, help!" The cry was faint but distinct. Without looking at each other, we took off in the direction of the call. It seemed to be coming from a pile of rocks at the base of a cliff. I couldn't see anyone at first. But I finally found her. She was a woman, probably in her early twenties, and there was a massive boulder on her foot. I was amazed that she wasn't screaming bloody murder.

She saw me looking with shock at her foot. "It's not as bad as it looks. The boulder has my foot trapped, but it's not crushing anything. I think I'm unhurt. I just can't seem to get myself loose!"

"I don't know… We might have to amputate." I said, my heart still racing. As you know, my sarcasm kicks in when I panic.

She looked at me carefully before realizing I was kidding. "Oh, you joker. Can you help me roll it off? Say, what's your name, anyway?"

"Sorry, that was rude of me. I just don't seem to know the protocol for introducing myself to a woman trapped under a boulder." I laughed. "I'm Zemma, and this is the Story Lady."

"Nice to meet you both. I'm Sally. I'm so glad you came along. I sure hope you can help me get out of here."

I bowed, "At your service."

I gallantly pushed; the boulder didn't budge. I pulled; nothing, no movement. I started looking around for a big stick or something I could use as a lever. "Joy, do you see anything we can use to help move this boulder?"

"Nope."

"Just, 'nope'? Any ideas?" I said, incredulous. Joy always had suggestions.

"Not really."

"Come on, Joy. What can we do to help?"

"Not much, it seems. I think this job is beyond us," Joy said airily.

"Then what, we just leave her here?" I was beginning to feel exasperated at Joy's lack of compassion.

"Well, we could do the sensible thing and go on to the next town and send someone back."

"Joy, we can't do that. It's almost dark. What if there are wild animals? What if some bad men come along?"

"Zemma, you're hysterical. When was the last time you saw a man-eating animal in these parts?"

"Are you two going to stand and argue all day? I honestly need some help here," Sally said.

"Oh, sorry." I patted her shoulder awkwardly. "I don't know what to do. Can you stay here until we get help?"

Slowly, she shook her head. "Well, I guess I'll have to, won't I? I don't see that I have an alternative unless you've got a crowbar or a genie in your pocket."

Joy looked thoughtful. "Hmmm, a genie? That could be just what we need."

"You have a genie on you, Joy?"

"Well, not exactly, but I think I know how to find one."

"Lady, I don't know who you are or what you're thinking, but I sure wish you did have a genie here," Sally said.

I could almost see the gears clicking in Joy's head as she touched and passed over most of the items dangling from her scarves. Curiously, I watched, wondering how she was going to conjure up a genie. Her fingers came to rest on the little bottle filled with purple iridescent liquid, and she nodded.

Joy walked over to the girl smiling. "Well, Sally. I think we can get you out of here. But you're going to have to help me out here."

"Okay," Sally said, slowly and cautiously. She didn't appear to be the most trusting girl I'd ever met. She looked at us both as if she were expecting some kind of trick.

"Very well, Sally. I want you to close your eyes tightly. Don't open them for any reason until I tell you to. If you do, the magic won't work."

"Magic? You have magic?"

"Well, yes, of course."

"What do you mean, of course? I've never met anyone with actual magic before. I'm not even sure I believe in magic!" She peered suspiciously at Joy.

"Now you have met someone with magic. It doesn't matter if you believe in it, only that I do. Close your eyes. Don't open them until I say so! I'm going to sprinkle my magic potion on you."

Joy uncorked the bottle and sprinkled it freely over Sally. Nothing happened. Joy tapped Sally on the head with her finger. "Don't open your eyes yet. I want you to imagine with all your might that there is a genie strong enough to lift the boulder like a pebble. But he's gentle and wouldn't hurt a fly. Imagine him easily lifting the boulder from your foot."

"Okay." Sally closed her eyes tightly, squeezing them, looking almost comical.

"Can you see him?"

"Oh, yes. The genie is enormous and super strong."

"Good. Ask genie to lift the boulder just enough for you to pull your foot out."

I swear I still didn't see any genie. That boulder seemed to lift in the air ever so slightly. Sally pulled her foot out and collapsed on the ground. "Can I open my eyes now?" Asked Sally

"Yes." Replied Joy.

She opened her eyes and looked around wildly, clearly expecting to see a genie. "Where is the genie?"

"Oh, he's already gone. He doesn't like to stay around for thank you's. He's quite shy. You'll have to forgive him for being so rude."

"Oh. But I wanted to thank him!" Sally said with evident disappointment.

"He knows."

"Oh, that's good," said Sally.

"Sally, you were fortunate that we happened to come along to help you."

"I sure was. I'm always getting myself into scrapes, and it's not usually so easy to get back out."

"This frequently happens?" Asked Joy.

"Well, not this exact thing. I've never gotten my foot stuck under a boulder before. But I am rather clumsy. People tell me I just don't pay attention, that I shouldn't be such a scatterbrain, be grounded, all that stuff. But I do pay attention. I don't know why these things just seem to happen to me. I guess I'm jinxed."

"Sally, this is your lucky day. The magic potion I sprinkled on you has lasting properties. It's not just a one-time thing."

"Lasting? What will happen?" Sally asked with curiosity.

"It removes your bad luck. You won't be jinxed any longer. But if something does happen and you need help, you can close your eyes, and the genie will be there to help you. Genie can only appear in the physical like he did today, just this once. From now on, though, he'll be able to talk to you and give you advice. All you have to do is ask for his help, then get quiet and listen for the answer."

"Wow, cool. I've always wanted to stop being such a klutz. But the more I tried, the worse I got."

"That happens a lot. The more you concentrate on not doing something, the more it happens. That's because whatever you focus on continues to grow in strength. It's an attention thing. If you focused on being graceful instead of trying to 'not be a klutz,' I think you'd find things would go a lot differently."

"You're saying I shouldn't think about 'not being klutzy.' I should pretend I'm graceful. And that will make a difference? Why?" she said, looking suspiciously at us once again.

"It's the way the Universe works. Whatever we resist persists. If you want to stop something, you don't think about not doing it. Don't resist it. Concentrate instead on a positive action that you do want. In your case, concentrate on being graceful. I think you'll be surprised at what a difference it makes. You've got a head start since you don't have a jinx to trip you up any longer."

"Sally, I am curious, though. Do you remember what was happening in your life at the time you first started being clumsy? Or were you always a klutz?"

"No, when I was a kid, I didn't have any problems at all. I think it all began about the time I started 7th grade."

"Did anything that happened that year stand out?" Queried Joy.

"Well, I don't know if you'd call it significant, but to me, it was everything! I got accepted into an art class. To get into the course, I had to enter several things for judging. They were only taking pupils they felt had promise. I was thrilled when I got the letter telling me I was accepted. I was so determined to show them that they'd made the right choice, I spent all my time looking at everything around me, paying close attention to its form, color, how it looks in the light, the feel of it. It's surprising how beautiful even those most mundane things can be. Everything was captivating to me. I was astounded at the artfulness around me that I'd taken for granted."

"Is that when you started having problems, Sally?" Asked Joy.

"Yes, I think it was. Geesh, I was continually walking along while looking at the construction of a leaf as I passed it by, and the next thing I knew, I'd be flat on my face in the dirt."

"Sally, you're not a klutz at all! You're just distracted by the art around you and not paying any attention to where your body is. When your mind and spirit are elsewhere, you're not fully present in your body at all."

"That would explain so much! I do sometimes feel a little spacy, and I'd just love to be able not to be falling up, down, and over everything."

"Sally, I believe this awareness, as well as focusing on being grounded, will put you back on much more even footing. Sorry for the pun; I just couldn't pass it up."

"How can I thank you? By the way, what's your name? I was so busy recounting my problems that I didn't even ask your name! I am so sorry."

"You can thank me by sharing this idea with other people. Help them focus on the positive actions and thoughts instead of the negative."

"And your name?"

"I go by many names. If you didn't know my name, what would you call me?"

"Hmmm, let me think for just a moment. I would call you Connie."

"Connie?" Joy tilted her head quizzically.

"Oh, yeah, I guess I should explain. It's short for confidence. That's how you make me feel. Confident, like I can handle things, and I'll be alright."

"Okay, then, Connie, I shall be."

"Connie, if I just need to pay attention to where my body is and think gracefully, why do I need a spell?"

"You don't need a spell. I said that just to give you a little extra confidence. But you can still call on the spirit of the genie whenever you need help. Just remember to listen for the answers, and you'll have all you need."

Joy's eyes lit up again as she reached into her pocket and pulled out a heart pendant of vibrant orangish-red color. Again, we both explained the Unmakers, the Crystalline Heart Family, and our reasons for asking her to join us. As Joy put the necklace around Sally's neck, she told Sally that the heart was Red Jasper and was an excellent stone to ground and stabilize both her body and emotions, allowing her to handle challenges with strength.

"Thank you. Oh, thank you so much." Sally exclaimed, and she hugged us both.

"You are most welcome, Sally. I hope you're still doing art. Art opens people's minds to help them see things in new ways. It sometimes goes as far as to touch a person's deepest heart."

"Of course, I am still creating art! I'm the school district's art teacher. I love seeing the faces of the kids when they finish something that pleases them. They light up from within. It's too easy to dismiss art as something frivolous and insignificant."

Joy looked intently at Sally, "You don't believe that, do you?"

"No, it's like life-blood to me. But when I'm fighting to keep art in the school and keep at least some budget for supplies, I sometimes begin to doubt after repeatedly hearing how the students need to learn something useful and practical. It feels like a continual battle to stay clear and that it's important."

"Sally, it's essential that the students have art and other things in their lives to keep them connected to a critical part of Creation and their souls."

"Connie, that's so encouraging. I'll never forget what you've said. I can't thank you enough. But I've got to get home before my father starts to worry."

Sally headed off, limping a little. Joy and I pitched her skirt tent right there next to the rocks. I sat down on the mysteriously moved boulder and gave her a long look.

"Joy, what happened here? I didn't see a genie."

"Well, of course not. There are no genies."

"How am I to know that? I've already seen lots of other things that don't exist, so why not a genie?"s

"No, you've seen things that you thought did not exist. But genies don't exist. Well, at least, I don't think they do."

"Then why on Earth did you tell her to imagine a genie?"

"That was just to give her confidence. Once she believed the genie could move the boulder, it moved."

"Ah, so it was the magic potion that did it."

"No. That bottle was nothing but glycerin water and food coloring."

"What?! Then what happened here?"

"Sally believed that the bottle had magical properties. It was her belief that made things happen."

"Then, you didn't actually remove her jinx?"

"There never was a jinx, Zemma. Sally became convinced over the years that she had a jinx and because she passionately believed it to be true, she was jinxed. Now that she equally believes it to be gone, it is."

"So, we're back to seeing what you believe again?"

"Yes, it appears so," said Joy nodding.

"Is it that important, that powerful?"

"Yes. You'll see. Your thoughts are immensely powerful, and when you add feelings and emotions to them, anything can happen."

Gratefully, I realized I was tired. "Joy, I don't know about you, but I'm ready for food and sleep." She smiled and nodded, reaching to undo her skirt to make camp.

We shared an endless energy bar, some water and prepared the tent. I crawled into my sleeping bag and was asleep almost before I'd closed my eyes.

CHAPTER 21:

Promises Made
To & From a Bicycle!

Morning arrived without fanfare. We ate, packed, and went on our way. I was getting bored with backcountry roads. Joy seemed to like walking the slower-paced routes without worrying about traffic. She said that the people you meet on the back roads are a lot more likely to stop and chat than those rushing by in their cars on the highways. I knew all this, yet I felt nostalgic for the days of getting there quickly, riding in fast cars. I knew I was being silly. I couldn't imagine any of the adventures we'd had taking place alongside an interstate highway. Nevertheless, I missed wheels even though there was no place, in particular, we needed to be and no reason to hurry.

In case you haven't noticed, I hadn't yet mastered the fine art of hiding my feelings. I was a little better at letting them go, but at the moment, everything I felt was still evident. Some of my friends are good at hiding their moods and pretending to be happy even when they're upset or worried. I've tried, but it somehow never works for me. I couldn't decide if this lack was a good thing or a bad thing. Maybe it just was.

On the plus side, I have always been real! My friends knew they could trust what I said was what I meant. If I told them I was okay with something, they knew I was genuinely fine with it. If I was angry, sad, disappointed, happy, joyous, they always knew that, too. I've known people who can put on a convincing face, and I never know if what they appear to feel is authentic or just a mask. It was disconcerting to have taken someone at face value and discover later that they were upset or mad about things. I frequently felt confused and betrayed by this lack of honesty and integrity.

The downside of this inability to cover my true feelings and pretend was that I couldn't hide anything. I don't mean I'd blurt out confidences, I was good at that kind of secret, but I never left anyone guessing about anything I was thinking or feeling. Most girls try to maintain some aura of mystery, keeping people guessing (especially boys). Not me. If I liked a boy, he immediately knew by the goofy look on my face or the blush creeping up my neck. Some boys found this endearing and sweet, but not most of them. Sometimes I thought I was cursed to be emotionally transparent.

Suddenly, Joy burst out laughing.

"I'm sorry, Zemma. I don't mean to laugh at you. I've tried, really tried, to ignore your melancholy mood. You are extremely funny at times. What is it that's bothering you today??"

"Joy, I hate to say it. It's silly. I know we're on the right road, but I feel nostalgic for the old days when I had my wheels. I miss being able to jump on a bike or into a car and go a little faster."

"You, my friend, are predominantly right-brained and heart-centered, and to add to that, you get a lot of your information through your perceptions. You lead with your heart. Right-brained, we call you. Feeling/intuitive. Most of your decisions about the world are based on what you feel with your five senses and perceive through your other senses."

"Other senses?" I braced myself for something unexpected.

Joy continued as we walked. "You're familiar with sight, smell, touch, hearing, and taste. These five senses are connected to the physical, knowable world and help you interpret what's tangible. Everyone has other senses, as well. We talked earlier about a sixth sense. Usually, the sixth sense refers to intuition, and, as you know, this sense is more developed in some. Those with a heightened sixth sense have strong 'gut feelings' about things or intuitive understandings about others' feelings and motivations. Some perceive future events through visions, dreams, or a sense of knowing, which can be a helpful skill at times. Many people with this ability find it challenging to explain why they decide the way they do. They often have no rational explanation for their choices and find themselves deeply frustrated in their attempts to justify their actions."

"Joy, I know this! Gosh, most of my life, I've been trying to explain myself and why I think and do things that are often out-of-step with what most people consider the norm. I've never had words to explain it. Somehow the way I learn and understand things seems different from how most of my family and friends do. Is it just I have more information? No wonder I've had so much trouble explaining my ideas!" I was practically jumping up and down. I was so excited to have an explanation.

"Exactly. You listen to your sixth sense, and it has guided you throughout your life."

"But I've spent most of my life feeling strange and out-of-step."

"Zemma, I'm sorry to tell you that probably won't change. Don't look so unhappy about it. If you lost your sixth sense, you would feel completely lost. That's one of the reasons you've been so resistant to protecting yourself. You think you'll lose the ability to communicate and know deeply. Being aware of your sixth sense and how it works will help you find ways to explain your actions to others and trust your choices. I think you'll find yourself less frustrated as time goes on."

She looked at me to make sure I was listening and went on, "What I want to talk about today, though, is your 'other senses,' not just the six you are aware of."

"I don't have any other senses!" I stated with finality and assurance.

"Hmmm, you think not? Zemma, I am surprised that you can still make definitive statements about anything, after all you've learned recently. Don't you understand yet that just because you haven't experienced something doesn't mean it doesn't exist?"

"I guess I deserved that," I apologized. "It's a lot to get my head around."

"Zemma, you ain't seen nuthin' yet,'" she quoted from an old song with a wry grin.

"What? What do you mean?" That old fear feeling was starting to cramp my stomach.

"Remember the unicorn?"

Cautiously, "Yes."

"Don't look so afraid. I assure you that the abilities the unicorn passed on to you aren't scary or dangerous unless you make them so."

"Unless I make them so?!" I yelled, coming way too close to screeching like a little girl. "They are either dangerous and scary, or they aren't. Right?"

"Wrong. We've talked before about attitude, intention, and consciousness. If you resist your new gifts, or fear them, or otherwise brand them as negative, then they can become so. You must begin learning to control your emotions."

"I thought you said I was in the group of people who couldn't just 'think' themselves into a better mood."

"I didn't say you should control your emotions by thinking. That won't work for you. But there are other ways of learning control by working within your normal abilities."

"How then? In the past, every attempt I've made to change my mood has failed. Sometimes things get even more out of control."

"That's because you're trying to change from the outside in. You need to make the alterations from the inside out."

"How?"

"Zemma, I can't tell you yet."

"What, again?! Can you give me a hint?" I felt as if all my energy had left me.

"I merely brought up the subject because I want you to think about it for a while. See if you can remember instances where you could shift your attitude or change the way you felt about something or someone. We'll get a chance to put this into practice later."

"You are infuriating, you know?" I just shook my head at her.

"Yes, I am, aren't I?" Joy laughed.

I looked at Joy's smug smile and took off running. I was tired of her secrets and roundabout ways of telling me things, or maybe I should say, not telling me things! Why couldn't she just come out and tell me something? I have more than six senses; I can make my gift bad, but I don't have to, and I have to figure it all out myself! From the inside out! Ridiculous! I'd been trying desperately to stay positive and happy, but the crazy funks caught up with me again. This time it was only a mild funk and was dissipating as we walked, me a little ahead of her. I was learning that sometimes I just needed a little space.

I began to look around, enjoying the scenery. I forgot my nostalgia for faster modes of travel, appreciating that I could stop and enjoy nature. I watched rabbits and mice scampering among grasses. I saw much that I would have missed speeding on the interstate.

As we rounded the next corner, I spied a bicycle leaning against a sturdy oak tree. I looked around, expecting to see its owner nearby. I didn't see anyone. The bike was beautiful metallic red, which somehow appeared to be glowing in the sunlight. The longer I looked at it, the brighter it got. It was positively pulsing with light and energy.

Curious, I walked up to within about a foot of the bicycle. I didn't touch it. I just stared, looking around in all directions for the owner. I was amazed that someone would leave it in the open without chaining it to the tree. Leaving a bike unchained and unprotected was a surefire way to get it stolen.

"Ride me."

I turned around wildly. "Who said that?"

"Ride me."

"Who's there? Come out, whoever you are!"

"Ride me."

I turned around and around, looking everywhere, not seeing anyone. I walked around the tree; looked up into the branches; nobody was around.

"Ride me."

I looked more closely at the bike. "Are you talking to me?"

"Yep. Are you always this dense?"

"Well, no. But I don't normally run into talking bicycles."

"Really? I believe you are mistaken," said the bicycle in a somewhat tinny but appealing voice.

"Look, I think I'd know if I'd seen a talking bike before."

"Really?" the bike said again. "Just because a man is deaf doesn't mean someone is not talking to him."

"I'm not deaf."

"Not entirely deaf. However, you have managed to tune out a lot of the life going on around you until now. I bet until recently, you only had conversations with other humans."

"Well, of course."

"See! There you go with the 'of course' bit."

"Ahhh, I'm beginning to see what you mean." I shook my head, feeling somewhat bemused. "Well, you're my first talking bicycle. Can all of you talk like trees and birds and fairies?"

"No, not all of us, silly. That would be ridiculous. Some 'inanimate' objects are inanimate. Others can communicate but not in words; some use feelings, images, even music or other sounds."

"Why can you talk, and they can't?"

"It has to do with their creator's intent. Some things just aren't made with the conscious knowing or understanding that they can communicate. If the person, or people, making an object believes in or loves it, then that item becomes endowed with consciousness."

"So, basically, you're saying that the feelings of the makers go into what they are making?"

"Yep, that's pretty much the way it works."

"How do I know which items are animate and which aren't?"

"That's simple. The ones who communicate are, and the ones who don't aren't. So, who has been opening your eyes lately?"

I looked at Joy, shrugging my shoulders and raising my eyebrows. We both laughed and nodded.

"Joy. I guess I'd say, Joy," I answered.

"There's your answer." The bike rattled a little, restless.

"Now that we have that settled, where is your owner?" I asked the bike.

"I don't have an owner."

"Then how did you get here?"

"Gee, let me think…Oh yeah, wheels turned. Road went by underneath me. Here I am."

"You know, you're a bit of a smart-aleck."

"I'm glad you noticed," responded the bike.

"You came here on your own? Why?"

"Because this is where you were going to be."

I felt a small thrill go through my body. "Me?"

"Yes, you. I came from a bicycle factory like most other bicycles. However, what's different about me is that I am one of a dozen or so made by old Tom during his last week of work before he retired. During that last week, he put all his love for bicycles into everything he did; Tom turned every screw with loving care. All the bikes he made during his career are conscious. But the last twelve are much more than merely animate; we are truly alive. I was the last bike he ever made."

The bike seemed to pause for effect and then continued. "While he was putting me together, Tom was thinking of how much he'd loved his first bike as a boy. He thought about the person who would ride and care for me and decided it should be an adventurous youngster much like he had been. You and old Tom have never met, but somehow he could sense your spirit out in the world. Through him, I, too, could sense who you were. Over the last week or so, it's continually gotten stronger. Yesterday, I managed to pick up a decidedly clear signal of exactly where you were. So, here we are, together at last."

"What about the factory owners? Aren't they looking for you?"

"Nope. Old Tom used his last paycheck to purchase all the bikes he made that last week. He sent all of us out to find the boys or girls who were meant to ride us."

"So, you're mine?" I asked with delight and hope.

"No. I don't 'belong' to anyone. I am conscious and alive; I do choose, however, to be with you. I am happy to have you ride me in rain or shine, for richer, for poorer, in sickness and in health, as long as we both want to."

"Those words remind me of wedding vows!"

"Well," said the bike, "I am pledging myself to you, but you have to make promises as well."

"What kind of promises?"

"I promise to give you transportation. You, in turn, pledge to keep me clean, oiled, and well maintained. As long as we keep our promises to one another, we'll have a happy life together."

"Sounds fair enough. What do we do now?"

"Well, gee, let me think! Duh! You get on and ride."

"Oh!" Happily, I started wheeling the bike to the road, oblivious to what Joy was up to for once. "Hey, what's your name? I can't just keep calling you 'bike.'"

"Flicka."

"That's a horse's name!"

"Really? Wow! Does that mean I'm a horse, oh literal one?" The bike could dole out sarcasm as well as the next person, almost a match for me. "Just because someone else has had the name before, does that mean I can't use that name? There are other Zemmas in the world. Well, I'm not so sure about that, but I've met other Joys."

"Well, no. It's just that I used to watch reruns of 'My Friend Flicka.' She was a horse."

"It sounds like this Flicka was a good horse to know."

"She was the boy's best friend," I said, remembering and smiling.

"Didn't you pretend that you were the boy and were riding Flicka?"

"How did you know? But I pretended I was a girl riding Flicka."

"Haven't you learned yet that there are no secrets? We can read your mind."

"What a frightening thought!" I declared.

"It's only scary if you want it to be. I, on the other hand, believe that it's rather comforting to feel connected. Zemma, aren't you tired of talking yet? Don't you want to go for a ride?"

"Yes!" I looked over at Joy. "Joy, I don't want to leave you behind. You don't have a bicycle!"

"That's sweet, Zemma. Don't worry; I have transportation."

"What is it?"

"You'll see. You and Flicka go on ahead. I'll catch up."

I jumped on, and before I even started pedaling, we were speeding down the road, kicking up dust in our wake.

"Flicka, I hate to say this, but can you make less dust? I don't want Joy to be choking on it."

"Certainly." I looked back, and there was no dust at all. Puzzled, I looked down to see we were about one inch off the ground!

"Um, Flicka, we're not touching the ground."

"You didn't want dust. Now there isn't any."

"Are we flying?"

"Do you want to fly?"

"Yes, oh, yes! I love to fly."

"Then we can fly," Flicka said in a matter-of-fact voice.

"So, whether you can fly or not depends on me, not you??"

"Yep."

"How can that be?" I was incredulous once again.

"It's another consciousness thing. If you want to fly, you must believe it."

"How can I believe something I know is impossible?"

"Impossible? Hmmm, look down, trees talk, fish speak, dragons are real, unicorns aren't extinct or a myth. A woman can move boulders because she thinks she can. We aren't on the ground. Should I continue?"

OK, I thought, let's give this a try. "Flicka, let's fly."

"It's not quite that easy. You can't just command me. You must feel it."

"Feel it? What does that have to do with flying?"

"Remember your conversation with Joy this morning about controlling your emotions?"

"Yes, but how do you...?"

"Zemma," Flicka spoke firmly with just a hint of exasperation.

I was beginning to feel extremely slow on the uptake. "I think my brain is still trying to catch up!"

"Right."

"So, how does controlling my emotions make us fly?"

"If you visualize flying and feel it deep down in your bones, then we can fly."

I closed my eyes, imagining we were flying just like the boy on the bike in the movie E.T. Nothing happened.

"Why aren't we flying?"

"You're thinking it. You can see it in your head. But you didn't FEEL it."

I closed my eyes again and saw us flying. I took a deep breath and began to feel how it feels to fly. I remembered what it was like to be an eagle. I was free.!

I opened my eyes, and we were flying about five feet off the ground. I was so shocked, I instantly thought, 'Bikes don't fly!' We crashed to the ground.

Untangling myself from Flicka, I said, "Oops. Are you OK?"

"Try again. Do better!" Flicka rolled forward and back, testing her wheels.

This time, I closed my eyes and accessed the sense of flight and freedom much more smoothly. When I opened my eyes, we were soaring about eight feet off the ground. "Flicka, this is awesome!"

We flew up, down, and around. Then, just behind me, I felt a presence. I turned to look and did a double-take. Joy was riding a giant white swan!

The shock of seeing Joy behind me jolted me out of flying consciousness. Once again, we plummeted to the ground. We'd fallen from a greater height this time, and the landing was jarring. I rolled into the dirt. Flicka laughed as I jumped up, angrily dusting myself off.

"Be careful, will you? I can see we're going to have to stay closer to the ground until you learn better control."

"Maybe that's a good idea. Wow, talk about instant feedback."

A gentle voice wafted over to me. "Yes, Zemma, your thoughts can be powerful. It'll get easier to control them as you and Flicka practice more," Joy and her swan landed smoothly nearby. "I think you've had enough for right now. Why don't we have some lunch?"

Flicka rolled into the shade of a nearby tree, and I swear she leaned over and started to snore. I started unpacking lunch, tempted by a nap. Controlling my emotions turned out to be hard work!

CHAPTER 22:

Scary Monsters, Oh My!

Imust have dozed off after lunch. I don't usually take naps. The excitement and stress of the morning took their toll. Finding Flicka was astonishing, and I was beyond pleased and excited. But I knew I had a lot to learn.

I'm not sure what woke me. I only know that I was dreaming of flying with Flicka one minute, and the next, I was awake and afraid. I had an intense sense of danger. My heart was pounding, and my palms were sweating. I looked wildly around and saw nothing. I mean really nothing. No Joy. No Flicka. No swan.

It took a moment to sink in that not only didn't I see those things, but I didn't see anything. Everything was a complete blank, as if I were in an empty room, except that this one was so huge, I couldn't even see the edges—blank gray walls without angles. I opened and closed my eyes several times, expecting things to be back to normal. Gray, everywhere I looked was just gray. The grayness began to vibrate as shapes and colors appeared and disappeared. It was hypnotizing but scary.

"Everything is fine, " I said aloud. "Everything is fine." It didn't help; my knees were shaking; fear filled my whole body. I was breathing hard as if I'd been running. I watched the place where the colors were emerging into one shimmering mass.

Tall. It was tall, at least seven feet, thick and menacing. I saw a thick black mouth with sharp teeth, gnarled muscular limbs, and torso emerging. It was a monster from my childhood, the thing that kept me awake at night when I was six. A friend had been staying over, and we'd told stories for hours about my closet monster. For months, I lay in bed prepared to die whenever the light shifted in that corner of the room. Sometimes I heard it slithering underneath my bed.

It now stood before me, every feature precisely as I'd feared. Had we somehow known it was there, even though we couldn't see it? Had we sensed it? I froze, unmoving, scarcely breathing, a childhood trick I hoped would work even though it was only him and me. There was nowhere to hide. If I pretend to be dead, maybe it'll believe me and go away. If I don't breathe, perhaps it won't notice me.

Suddenly it roared! My ears felt like they'd burst. I covered my ears and closed my eyes. It roared again. The sound penetrated the very marrow of my bones. I was gasping for air. I tried to turn and run, but my legs refused to move.

It took a lot of effort, but I willed some energy to my legs, and I managed to run. I ran and ran until I could hardly breathe. I turned, and it was right behind me. I ran again. It kept up with me; I was terrified!

Inwardly I began to pray. "Please don't hurt me. I'll be good. I promise. Please, just go away."

As I prayed these words, the phrase 'scary monster' flashed in my mind. Where had I heard that phrase before? I was terrified and seemed to be unable to grasp the thought. I almost remembered someone saying… It would flash through my mind; I could almost hear someone saying the words, but just out of conscious reach. Then the thought would be gone again. In my frustration, I screamed, "There are no scary monsters! Go away!"

"Hey, wait a minute," I thought. Scary monsters. Scary monsters and fairies. Good things and bad things. I get it. I made jokes about this! I'm not scared of scary monsters! Right…. But I reached for another thought: what if it's another manifestation of my beliefs. If I believe it is, then it is. If that is true, then if I believe it is not so, it is not. But I see and hear it now. How do I stop believing in the monster? How do I shut out the evidence roaring before me?

I took several deep, shuddering breaths. I wondered if the pillar of light technique would help. It certainly couldn't hurt. I visualized the golden light streaming in through my crown. However, this time, instead of sending it out my solar plexus, I pushed it down through my feet into the ground. The light was a steady stream through my body, connecting me to the heavens and the Earth. I felt better. I no longer felt like running away.

I opened my eyes. The scary monster roared and waved his talons; I closed my eyes again. I imagined that the pillar of golden light not only moved through me but was now wide enough to fill and surround my body.

I peeked out between my fingers. It was still there, although I believe it had moved back a foot or two. Encouraged, I started chanting in my head. "Scary monsters do not exist. Scary monsters do not exist. Scary monsters do not exist. Scary monsters do not exist." When I opened my eyes next, there were two of them.

Desperately, I wondered what I was doing wrong. I heard Joy in my head, "What you resist persists."

"Okay, okay. If I want to make my lifetime nemesis disappear, I've got to focus on something else. It's not enough to say it does not exist. The Universe doesn't hear the 'not,' so what it hears is *scary monsters Do exist.*"

Confident that I'd hit on an important clue, I began searching my mind. I remembered Sally trapped by a boulder and her genie. If the genie came because she believed it was possible, then I should be able to do the same.

I needed a protector who would gobble up the scary monster. No sooner than I had the thought, he appeared. He was huge and green, just like the Hulk. Yes, that would be great! "Wow, the Hulk is real." As soon as I said it, I understood. The Hulk and the scary monster were both real only in that I believed in them. Did it make sense that I could conjure up the Hulk to protect me from the terrifying monster? Were they both figments of my imagination?

If I could conjure up The Hulk, then I knew I could protect myself. I closed my eyes and thanked the Hulk for coming and told him I released him from the job of protecting me. When I opened my eyes again, it was just me and the scary monster! It roared! It threatened!

I looked it straight in the eyes; it had the dead, blank eyes of the Unmaker. Had my scary monster always been the Unmaker, or was the Unmaker using the specter of my scary monster to get to me? As my mind started going down those rabbit holes, I stopped myself. Letting myself get sidetracked would weaken me, and he'd win. Questioning my previous perceptions would also diffuse my confidence and focus.

I realized that all these things are tools that the Unmakers and other manifestations of darkness use. They cause us to shut down, close off our hearts and lose sight of the immense strength of our light, strength, and power.

Even with this realization, I was still shaking in my sneakers; after all, it was still a big scary monster, and I felt like a frightened little girl in front of it. In my mind's eye, I changed its appearance to that of a cartoon figure that, like the Purple People Eater, was trying hard to be a big scary monster. I started to laugh! It roared and gestured crazily, not realizing it no longer appeared in the same way. I was gasping for breath, slapping my knees, tears in my eyes, unable to stop laughing. If I'd been drinking milk, it would have been snorting out my nose. The dread I'd carried all my life left me.

I stopped laughing, stood straight, feet apart, and felt my energy ground into both the Earth and the Heavens. I let my core energy build up and then opened my heart, allowing all the love I had for the Universe, the Earth, Humanity, all of Creation to stream from my heart in brilliant light.

I hear you asking questions. So, I'll answer them now. Did I push that light at him like a weapon? Did I try to make him feel the love and the light?

No, to all those things. Darkness is the absence of light and love; if I tried to push it on him, then I would no longer be coming from a place of love. I allowed my love to shine brightly but softly, illuminating all around us. The energy was there for him if he was open to it, but it was his choice. Darkness cannot be overcome by resistance, only by inviting it to open to the light.

The Unmaker began to waver. I held the love in my heart, feeling it fully, welcoming him to join me. It tried to roar but was only able to get out a squeak.

And it disappeared in a puff of dark smoke.

I collapsed onto the ground, gasping for air. I had done it; I had conquered a monster!

I stood tall and roared!

It felt so good to have stood up to my fear. I pondered for a moment, wondering if he was real or imaginary? I was hit with the realization that it didn't matter. The critical part was realizing I wasn't helpless and refusing to be a cowering victim. The minute I grounded myself and stood firm, he lost power over me and vanished.

I ROARED once more.

CHAPTER 23:

The Giant One-man-band

It was already late afternoon when I opened my eyes. Where had the day gone? How long had I been fighting? I looked around, relieved to see Joy peacefully sitting on a rock, watching me.

"Did I fall asleep again?"

"Again? You nodded off right after lunch and have been asleep ever since."

"I have? I didn't wake up and run around or anything?"

"No. But you roared twice."

"That was all just a dream?"

In an almost remonstrative voice, "Zemma, I wouldn't go around writing dreams off as not being real."

"Yes, this sure felt scarily real." I laughed nervously.

"Then it was real to you. Anything that takes place in your dreams is as real to your mind and emotions as if it happened while you were awake to my vision."

"Awake to your vision?" I wondered.

"Just because I see you were sleeping doesn't mean that it's necessarily so. I could be dreaming that I'm watching you sleep. There are many levels of reality. Who's to know which one is real? Maybe they all are. Perhaps none of them are."

"Ayeee! Joy, this could make me feel very crazy!" Maybe I should go back to sleep again and start the day over.

"I know, it's a lot to take in," she said soothingly.

"Fine. Can we make camp and stay here for the night?"

"Certainly. We are running a little short on food. Do you want to see if you can catch a fish?"

"Is that a trick question?"

"No. Why?"

"Last time I caught a fish, I had to listen to a dissertation on reincarnation before breakfast. I don't feel like I'm up to all that right now. Can I fish, and we just eat?" I asked.

"Sure. Just remember to send out a request for volunteers and to thank them for their sacrifice."

"No problem." I took the proffered needle and thread and headed in the direction of the stream I could hear in the distance. I walked carefully; I didn't want to be responsible for inadvertently causing harm. Then I heard a strange noise behind me. I tried to place it and couldn't quite make it out. After the day I'd had, I wasn't too anxious to turn and look. My curiosity won out, and I turned. Following at my heels was Flicka!

She giggled gaily at my surprise. "Did you forget about me already?"

"No, I didn't forget you. But I hadn't expected to see you trotting, or rather rolling behind me like a puppy."

"A puppy, huh? You wouldn't leave me behind if I were another girl, would you?"

"Noooo," I answered slowly, not quite knowing where this conversation was going.

"I'm your friend. Take me with you everywhere you go."

"Flicka, that's fine out here, but that could raise some eyebrows when we get to town."

"You think so?" she asked.

"Well, yes. I can't take you into stores or restaurants. Some people might be downright afraid of you."

"Me? Why?"

"Well, see, bicycles don't normally go following along behind people. Usually, when they move, it's because they have a pedaling rider."

"Well, then, I imagine you'll just have to get on and ride when we come to a town."

"I don't want to cause problems."

"Good, that's settled."

We were almost at the stream when an intense feeling overtook me that we needed to get to the next town right away. I shrugged my shoulders as if that would get rid of this strange sense of urgency. It remained and, if anything, became even more insistent. I jumped on Flicka, and we bounced back over the field to find Joy packing up the camping stuff.

"You, too?"

"Yes, I heard it too. I've called Swanee, and she'll be here in a minute. We can fly if we're careful not to be seen and then walk the last little bit," Joy said matter-of-factly as if flying to town on the back of a swan or seat of a bicycle was an everyday occurrence.

We made it to town in under ten minutes. Joy dismounted from Swanee, who flew off, honking her goodbye. I walked beside Flicka, taking care to keep my hand on her seat, so it appeared I was walking her.

The town seemed calm in the extreme, almost asleep. There was no apparent reason for any urgency. We walked down the main street, looking carefully to see if anything was wrong. In the distance, down one of the side streets, I could hear what sounded like a brass band. It appeared to be getting closer.

We turned the corner and stopped in disbelief. Coming toward us was the wildest one-man-band I'd ever seen. At least seven feet tall, the man was huge, with bright orange hair sticking out in all directions. His bulbous nose was sunburned. His eyes seemed to spin around independently of one another. Tattoos covered every visible surface of his body. He carried an enormous drum, with dangling tambourines on each side, cymbals, a harmonica, and a trumpet, each on flexible wires just in front of his mouth, a bell, a triangle, a set of bongos, and several other instruments I couldn't place. A smaller man couldn't have even lifted that set up, let alone walk and dance. He alternated between playing the harmonica and the trumpet. The drum, bongos, and tambourines seemed to be playing themselves. A cacophony of children and dogs surrounded him.

His music was spirited. The best part, though, was watching the faces of people as he walked and danced down the street. Joy and I fell in behind him and went with the crowd for several blocks.

Villagers of all ages came out of their doors to listen. Some didn't appear at all happy about having their peace disturbed. But most smiled and waved at all the commotion. I could swear I saw one couple step out onto their lawn with a frown. Mind you, they weren't fully blank-eyed but looked like they were getting close. It seemed that the one-man-band slowed down, taking longer to pass and that he made even more of an effort to put joy and delight in his music. Joy and I stopped on the edge of their lawn. Was there now a bit of shine in their eyes and a hint of a smile?

He saw us, smiled, and stopped. "Ah, here you are."

"You were expecting us?" I asked, amazed.

"Yes, I've been expectin' you since early afternoon. What held you up?"

"Nothing really, except that we didn't know anyone was expecting us."

"Why ever not? Don't you listen for your messages?" Asked the giant.

Cautiously, wanting to humor this man I was beginning to suspect of being a little addled, I tried a simple question. "Messages? Which messages would those be?"

"Well, silly girl, the messages that people send out into the cosmos callin' you."

"How could you call us when you don't even know us?"

"What makes you think I don't know you?" he said with a grin.

"Sir, I have never met you in my life." I felt the need to be extra polite. "Maybe you already know Joy, though."

"Nope, we've never met." He bowed politely towards Joy. "No, it's you I was callin' to."

As we paused to talk, small children crawled all over this gentle, mountainous man. It didn't seem to bother him at all for the kids to climb on him like he was a jungle gym.

"If you must know, I dreamed about you," the giant stated in his resonant voice.

"What happened in your dream?"

"You came to town, and we met and then, and then....." He paused, looking around carefully. He seemed not to notice the ten or so children crawling around on him. "Well, see here, we met, and you told me somethin' very important. Somethin' I've been waiting a long time to hear."

"What did I tell you?"

He wailed in frustration, "I don't know! I woke up just then, and it went clean out of my head. You know how that happens with dreams; things can just blip away, and you can't seem to call them back. I tried, honest I did, but the answer keeps slippin' away from me. I was hopin' you could tell me now while I'm awake."

"But I don't know what you imagined I said in your dream," I told him, almost feeling his dismay.

"Dang, so you don't remember neither?"

"No, sir, it was your dream, not mine." I was speaking carefully, as one does to the mentally ill.

"Are you sure of that? Weren't you asleep a couple of hours ago?"

"Yes. How'd you know that?" I asked, astonished.

"Well, see, there are dreams that are just dreams, kind o' like cartoons to entertain your mind while you sleep. Then there are them dreams that are real. Most people don't know the difference and think dreams aren't important. Then there are those folks who think dreams should all be analyzed, and so they made some kind of sense. Some o' us know that some dreams are as real as you and me are here. Now, mind, they aren't all like that, and you've got to pay attention to know the difference."

"This here dream today came on me just all of a sudden like. I was busy playin' for the kids, and then I just got so sleepy, I had to lie down. It was as if the dream world was callin' to me. So, I told the kids to play somewhere else for a bit, and I laid myself down on a quiet spot of grass in the park. I was gone asleep in just a blink of an eye, and then whilst sleepin' had this dream that I swear was real important. You were there." He paused for a moment, looking me over from head to toe.

"Are you sure it was me?"

"Yep, positive. You even had that there flyin' bicycle with you."

"How'd you know about that?"

"Well, 'cause I saw you both flyin', silly." He looked meaningfully over at Joy. "And that there lady was wingin' on a swan. I mean, that's somethin' you don't see every day, so it kinda stuck in my mind, see."

"Well, mister. I don't remember your dream, so I don't think I can help you," I said.

He looked crestfallen for just a moment. Then he brightened up. "Hey, that's fine if you don't remember now. We'll just spend some time together, and maybe you'll remember and help me figure this whole thing out."

Thoughtfully, I said, "I guess that could work. We were getting ready for dinner when you went to calling us here. Would you care to join us? Could we buy you dinner?"

"I know I look kinda strange, but I ain't no bum. I got money to pay my own way. Willie don't take charity from no one."

"Fine, you pay for your own. I'm starving and want to eat soon."

Joy and I let Willie lead the way to a diner tucked away on a side street. His drum set wouldn't fit in the door, so he carefully took it off and patted it. "Now you wait here, you hear me? Don't go wanderin' off or making any racket. The last time I left you, you made so much racket I got kicked out of the place. Don't you go makin' anymore kinda trouble."

I swear that the tambourines, cymbals, drums, trumpet, and harmonica all made little noises of agreement.

We went in and found ourselves a cozy little table in the corner. The waitress came right over. I was about to comment on her quick service when I understood that her swift approach was because she had a different purpose in mind. "Willie, now I don't want you making no trouble! You keep those drums and all those kids outside. I don't want you levitatin' plates and saucers or doing any of your fancy tricks. This cafe is a place for eatin', and you just settle in and do that and then go. Nothing else," she concluded emphatically.

"Yes'm."

She tossed menus on the table and strode off to fill someone's coffee cup.

I gave Willie a curious look. "Levitating?"

He leaned over and whispered confidentially, "Well, yeah, sometimes that happens. I don't mean it to or nothin'. I just never managed to get good control over it. When stuff happens, like, I try to pretend I was playin' around and meant to do it. It makes people mad, especially Jane, there, but it's better to have them mad than scared. If they knew the stuff just happened by accident, I'm worried they'd be afeared o' me."

"Maybe you aren't the one making stuff move," I said in an almost placating voice, trying to make him feel better.

"Well, that's nice o' you to go tryin' to set my mind at rest. But I know I am doin' it, 'cause it happens when I'm at home, too. Sometimes even when I'm sleepin'. I'll wake up the next mornin' an' go in the kitchen an' it's all rearranged, stuff is out on the counters, plates broken like someone threw them against the wall. Food that's supposed to be in the freezer is thawin' in the sink. It's right unsettlin', it is."

I looked to Joy, hoping she'd say something and provide some answers. But she just smiled rather absently.

"Willie," I said, "I've heard of things like this happening. They call it poltergeist activity, I think. It seems to happen more often to disturbed tweens, but that doesn't seem to fit you at all."

"No, not the tween bit. But I'm plenty disturbed if you ask me."

"Why are you disturbed?" I asked, really wanting to know.

"Well, see, it's like this. My Mum, well, she wanted me to be a classical musician like. I tried. I really did. I went to her big fancy school, and I played that there grand piano, even did some big concerts wearing a fancy long tux and ruffled shirt. Can you imagine me dressed up like a fancy dandy man? But it were just plain borin'. I wanted to curl up and die there in that school. Besides bein' bored, I just din't have any friends. The other kids, well, they thought I was too big and too strange."

"Didn't they like your tattoos?"

"Aw, that was way before I got myself all prettied up with pictures. They thought I was too big and too clumsy. They made fun of me all the time. If I'd nod off in class 'cause I was just so stupid-bored, I'd wake up and find someone had climbed up me and was a sittin' on my shoulder like I was a big rock or sumpin. A day came when I just couldn't stay there any longer.

I was about to die from boredom and bein' made fun of. I upped and left school" He peered at me to see if I was getting all this.

The big man continued, folding and unfolding his huge hands on the tabletop. "I tried to tell me Mum, why, but she just couldn't hear me. She acted like I was doin' it just to hurt her. She couldn't hear me at all; it seemed like. It was like I wasn't even a-talkin' to her. I left town and went a travelin' around. I didn't know what I was gonna do next."

"Then I met this old guy they called 'The One-man-band'. He was puttin' up quite a racket, and it weren't too musical at all, but he sure looked like to be havin' fun. I could see on his face that he was real happy. So, I went over and talked to him, and he told me he just loved travelin' and making people happy, but ol' one-man-band was gonna have to quit soon on account he was getting old, and it was hard on his old bones a travelin' an' sleepin' on the ground. Well, he and me we made a deal right then; I bought that drum set offa him and started my career." A proud grin spread over Willie's weathered face.

"Willie, that still doesn't explain why you're feeling disturbed."

"Oh, yeah. Well, see, me Mum, she never forgave me. I went back to see her a few times, and she'd just shut the door in my face and tell me she din't have no son." Willie looked like he was going to burst into tears at any moment.

"Well, that just about broke my heart," he went on. "After a while, I was goin' back less and less often, maybe just once a year or so. Now maybe a smarter guy woulda stopped goin', but I just couldn't give up. I kept a hopin' she'd see her way clear to forgive me."

"She didn't?"

"No, siree. See, I'm not much for writin' and all that kind o' nonsense. Someday I wanted t' be able t' tell Mum 'bout all the places I'd been an' the pretty things I'd seen. So, I started havin' pictures put on me. That way, I can remember every place I been. There's a record here on my body about everything that's happened t' me that I thought was important. It's better'n a travelogue 'cause I can't lose it or nuthin'."

"Wow, you must have been just about everywhere!" I exclaimed, looking at the colors and images swirling over his immense body.

"Yep, I think maybe I have. See, here, there on my arm, that's Borneo. Then here on my cheek, now that's Sally." He got a dreamy look on his face. "Sally was one swell gal. She didn't seem t' think I was strange or ugly. She liked me 'cause I was different than the other guys she'd met."

"What happened?"

"Well, Sally liked me, but her daddy was another matter. He chased me off with a rifle. That made me real sad. It's been a few years, and I still see her face all smilin' and dimpled and ah so sweet when I go to sleep at night."

"Willie, where did Sally live?" I asked, something strange coming up in the back of my mind.

"Hmmm, let me think on that a minute. Hey, you know, it weren't far from here!"

"Willie, I think we met Sally on the road yesterday. She lives in the next town back. Maybe you could go see her?"

"Yeah, an' her old daddy'll just run me off with that shotgun again."

"You don't know until you try," I said, again not entirely sure why. "Did you ever make up with your mother? You don't seem like the kind of guy to give up on either the girl or your dreams or patching things up with your Mum."

"Yur right, I'm not. I tried, but Mum just couldn't get over being upset that I din't live proper. It hurts no end to think that she'd rather never see me again than t' accept that my way wasn't necessarily the same as hers."

"Maybe we can go with you to visit her and tell her about all the joy you bring to people in your travels."

"Well, that's right kind o' you, but she died a while back. That's why I'm so perturbed. I never got t' make it up with her, and now she's in her grave, and I never got t' say goodbye." He looked up, a shadow of despair in his green eyes.

"That's so sad, Willie. I don't wonder that you're disturbed and all that. Do things levitate all the time?"

"No, just if I been havin' a bad day, or if I see a lady that looked like my Mum and I get t' thinkin' about her. Then stuff starts movin' and jumpin' around."

Joy leaned forward intently. "Willie, do you think it would help if you could talk to your Mum one last time?"

"Well, yeah, but that ain't rightly possible. You did hear me say Mum's in her grave, didn't you?"

"Yes, I heard that part. Willie, even after people's bodies die, their spirits continue to live. We may be able to contact her, and you can talk to her and say what's in your heart."

"I thought that kinda stuff was just in movies and such."

"No, it's real. Do you trust me, Willie?" Joy asked.

"Yeah, you seem like a real nice lady."

"Good. Let's finish up our dinner and get out of here." Without another word, we cleaned our plates, paid our check, and left.

Where he'd been talkative before, Willie was now silent. He picked up his drum set, and even it didn't make a sound. Joy led the way out of town. Willie followed quietly at first. Then he plucked at Joy's sleeve, holding her back. "Lady, how are we gonna do this? Don't we have t' go t' her grave or somethin'?"

"No. Her spirit doesn't remain in her grave. She's gone on to other places and experiences."

"If she's gone on, then how do we talk to her?"

Joy laughed. "I have my ways. Don't you worry."

We went a little further in silence. When the town was behind and out of sight, Joy led us off into a grove of beautiful old oak trees. When we were all seated, Joy leaned forward and touched Willie on the arm.

"Willie, I want you to picture your Mum standing here in front of you. See her clearly in your mind. When you've got her picture, open your eyes."

He sat for a few minutes, screwing his face up and concentrating. Suddenly, his eyes popped open and looked like they were about to pop out of his head. "I'm ready."

Joy held out the golden wishbone that had been hanging from her belt. "Willie, I want you to close your eyes again and see your Mum. Think intently about wanting to see and talk to her. When you have it clear and feel it in your heart, reach out and pull on one side of the wishbone."

Willie went through the screwed-up-face, concentration bit again. He was faster this time and was grinning as he reached out and gave that wishbone a yank. It snapped in two, and he held the larger piece there in his hand. "I won. I won!"

Joy smiled and motioned for Willie to turn around. A wisp of cloud had formed behind him. Within moments, the misty form took shape and became a woman. She was almost as big as Willie, but her clothing and manner were formal. It was clear from her demeanor that she'd been a society lady.

"Willie!"

"Mum, you're talkin' t' me?" He couldn't stop staring at the apparition before him.

"Yes, and I'm sorry I was such a pill."

"What changed your mind?"

"Well, when I died, I got to go back and see an overview of my life. It was horrible because each time I'd been unkind to someone, I became the other person for a moment. I felt how much I hurt them. I didn't realize that my high and mighty ways caused so much hurt to so many people. Then when I was sure I couldn't take anymore, there you were. I got to feel how you felt. I now know how much I hurt you." She looked straight at Willie, who had tears – whether of joy or sadness or something else – running down his cheeks. His mother continued, "I know how unhappy and bored you were in that school and how badly the other kids teased you. Willie, then I got to feel how you feel when you play your music. And I got so happy. I felt the joy you bring the kids that crowd around you. You have a wonderful gift for making people happy. I'd never realized that it could be an honest calling. Can you forgive me?"

"Mum!" The ground shook as they ran into each other's arms. Mother and son stood crying and patting each other on the back. They went away from us and sat down under a tree.

Joy and I watched their reunion from a distance. It wasn't necessary to hear their words to feel the delight. Willie spent a good hour pointing out every tattoo on his body and telling his mother about all his adventures. The sun was going down as they came walking back towards us to say goodbye. They hugged one last time, and then she was gone in a blink.

Willie was grinning like a schoolboy as he hugged Joy. "Thankee, thankee. I can't even tell you what you've done for me."

"Willie, you're quite welcome."

He turned towards me, started to say something, and stopped. He slapped his forehead hard. "I almost forgot. You were tellin' me that you mighta met my Sally."

"Maybe. Don't get your hopes up, but it's possible."

"Can we go see now?"

"Not tonight, the sun's gone down, and we all need some sleep."

"Tomorrow? Can we go tomorrow?"

"Willie, yes, let's go tomorrow. Sally is a sweet lady. I just know she'll be happy to see you." I said, looking forward to the next day.

Well-practiced, we made camp in no time, crawled into our sleeping bags, and soon were dreaming our own dreams. This time they were happy dreams.

CHAPTER 24:

The Klutz, the Musician & the Wedding

Morning came. Even the bright summer sun was unable to match Willie's shining face.

His excitement was infectious. Although I was inwardly worried that the Sally we'd met wasn't Willie's Sally, I kept practicing trust in synchronicity. We gobbled breakfast and packed up camp.

Joy and I couldn't keep up with Willie's long strides. He was a man with long legs and a purpose. Joy called Swanee, and I hopped on Flicka to all arrive at Sally's about the same time. In his excitement, Willie's instruments played as he walked. I whispered to Joy, expressing my fears that he would draw unwanted attention to our unconventional means of travel.

"Don't worry, Zemma, Willie is making so much racket and is such a spectacle that no one will even notice us."

I was dubious, but Joy was right, as always. We managed to get to the town without anyone giving us as much as a second glance. Willie stopped when we got to the main street. "Well, where does she live?"

"Willie, I don't know!" I said in dismay. "We didn't see her at her house. We saw her alongside a cliff where she'd gotten trapped by a falling boulder."

"Yep, that sounds just like my Sally. She was might pretty, but the clumsiest gal I ever did see. Somethin' awful was just always happenin' to her. If you don't know where she is, then I guess I'll just go drummin' up and down every street in this town until I find her. Sooner or later, she'll get curious about all the noise and come out."

Willie did just that. Joy and I followed for the first hour. Eventually, we parked ourselves in the village square. We kept track of his whereabouts effortlessly by the noise and the groups of children and a scattering of adults, even a few dogs, running to join an impromptu parade.

Three hours later, I was beginning to fear that we'd made a mistake. If Willie didn't find Sally, he might be disturbed and start levitating things. Besides, I wanted to see another happy reunion. I'm such a sucker for stuff like that, making me smile and cry at the same time. At least, I hoped it would be happy.

Then there was silence. It took me a minute for the reality to register. Quiet, that meant that Willie had stopped playing. Joy and I jumped up, running toward the last place we'd heard him play. We rounded a corner and stopped. Willie was in full musical regalia, Sally before him wringing a towel in her hands, and an older man with a shotgun.

"Oh, dear! Joy, he's going to kill Willie."

"Not so fast. I don't think so."

I looked closer. The man with the shotgun was smiling. Willie was smiling. Sally was grinning from ear to ear. With an earsplitting cacophony, Willie started beating his drums and blowing on his trumpet. Next, he started yelling. "Hear ye, hear ye! There's going to be a wedding today. Come one, come all!" He started pounding his drums in tune with his shouts. We laughed as he went up and down every street in town, announcing a 3 o'clock wedding.

We couldn't get Willie's attention. Sally saw us and came running over. "How can I thank you? You've brought my Willie back to me."

"But what about your father? I thought he hated Willie." I exclaimed, worried she'd be disappointed again.

"He does. But my father also loves me. It's been three years since he chased Willie away. I haven't so much as looked at another man. My father despaired of ever seeing me happy. He was sure he'd die without the grand-kids he wants. My dad saw Willie today before I did, and he came and got me! Can you believe that? He loves me enough to let me marry a man he can't stand! Isn't that wonderful?" She was crying and laughing at the same time as she told us her story. She hugged us and went running down the street after her father. She turned back and yelled when she was still close enough for us to hear. "Come to the wedding. It's in the town square today at three. Oh, my, I've got so much to do!" As she ran, I could just barely catch her muttering to herself. "And what am I going to wear?"

Joy turned to me. "Zemma, go find Willie and help him get ready. I'm going to help Sally." Without waiting to hear my answer, Joy was off, running down the street after the bride-to-be.

Willie, as always, was easy to find. I caught up with him and convinced him that he had important things to accomplish with only two hours until his wedding. We went to a nearby hotel, and I got a room, overriding his protests about the expense. "Willie, you only get married once. Joy and I want to pay for this room so you can have a proper soak in a tub and get dressed. While you're doing that, I'll send out your spare clothes for a quick cleaning at the laundry next door. By the time you get to the Village Square, you'll be looking like a proper bridegroom."

With Willie gratefully sunk into a sizeable steaming tub, I took his clothes to the laundry and ran a few more errands. The clock was just striking three as Willie and I arrived breathlessly at the village square. Willie looked around wildly as if he was afraid Sally had disappeared again. I caught sight of Joy peeking out from behind the clubhouse building on the square and reassured him, "Willie, they're over there. Now you can't see Sally before the wedding, so stay here and wait." Which he did, shifting his bulk from foot to foot like an excited little kid on Christmas morning.

Sally's father arrived with a preacher in tow. The square was filling up. The entire town appeared to have turned out for this wedding. Tables were laden with gifts and food. I don't know how they did it, but the townspeople had managed to put together a full wedding feast in a few hours.

Sally was the most beautiful bride I'd ever seen. It wasn't what she wore that made her lovely. It was her joyous smile. Her dress was unembellished, and I seemed to recognize the fabric as being from Joy's underskirt. In her hair, she wore a crown of daisies. She was glowing with happiness, as was her groom.

The ceremony was brief but moving. There wasn't a dry eye to be seen, especially when her dad gave her away with a bow to Willie. We ate, drank, and danced in the square well into the wee hours of the night. I don't think anyone noticed that Willie's drum set was making music by itself! His one-man-band even managed to play a waltz or two so Willie and Sally could slow dance.

When we'd eaten all the food, and the wine had disappeared down dozens of throats, the townspeople told Willie and Sally it was time for their wedding night. Willie looked around in a panic. "Oh no! I was so happy to be gettin' married; I forgot to figure out where we were going to go after the wedding."

Joy whispered in his ear. He grinned widely as she handed him the key to the hotel suite we'd used earlier in the day. During the feast, Joy and I had stolen away briefly and decorated the suite with flowers. Champagne cooled in an ice bucket, next to a plate of chocolate-covered strawberries and a full tray of snacks for late-night nibbles. They would have a wedding night to remember.

CHAPTER 25:

Love, Compromise & Happiness

Light streaming through the leafy arbor woke me from a deep sleep. I sat up in my sleeping bag and looked around sleepily. Joy and I weren't the only ones who had slept in the town square. There were at least a half dozen others scattered about, under arbors, on and under benches. Even after the bride and groom had retired for the night, the celebration went on until early morning. People were having far too much fun to go home.

Ragged and rumpled, people started waking up. Soon practically the whole town reconvened in the local diner for a hearty breakfast. The party was so large we spilled out onto the street, using the tables from the wedding feast. We toasted each other with steaming cups of strong coffee and fresh-squeezed juice. It was apparent that Sally was loved. I overheard many conversations in which people were speculating that Sally might leave town and go traveling with Willie, and they'd lose a good friend and the best teacher their kids had ever had. I was curious as to what the newlyweds were going to decide to do.

Joy and I polished off a healthy breakfast and were just leaving the diner when we saw Sally and Willie coming out of the hotel's front door. Running hand in hand towards us, Sally was bubbling over. "Joy, Zemma, thank you so much! Nothing I can do will ever be able to repay you for bringing Willie back to me."

"Just live a happy life. That's all the thanks we could ever need. I know you probably haven't had a chance to think about it, but where are you going to live?"

Willie looked positively crestfallen. I could feel his panic as reality hit him. He didn't have a clue as to how he was going to take care of himself and a wife.

"Gee, I don't know. Oh Sally, how could I marry you?" Willie said, looking at his beautiful new bride in dismay. "I can't ask you to go on the road with me. Traveling isn't a fit life for a lady."

"Willie, I'll live in a shack. I'll travel every road in this country. I'll do anything it takes to be with you."

"That won't be necessary, Sally." Her father spoke up as he arrived at the edge of our little group. He tipped his hat to Willie. "Willie, let's have a little talk. I've got some ideas for you. Now, don't worry, I'm not going to be telling you how to live your life. I've made some inquiries and have some suggestions I hope you'll like. If not, you're free to make other plans, of course."

"Ok, I'm listening." Willie's face had a touch of caution to it as he moved toward his new father-in-law. It was apparent he wasn't wholeheartedly sure of the man's good wishes.

"There's an opening for a music teacher at the local school. They've been looking for someone for a couple of years. Not too many people want to move to such a little town. When I told the superintendent you might be interested, he said he wanted to meet you."

"When can we meet?"

"Right now! His office is just around the corner," said Sally's dad as he motioned Willie to follow him.

The superintendent was waiting at the door to the office and greeted them heartily. "Willie, I hear you might be interested in teaching music. I know you just got married and need to settle down, but I have some questions before I let you teach our kids. First, why do you want to teach?"

"Well, sir," replied Willie, "I love children and how they enter into new things with so much enthusiasm. I want to teach them music for the sheer joy it can bring to a soul, not so they can go on and do concerts or get all serious about it. My mum did that to me, and it just about killed me. It took the most beautiful thing I could think of doing and took away the life and spark. Have you ever seen those people with the dead eyes?"

"Yes, I don't know what to make of them."

"I almost became one when I was trying to fit myself into life as a concert musician. I believe if you'd seen me then, you would have seen my eyes be just dead and blank as all that. When the joy of doing and being is destroyed, people lose their connection to the magic and love that gives them life. The fire behind their eyes just goes out. They're like walking dead. If I can help them find their connection to joy through music, then I'll be a blessed man."

"Willie, I think that's just about the best reason I've ever heard for wanting to be a teacher. Would you agree to a one-year trial? Then, if either of us doesn't like the arrangement at the end of the year, you find something else. The job doesn't pay much, but it comes with a little cottage out at the edge of town. You won't have much money, but you'll have a place to live, and you can have all the vegetables and chicken and eggs you need from my farm. The other plus to all this is that Sally is the art teacher, so you'll get to work together in the same place. Maybe you'll even come up with some creative ways to bring music and art together."

"Sir, I would be more than happy to be the music teacher. I'd get to do the two things I love most in the world. Make music with kids and build a life with Sally."

They shook hands, and within minutes, the school superintendent handed Willie the keys to their new home.

Sally turned to Willie. "I know you love playing music, and the job as a teacher will let you do that. But I've seen the joy when you entertain in front of a crowd. I don't want you to give that up for me."

"Sally, I'd do anything to be with you."

"Thank you, but I won't allow you to give up something you love so much. I know that eventually, you'll miss the fun. I also think that maybe there's a reason for you to be traveling around the countryside. You can keep the sparks bright in people's eyes. Can we compromise? We can both teach during the school year, and in the summer, we'll go on the road with your one-man-band. We can have the best of both worlds."

I swear there were rainbows of joy coming from Willie as he grinned and swung his wife around. "Yes, oh, yes!"

Joy and I seemed to spontaneously realize we needed to tell Willie about the Crystalline Heart Family and invite him to join us. In all the commotion, we'd nearly forgotten. As expected, his eyes lit up, his one-man-band played joyously, and he smiled and laughed. "This was my dream, Zemma. You were telling me about this family of yours! Don't you remember?"

I thought for a moment and had a flash of a dream I'd been dreaming that night. Often the dream comes back in tiny bits during the following day. That's what was happening here; I wasn't seeing anything clearly, just flashes of things. I seemed to remember inviting several people to join the family. "I don't know how I could have forgotten!"

Joy once again reached into her pocket and pulled out a heart pendant of spring green with a brown band running down one side. "Willie, this chrysoprase is a stone of joy that activates your heart chakra allowing you to emanate your loving, joyful energy into the Universe even more than you already do. At the same time, it asks you to let go of any past hurts or resentments with forgiveness and love to both yourself and the other. The brown stripe you see is grounding and also represents the path you are on."

"Miss Joy, I'm honored that you have asked Sally and me to be part of your beautiful family." He looked lovingly at Sally. "We'll do our best to inspire others and keep love and creativity alive in our part of the world."

I could see that Sally and Willie were preparing to get settled. I had to know the answer to a question that was burning in my mind. I got Willie aside for a minute so I could talk to him.

"Willie, I'm curious. Yesterday you talked like a country bumpkin, all slang and dropped consonants. Today you're speaking proper and correct like an educated man. How? Why?"

"'Talkin' country' was part of the whole act I was putting on. It was all for show. People liked knowing the no-account traveling one-man-band. By talking rough like that, they figure I'm harmless, kind of straightforward, you know? I'm not a challenge to anyone, and it makes them feel good about themselves. But now that I'm a married man, I've got to be the man my Sally deserves. I learned from my Mum and at school to talk all nice and proper."

"Willie, you're a mighty good actor. If you ever want another career, you might consider the stage." I slapped him on the back.

208

"Yeah, I might look at that. But for now, I'm going to be happy to be a school music teacher and Sally's husband, William. I'll be Mr. William during the school year and Willie when we're traveling." He walked over and gave her a gigantic hug and started to give her a peck on the lips. She wasn't having any of that as she pulled him to her and kissed him very thoroughly on the lips.

People cheered as Sally and William walked down the street and opened the front door of their new home. Joy and I turned away, extremely happy for them both. I wondered what the chances were that we'd met them both and been able to bring them back together. Then I laughed at myself, knowing the chances were pretty darned good when love, magic, and synchronicity were at work.

CHAPTER 26:

Cricket Call, a Warning in the Night

I rode Flicka in the time-honored wheels-on-the-ground method until we were out of sight of the village. When it was safe, we took off flying low. I was on Flicka, Joy on Swanee. The scenery had changed dramatically, and we were rising into red hills dotted with cliffs and tumbling into rusty soil and bright green plants. It was like being on another planet.

I lost track of Joy and didn't realize it. Initially, I was unconcerned; she was always just around the corner. An hour later, I was somewhat panicked. Nothing like this had happened before. I couldn't imagine that she'd just go away and not say anything.

I needed to focus and stop running around looking for her. Had she abandoned me? Was I on my own?

"Bet she's out having fun. Wonder if she'll stay away for a few days?" Flicka echoed my thoughts.

"No, she's just – oh, stop it! You're just echoing me…."

Flicka snickered. We stopped on the side of the road near a stand of trees. They were irresistible. I thought she must be there, so I ran to the grove.

"Joy! Joy!" I looked for where I thought she'd be sitting in the shade, with a full picnic basket. But she wasn't there. I leaned my back against the largest of the trees, instantly feeling more relaxed. I closed my eyes and took several deep breaths, willing myself to tune in and fill with light. I saw Joy's face in my mind's eye. She was smiling as she worked, but I couldn't see what she was doing. I attempted unsuccessfully to speak to her mind-to-mind. I don't know if my worries kept us from connecting or if something else was in the way. I finally felt all was well and that I should keep going.

Satisfied but frustrated, I scuffed back to the road and mounted Flicka. I started pedaling rather than taking the easy way and flying. The rhythm of pedaling made me happy: no thinking, no worrying.

Then a boy about my age seemed to appear in the middle of the road. He was waving his arms wildly and running towards me. "Stop! Stop!"

When I dismounted, he caught up to me, out of breath and panting. He leaned forward, hands on his knees to catch his breath. I waited.

The boy looked up under his lashes before straightening up. I felt that he was assessing me, testing, checking me out before speaking, trying to decide what to say. He appeared to resolve something within himself and stood up and held out his hand to me.

"Hi, I'm Josh."

"Zemma."

"You must be new here, or you wouldn't be on this road. No one goes on this road."

"Really? You're here."

"Well, I had to meet you," Josh said.

"You're here for me?"

"Yep."

"Why?" I asked, puzzled as to why another person was waiting for me in a place I hadn't even known I'd be.

"I dreamed about you last night. I've been waiting all day."

"Again, why?

"I think you can help. There's danger needs fixin."

"I don't see any danger." The red hills were quiet and beautiful.

"You can't see it!"

"Is it here? If I can't see it, then how can it be dangerous?"

"I thought you were smarter than that. Some of the scariest things ever are invisible."

"What is it then? A monster?"

"Not that easy. Average scary monsters are easy; children can drive them away."

"They can?"

"You already know that. Why are you pretending? Are you testing me to see if I'm a complete ignoramus?"

"No, the idea hadn't crossed my mind. However, if there is something invisible and threatening, I need to get a better sense of what you already know and understand."

"We don't have time to play games. I need you to listen to me."

"I'm all ears," I said.

"This is a long story. Can we sit?"

"Of course." We walked up a hill and settled under a wide-spreading shade tree.

"Here's my story. It's a long one, so get comfortable."

I didn't interrupt. I was instantly fascinated by Josh's tale.

"This morning, crickets called me. I tried to stay in my warm bed. I snuggled down deeper into the covers. I even pulled the pillow over my head. But their noise tugged at me continually and kept gettin' stronger. Me and crickets have a kind of freaky relationship. They warn me of danger and talk to me when I'm lonely. They make me smile when I'm sad. When I need someone to tell me what to do, I go down to the pond, and there's always a cricket somewhere, on a log or a nearby branch. It looks to be the same cricket, but I could be wrong. I wouldn't swear to it. It's the first time they called me out.

"My curiosity got the best of me. I tossed the covers into a heap at the bottom of the bed and sat up. I searched under bed and found the sandals I'd tossed on the floor the night before. It was barely daylight, so I threw on the clothes in a pile at the bottom of the bed, so I didn't need to turn on the light and wake up my little sister. I tiptoed down the hall and went out.

"I was surprised that the wind was warm. It's been cold and damp. Now it was almost balmy. That could explain the crickets' call. But it was surprising to hear them so early. Lately, it had been too cold for them to chirp even during the height of the day. I waited a bit, thinking they weren't calling me at all. Maybe they were just happy it was a beautiful day. As if they heard me thinking, their chirping became even louder. I had to know what was going on. I took off for the pond at a trot.

"The air seemed extra still and heavy. I got goosies on my arms like when I know somethings wrong. I didn't see anything odd. I ran faster as I went. I'm usually kind of quiet; not much gets me rattled—no idea why, but I was feeling both rushed and rattled.

"As I got close to log where Cricket and I meet, I slowed so I wouldn't scare him. There were not one but three identical crickets waiting. I crouched down low to look them in the eye. I was polite and waited to hear what they had to say.

"They spoke all together. "We greet you, young friend. Thank you for rousing yourself to answer our call. You must know we would not disturb you if we did not feel it was important. There is a great calamity about to come to this place. We have called to warn you."

"Warn me?"

"Did you not notice the heaviness in the air?"

"Yes, I thought a storm was coming."

"No, young one. This storm is not from the weather, but of powers and energies beyond comprehension."

"But what can I do? I am only twelve. I'm not smart or talented. Why aren't you telling the elders or priests; they'll know what to do. I can call them for you!"

"But the elders are the problem, and the priests do not know the matters of which we speak, although they believe they know everything. They would not see the truth until it was too late."

"But what can I do?"

"A great deal. There are stories your grandmother has told you of the heroic deeds of young ones who have saved whole families, even whole villages. Aren't those some of your favorite tales?"

"Yes, but they're legends. Cool stories, but that's all."

"Are you telling us that you have never believed those stories? Didn't you wish you could be one of those heroes?"

"Well, sure, but I knew it wasn't true. and it wasn't going to happen."

"Many of those legends are true. Most come from a time when people still talked to us. In those times, things were more connected than they are now. Ideas, feelings, and knowledge passed easily from person to person and even between people and the animal and plant kingdoms. You are one of the rare ones who still have some of those old abilities. That's why we have called on you."

"'I'll do what I can. I can't think how I can help anyone."

"We will guide you and be behind you all the way."

"Great, behind me. Don't I get someone to be in front of me? What is this vile threat?"

"You've got the wording right. This threat is vile. The being coming here is the very antithesis of who and what we are. Its energy deadens all in its way, causing lethargy in every person, even every animal it meets. This apathy causes its victims to have no willpower, no desire to fight; they simply give up their dreams to it."

"Why don't they fight?"

"Most of the time, the victims never realize anything has happened. They fall into an apathetic stupor in which they are happy to live a gray existence. They have no excitement, no new ideas. And they are content with whatever comes their way. Some remember the way they used to be but are sure in their minds that the old way of always trying to accomplish something or make a difference was wrong and silly, and they're better off now. Because they no longer feel the old inner passion and longing, they think that they are at peace."

"That is terrible! How can it be so strong, and why? Who is coming? What's he look like? What can I do? "

"The one coming takes on many forms. Sometimes as a false priest or prophet, a salesman, a teacher, or even an angelic messenger. We cannot tell you what his form will be. We can only warn you to be aware, to look into the eyes of all you meet. When you meet this one, you will know it immediately by the blankness in his eyes and the pain you feel when he starts to suck your dreams from your heart. The why is something we can only guess. We believe they are part of the group that seeks to control everything.

What better way to do that than to weaken the resolve of many. You must stop him."

"But what's this got to do with me!?"

"We cannot say. It is up to you to find that answer, to discover the way," replied the crickets.

"But I am just a boy!"

"Now you are. But do not deny your history. Think back, way back. Don't you remember other selves, other lives, and other places? You have more than just the twelve years of this life available to you. You have centuries of living and learning to guide you. You also have the backing of all the kingdoms of the natural world. All you have to do is ask."

"But how can fight a beast like this with no weapons or powers?"

"This battle will not be about physical strength or stamina. It is who you are and what you know that will make a difference. Trust your inner feelings and guidance. You will know the answers and take the correct actions when the time comes. The time is not yet. You have a day to prepare, maybe two. Rest here and dream, and you will know what to do."

"I ran home and told my mom I was going fishing. She said I could pack a lunch and take a canteen, so I'd have enough to drink and eat. I went back to my quiet place by the pond with my rations.

"As I lay by the river, I dozed and dreamed of my many lives.

I saw myself as a boy, a runner, for an ancient Indian tribe. I thought of stories I'd read about the Incan tribes of South America. Then too, a threat was coming to the land. The priests had warned the people, but they didn't believe it. They said their gods would protect them. The priests sent me out to warn people. They only laughed and acted like I was just a crazy kid.

I ran, always ahead of whatever was coming, and I didn't see what was happening behind me. I didn't see the light go out of people's eyes in each village the guy passed through. I didn't see them quit going out to work in the fields. I didn't see people lose interest in even basic stuff like feeding themselves – well, they were still eating, but they sure weren't cooking anything that looked good, just what they could find. Finally, I got to the last village. No one listened, except for one older woman who looked at me and believed me. She listened carefully to every word.

She nodded seemed sad. "I've feared this moment. When I was a child, I dreamed of the grayness that would one day envelop the people and take away their dreams. I'd always hoped it was just a nightmare, but it was one I could never fully dismiss. That vision was worse than the scariest monster I could ever conjure up."

"Grandmother, what can we do? No one else will listen. They simply laugh."

"We will sing. We will get everyone else to sing. When the grayness comes, we will keep right on singing. The grayness can only live when it receives a constant flow of energy. It takes the dreams and hopes from the people it encounters and nourishes itself in the taking. What we must do is keep the people-centered in themselves, in a song that keeps their spirit intact."

I doubted her. How could a song fight evil?

But she told me, "Songs have great power; songs can heal and awaken. Music can bring forth one's deepest hopes and desires. We need a song to strengthen us and keep alive our hopes, dreams, desires, and inner fire. Go among the people; tell them to come to the square as the sun goes down tonight. I need them all here. I will share the song with them, and we will survive."

The song just repeated the same words, over and over. "We Are One. We Are One. We Are One." They sang for about an hour until they had the rhythm in their hearts. It seems like everyone was singing the song all the time, no matter what they were doing.

A harmless-looking guy with a few things in a pack arrived a few days later. He dressed like the traveling priests and holy men. He had a kind face and a gentle walk. He sure seemed harmless. Some started to go to meet him and welcome him. The woman got there first and saw the blankness in his eyes. This man was not a holy man; there was no love or kindness in his eyes. Her skin prickled, and she wanted to run. But she held firm. She called out loudly for the others to gather and sing!

"We Are One. We Are One. We Are One." All the villagers sang together.

The blank-eyed man asked for food and water, insisting she talk and listen to him.

She gave him food and water, but still, we sang, "We Are One, We Are One, We Are One."

He covered his ears. "STOP! Old woman, I am ill. Please help me."

She gave him hot tea and a warm cloth to clean his hands and face. We sang, "We Are One, We Are One, We Are One."

All the people joined hands, making a circle around the grandmother and the stranger. They sang, "We Are One. We Are One. We Are One."

The traveler collapsed on the ground as if he was really hurting. They continued to sing.

The man struggled to his feet and called to them. "Stop it. I am the one! I am your salvation; I have come to bring you to God. Open to me, and I will give you great treasures. I bring you great knowledge. Come to me; I am the love that you seek."

The villagers sang, "We Are One. We Are One. We Are One."

She looked him in the eyes and shuddered but spoke loudly so he could hear over the singing. "Sir, you do not speak for any God that I recognize. Please leave us in peace."

The stranger raised his staff, and it spouted lightning to break up the circle. "I have been sent to save your wretched souls. I bring harmony to your lives. I am the messenger of God. Follow me, and your lives will be of peace forever."

She looked him in his blank, hard eyes. "The messenger of God would have love in his eyes. He would bring solace, not lightning. We demand you leave now."

The stranger screamed one last time and vanished into a cloud of gray and darkness.

The cloud disappeared, and the sun came out. The birds sang, the crickets chirped.

The grandmother started laughing. She looked at everyone with love and pride in her eyes. Her voice was triumphant. "We have met the face of evil, and we have triumphed."

The people hugged each other. They had fought off the doom that had taken all the other villages. They vowed to remember to sing the song. For many centuries, someone was always singing, "We are One, we are One, we are One."

"I came back from my dream and talked to the crickets again. I heard the song in their chirping.

"Zemma, I tried to warn everyone. The priest laughed, and others scoffed. 'This is the 21st Century. You don't honestly believe there are things like evil in the world! Go on. Go back to your mother.' I felt desperate.

"Finally, I found an older woman who had been here forever. Many in town were her descendants, and everyone calls her grandma out of respect.

"She called a meeting at sundown. Most weren't ready to believe her but afraid to ignore her words, so they learned the song.

"The stranger came the next day; he wasn't a priest or holy man but was a computer salesman promising to get us all online. He had some new kind of invisible frequency called 5G wi-fi, so we'd have faster access and see the world without ever leaving home.

"Some of the people got excited. 'Imagine faster access.' They said it was a dream come true. The woman stepped forward, saying not to believe everything they heard.

"It was the same as my dream. More and more sang, 'We Are One, We Are One, We Are One.'"

"Some told her to shut up so they could listen to his promises.

"The salesman covered his ears. 'Would someone shut this old hag up? I come with technology to connect you to the world. You'll never even have to leave your homes again. You'll be able to order groceries from your computer. Phone calls will be unnecessary; you'll just e-mail. Why go on vacation and put up with changeable weather when you can see all the sights on your laptop or big screen. With a big enough screen and our new faster access, it'll be just like being there. In a few years, you'll even have 3-D and virtual reality, and the Internet of Things will be yours.'

"She sang, 'We Are One. We Are One. We Are One.' While others sang, she spoke quietly to me. 'Can you say something to refute what he is saying? They can't all believe these promises would be good for us.'

"The man shouted louder. 'No need to go to work every day. You can trade stocks on the Internet, market your goods online. No need to ever talk to a customer or each other again; It'll all be electronic. It's the wave of the future.'

"I surprised myself and shouted over him, 'Do you want a world without human contact? Can you imagine how lonely you'll feel just in front of a computer all day? Think about it.'

"The stranger held up his laptop and his handheld device. "'You can be online anywhere. No need to suffer through boring picnics and family gatherings; you can be online the whole time. The Internet of Things is the future of humanity.'

"I shouted again, 'Don't give up being you and being with your friends and families. It's your families that keep you strong.' The grandmother sang. They loved all the fantastical promises. But what if the grandmother was right? They didn't want to lose their families or be out of touch on a personal level.

"More and more people started shouting back at him to go away; they didn't need what he was selling. They wanted time with friends and family. Doing things together made them happy. They wanted to travel; seeing it online just wasn't the same as being there.

"Our group got bigger than the one around the salesman.

"The stranger screamed in agony and vanished in a cloud of gray. His laptop shattered on the pavement.

"One boy called out, 'Do we have to give up the Internet forever? It can't all be bad, can it?'

"The grandmother's voice rose in answer to the boy's question. 'No, you don't have to give up the Internet or any technology. You have to remember it's a tool. It's there to serve you, never to take the place of human-to-human inter-action. It should not become your God or your only connection to the outside world. Use the Internet, but keep it in perspective, keep things in balance.'

"The gray cloud was gone, and the sun returned. The birds sang, and the crickets chirped happily again.

"We had one huge laughing, crying group hug. We'd beat off a threat. We promised to remember our song always."

Josh stopped speaking and looked at me steadily.

I didn't understand, although it was a remarkable story. If Josh had saved the town, why did he need me? "If the danger is gone, why are you here waiting for me?"

"Things have changed. Soon people started questioning why they drove him away. They forgot the horrible deadening feeling and that he'd disap-peared when they sang. All they remember is that what he offered began to sound good – speed, convenience, power."

"Josh, are you saying your village doesn't have computers or any wi-fi?"

"Oh, no, we have that. But not super-fast, like the man was selling. And we kept hearing from other towns about how much more we could see and know, and many people began longing for the lifestyle he promised. I kept reminding them that we'd be giving up our privacy. If everything is online, couldn't someone come in and hack the entire town and take control, leaving us defenseless? And that's just the physical part of it. That's not even talking about what could happen to our connections to each other, nature, and our own hearts."

"That's true. I've seen and felt what happens when people get sucked into their screens. Is he back? Have people withdrawn and given up their dreams? Is that why there's no one on this road?"

"The salesman has been seen around again. Maybe not the same guy, but he is the same if you know what I mean."

"I think I do."

"They're hard to banish when people call them in. What he offers appears so wonderful, so positive, it's hard to imagine or remember any threat within it. He can come in many guises, with different ideas, promises, or ideas, but always with the same purpose of stealing the light."

"How can I help?"

"Zemma, I dreamt about you. I think you are the key to a new answer. Sending him away was only temporary. We need a way to have technology safely, so it can't be used to control us. There must be a way to use the good of it without losing touch with who we are."

"That's an interesting problem, Josh. I like computers and use the Internet all the time."

"Have you ever felt the blankness?"

"Yes! I'd get lost for hours wandering. I'd completely lose track of what I was looking for."

"What did you do differently other times?"

"I'm not quite sure. I guess I did some research. Did you know that electromagnetic radiation and radio waves can harm our bodies and affect our thinking and moods? I couldn't find conclusive proof that EMF, 5G, or wi-fi causes cancer or other illnesses. But then I remembered how long it took to get people to see what smoking, asbestos, and DDT were doing to them; it can take decades for the damage to become so bad there's an undeniable connection. I decided to go with the 'precautionary principle' that says there's enough evidence to raise concerns, and we should use caution. I bought a shield pendant with a matrix of crystals (Appendix E) inside to help me stay clear, and I was careful about how I used the Internet. I guess I just paid attention."

"How did knowing that help?" Asked Josh.

"Josh, I don't know if this is significant, but after those first few experiences of getting lost in the web, I sat down and took a good long look at my computer and how it worked. I don't mean I took it apart or anything; I just looked at it, willing myself to see deeper into it. What I saw was a web, much like a spider web. It's a web on several levels. The first level connects computers through phone lines and cable networks. Everything beyond that is entirely different. There is a web of the energy of intent that spreads and motivates other people, often in not-so-good ways. "

"How do you fight that?"

"I don't think you 'combat' it at all. It seems when you go to war against something, you focus on it even more. My Aunt Joy says, 'What we resist persists.'"

"But what about the war on drugs and the war on poverty? We're at war against many things."

"Think about it. We've been battling those wars for a long time. Has anything changed? Have they been wiped out?"

"No. Sometimes it seems the things we are fighting have gotten stronger."

"My point exactly. Hey, I'm certainly no expert. I'm still learning about how things work."

"I can see you've got an idea."

"Yes, maybe, I do. It goes back to intent. I changed my intent and stopped seeing the Internet as entertainment. I focused on it as a tool. When I go to the Internet, I go with a purpose in mind. I search for what I want to know. I even print it out. Then I quit. I pay attention to how I feel when I'm searching. If it feels creepy, I don't stay. I don't get worn out."

Josh nodded and grabbed my arm. "Yes! Some sites seem to be doing something more than just giving information or helping us communicate."

I looked up at the sky. "What we resist persists. We have to protect ourselves; no one else will. We need to be clear about our intent and pay attention to what comes our way. Moment to moment, we are responsible for choosing what we will or will not interact with."

"What if our town makes laws to protect us?"

"That's giving someone else responsibility. That also opens the door to other Unmakers who kill dreams by censorship and too much control. I think we all need to be accountable for our own choices, good or bad."

"I hate having people tell me what to think or do."

"Exactly. Don't you tend to rebel and find out the hard way?"

"I have been known to do it that way from time to time." He laughed. I could tell by his face that he'd done it the hard way more than just a few times. "I still feel the Internet can be a threat to us. I know what I can do to keep my intent clear, but what about everyone else?"

"Josh, why not share your experience. Each person who turns on their computer has to choose for himself or herself. Perhaps with the information you share, it will be easier for them to see the negative influences. Maybe you can tell them about my shield and the importance of intent. For me, the two go hand-in-hand. Try to have them start thinking about mindless consumption as opening up to an energy vampire. Sing or fill with light. I'll teach you how."

There was a loud squawk from behind some trees a short distance away. I turned to see Joy and Swanee strolling towards us. I was so glad to see her I almost forgot to introduce Josh and share our conversation.

"Zemma gave you wise counsel, Josh. Use it well. I've brought us a snack and have a present for you."

I was beginning to love the suspense when Joy reached into her pocket for a heart pendant, eager to see and hear about the stone she chose. This time the gemstone heart was intensely orange with areas that seemed almost crystallized.

Josh gasped, "That's one of the most beautiful stones I've ever seen."

"This is carnelian; it's a form of agate that has many properties – grounding and courage are at the top. It's an excellent ally when you feel like you need the courage to start again. It helps you overcome and learn from the past. Carnelian is also an action stone, perfect for you! It will keep you motivated and strong to go on to whatever is next and next, facing it with strength and fortitude."

Josh held the heart to his own heart. "I could sure have used that! Thank you, Joy." Then he jumped up, leaning down to hug us. "I have to go! I have to tell them! I have to do it now!" And he was gone. Hugging me and then Joy, Josh rushed off, a boy with a purpose.

I turned to Joy. "Where have you been? I looked everywhere for you."

"Did you? That's funny. I would have thought that if you looked everywhere, you would have found me."

Her speech was so absurd I started laughing.

"Honestly, Zemma, I am sorry you were worried. I went to tend my wand garden. I knew you were going to meet someone on the road today and that you were the one to help him. You had the experience and wisdom he needed. The girl with the answers! Bet you never thought that'd be you."

With a smile, Joy sent Swanee away and started walking down the road.

I hurried to catch up. Flicka followed at a distance.

CHAPTER 27:

The Spirit of the Forest - Is he Merlin?

The next few days passed uneventfully. We met some fellow travelers and spent a day swimming in a pool near a waterfall. Somehow, though, I was full of questions. I tried to be patient and listen for the answers. I had a sense of being pulled inexorably towards a magnetic force. Even though I tried to relax and allow things to unfold, a strange mixture of anxiety and anticipation grew within me.

I loved riding Flicka, but I found myself more comfortable walking. Most of the time, I was on foot with Flicka following along. At first, she was unhappy because she thought maybe I didn't like her. I explained what was going through my head, and she relaxed. I swear if she'd been a cat, she would have purred. Instead, she quietly came along with me but was always ready for a ride when I was.

Joy, too, was uncharacteristically silent. She gave me the space I needed. I'd never had anyone do that for me. I loved my parents, but they were parents, trying extremely hard to do the job right. That never seemed to include allowing me to figure things out in my way. Although Joy's refusal to give me concrete answers about my purpose could be maddening in the extreme, I was beginning to see how much more I learned and how empowered I felt, gaining confidence as I went.

At the beginning of the summer, I was afraid I was trading my parents for a new authority figure, a babysitter. But Joy had turned out to be something new. She was there for me to bounce things off and offered wise advice when I asked for it. She never told me what I needed to do; she only pointed the way. It was refreshing, mostly. Of course, there were times that I longed for someone to take over and give me the answers.

In the quiet we shared, I became increasingly aware of voices almost out of hearing range. When I turned to look, no one was there. Joy had taken to walking either way ahead or behind me.

One day, when the sun was high, I realized I'd lost sight of Joy some time back. This time I wasn't worried. The road passed through a thick forest. I ignored its pull for a mile or so but was unable to resist. I walked curiously towards the forest. I got to the edge of the trees, and it seemed dark and a little frightening within. It was as if something or someone was beckoning me into the woods.

Then I saw the trail. I walked cautiously down the track. There seemed to be nothing or no one to fear, yet I had a deep sense of foreboding. The path was slippery with damp leaves. I walked carefully, not wanting to trip in the muck. Large overhanging trees deeply shaded the trail; everything was vibrantly green, either wrapped in leaves, moss, or ivy. It seemed like a forest of long-forgotten magic or living magic. Maybe if I turned quickly, I'd see…something. But there weren't even fairies among the trees.

I couldn't see where the path led; it kept curving just enough that I could never see too far in the distance. The forest was dense, full of underbrush and tiny little plants, flowers, mushrooms, and who knew what else; moss-covered rocks covered the forest floor, with only the slightest bits of actual rock visible. It felt as if it had been undisturbed for centuries, and yet that couldn't be true since the path was well-traveled. I felt like I was walking into a fairy tale.

I allowed my love of adventure to lead me on. Was I being summoned or guided in some way? I struggled with my old self, who was sure my imagination was working overtime, and my newer understanding of the synchronicity and perfection around us. I couldn't turn back without knowing what was around the next corner and the next and the one after that.

When I stopped to take a drink of water from the flask at my hip, I began to hear what sounded like low murmuring voices up ahead. Probably just a creek or something, I thought. Nevertheless, I needed to find who was speaking. As I listened more closely, the low murmur began to sound like singing, no, more like soft chanting, resonant and regular.

The breeze picked up, swirling leaves and bits of branches and dust around me. As I walked, it was like being in my tiny whirlwind. I found myself standing before two of the most massive trees I'd ever seen. They must have been over a thousand years old. I couldn't see their tops; they were so tall, and their branches reached out in a canopy of over 100 feet each. The trees stood just off to the side of the path. At first, I thought the way went between them, and then I realized that it turned and went around. I stood silently, looking at these ancient beings, awed and humbled. The silence deepened, and I began once again to hear the low chanting. It was so deep I'm not sure if I heard it with my ears or sensed it on a deeper level. There were no words, just a low, continuous humming that seemed to come from the trees themselves.

I pushed away my fear and walked towards them. A delicious shudder went through my whole body, and I felt as though I'd just been caressed by the most tender touches as I passed beneath their conjoined canopy. I had to stop and breathe deeply, or my heart might have burst out of my chest. No, it wasn't from fear; I felt an overwhelming love for everything that existed, seen and unseen. I kept walking and breathing until I was directly between the two trees. I wanted to wrap my arms around the rough bark of one of the trees, but I seemed held to this spot between them.

I stood silently, tears running down my face. At first, I had no idea why I was crying. Over the past several weeks, I'd learned not to question these experiences. I turned my attention to my heart. I could feel a deep, steady pulsing deep within me. It was as if my lifeblood were coming into my feet from the Earth and reaching out in all directions, circling, encompassing, sheltering, and nurturing everything that came under my power. I merged with the trees, and we became three beings that lived and breathed as one. They each held part of the whole...one masculine, one feminine. I could sense the separate energies and feel them as they came together in the center so much more powerfully than either alone. I expanded, beyond, way beyond the physical being of these magnificent trees. Together, we touched the Universe, spiraled through time and space, and became one with all. From that space of complete connectedness, the most intensely incredible love I'd ever experienced engulfed me. It was all I could do to remain standing. Only the powerful frequencies pulsing steadily through me managed to keep me upright.

Within these frequencies of love glowed a warm golden light with a touch of pink. At first, it glowed dimly but got brighter and brighter as I focused and gave it my full attention. It was brilliant and beautiful. It alternated between being before me and being within me. Back and forth, inside, outside, inside, outside. I was tempted to brush it all off as "just a vision" but knew that would be doing a disservice to myself and this incredible gift of love and grace. I touched my fist to my heart three times as I murmured my thanks. As I tapped my heart the third time, the light pulsed even brighter, momentarily blinding me.

I saw brilliant pulses of cobalt blue, emerald green, and deepest amethyst from within the previously all-golden light. A form began to appear. I must surely be delusional. The form standing clearly before me looked like my mind's picture of Merlin, the magician, from King Arthur and Camelot's ancient stories. My doubting Zelia tried to convince me it was only my imagination, but I heard the man say my name. "Zemma. Hello."

I blinked and closed my eyes tightly, then opened them again. The man before me still shone brightly in all the colors of the rainbow. His was a gentle smile, touched with laughter and humor. It was obvious he was used to and enjoyed such reactions immensely. As I peered at his wizened face, I could see his eyes were a brilliant blue, sparkling, and glowing with intensity. Words failed me. I couldn't have said a thing if my life had depended on it. I only hoped it didn't.

He spoke again, voice deep, seeming to come from outside, yet from inside my head at the same time. "I am the spirit of this forest. In the past, some have called me Merlin, but many names over the centuries have known me. Within this small forest, we hold the spirit and energies of magic; the magic that has been, the magic that is; and the magic that will be in the future. There have been periods when magic was revered and honored throughout time, and other times it was neglected or forgotten. Most terrible of all are the times when magic is reviled and persecuted or dismissed and disbelieved. We of this forest hold the sacred trust during the bad times to maintain magic for the future. If magic is allowed to die, we all die."

He began to hum. The tune had no detectable melody, but the tones had a power all their own. I felt veils lifting from me. I was swirling in a whirlpool of unimaginably powerful yet gentle energy. I closed my eyes and let things happen as they would.

Behind my closed lids, I saw a brief overview of the history of the Earth. I saw the times when magic was alive and honored...the land and the people prospered, and there was laughter and happiness upon the face of the Earth. I saw times when magic was persecuted and killed off, and I felt the death of the spirit, the hopelessness, and the despair of the people. It was like being plunged into a darkness that had no deliverance. There was war,

228

famine, pestilence, and disease, followed by recovery and rebuilding. There was an endless cycle of building and creation, followed by tearing down and destruction.

I was having difficulty breathing. Just as I was certain the world would die, and me with it, I saw a spark. That glimmer came from the heart of a child born without the veils of forgetfulness and life-poisoning hatred. The child remembered magic and wasn't afraid to develop that spark. That glimmer grew once more and sprouted up in cries of freedom, creativity, and love. However, it remained as only pockets of richness here and there among the darkness and despair. Some sensed it once and lost it but kept looking and searching. Some rediscovered it and gave up everything to live within its glow. I knew that it was only a hope...but it was also the only possibility to keep the darkness from crushing us. Some hearts always softly glowed with intense magic, sending out lightning sparks that ignited in the hearts of others who were ready.

Each heart touched another, and another, and another, and another, and a flood of light encompassed the Earth. The whole Earth appeared to explode into light. In that explosion, I could see the shedding of fear, control, hatred, and greed and a remembrance of the magic and love that is the fabric of existence. The Earth began to heal. The pollution left the rivers; green began to grow again in the deserts and eroded valleys, and from all this came a joyful song...a song of love, a song of humanity's hope.

I opened my eyes, the vision still reverberating through my being. I looked into the wizard's eyes, and he smiled gently at me. He took my hands and said, "Share yourself, your magic, and your love with others. Remind them of what has been and what can be again. You, Zemma, are a window into the soul of the Earth and humanity. Through that sight, you can share the truths that you have seen."

Waves of denial rose in me as I cried, "But I am not worthy!"

"Visionary. You have chosen to reawaken your connection to magic. In this lifetime, your quest has been to reconnect with this essential part of yourself. You feel at peace when you allow the magic to move within you. The times you experience pain and despair are the moments when you deny its existence, cutting yourself off in your imagined separation. Through those losses and experiences of lack, you have come to truly learn the value and magic of love and all that it holds within it," he explained in his beautifully resonant voice.

I felt the light pulsing. I felt stronger. "I don't want to deny the magic and love within me!. I want to know a feeling of deep abiding peace. But how can I remind people of the magic?" I asked.

Merlin touched my heart. "Magic, wonder, and true love are the same thing. When this energy is allowed and embraced in its fullness, all things are possible. Where there is love, there is willingness. Surrender to the All That Is. Let go of doubt, lack of self-worth, fear. The doubt comes in when you question that anything so simple could have meaning. When you give in to a feeling of unworthiness, you fail to see your power and beauty, preferring to look outside the self for something more; more powerful, more beautiful, and loving. If you could see yourself as I see you, you'd stop doubting," he said, looking at me with immense love in his eyes."

"Do you honestly want to know peace?"

"YES! With all my heart and soul," I cried.

"Then know it. Allow it to fill you. Be it!"

"It can't be that simple!"

"It IS that simple," he said, smiling. 'It's a moment-to-moment decision. WILL YOU BE THE MAGIC? WILL YOU BE THE LOVE? That's all there is to decide." He stopped, letting his words sink in. When he saw the slow comprehension spread over my face, he continued. "Breathe the 'Yes' back into your very soul. Practice. Practice. Practice. Darkness is always pushed back in the face of love. As more and more choose to be free, the love and magic available to all increases in strength and expands exponentially."

With that, he placed his palm against my forehead. I closed my eyes and felt the light go deeper into me, becoming more robust, more anchored, as if I had become one with infinity.

I closed my eyes and felt the infinite force moving within me. I was more completely at peace than ever in my life. I went to the trees, one by one, leaning my head against them, thanking them. I stood between them and felt myself surrounded by and becoming one with a more massive, universal infinity sign, in which the energy was moving and returning continually. I knew my search was over.

CHAPTER 28:

Magic, the Key & Destiny

I spent the night in the forest alone, giving myself time to absorb all that had transpired. I alternated between happiness, delight, and abject terror. Joy had told me that I couldn't go back to my life as it had been before. Now I was sure that was true.

I wondered, too, if I could remember my own past lives like Josh had remembered his. As I lay warm in my sleeping bag in the circle of trees, I began to think that even though I wasn't dying physically, perhaps I was finally dying to my old self and becoming a new me. I thought back on the thousands of experiences I'd already had during my short life. I remembered the times I'd felt or caused pain. I remembered the love I'd given, the love I received, and the love shared freely. I remembered times of joy and times of unimaginable depression and disenchantment.

I realized that the moments that stood out for me were filled with magic or love when all was in harmony and all things were possible. Others that still seemed vivid were marked by lack of magic or love and the despair and anguish of separation, cut off from Source, hope, and even life itself.

A spark ignited in my soul, and understanding came clear. I'd seen it before, but now I knew it deep in my soul. Magic and love are the same. Love is Magic, and Magic is Love and is the fabric and foundation of the Universe, All That Is, was, and ever will be.

How could I ever have denied it? Feared it? When I did so, it was as if I'd tried to deny the very essence of my being! I woke gently and slowly as beams of sunlight filtered through the leaves. I lay quietly with my eyes closed, feeling very settled. I knew I'd decided in the night.

When I finally opened my eyes, eager to find what the day would have in store for me, Joy's eyes smiled back at me.

"Joy! How did you find me? Where did you come from?"

"I never left your side," she said softly.

"But you weren't here yesterday. I didn't see you at all after lunch."

"That's true; you didn't see me. But I was watching over you all the same."

"How?"

"Zemma, why do you keep asking? You know now that anything is possible for those who believe and keep the wonder and love alive inside themselves."

"But there's more to it! LIFE IS ALL MAGIC. IT IS ALL LOVE. LOVE IS THE MAGIC THAT IS ALL THINGS!"

"Indeed?"

I took one look at her arched eyebrows and started to laugh. When I finally collected myself, I looked at her levelly and stated in a sure, steady voice. "Indeed."

"Good," she smiled and nodded decisively.

"Just 'good'? That's all you have to say, Joy?"

"Yes. Is there more to be said? Don't you understand now what it is you've been longing for all these years? What you want to do?"

"Well, I believe it must be something about sharing what I know about how the deadness comes when we lose our connection to love, to our very essence. But how can that be a purpose?"

"Do you remember all you've learned about how fear can cloud your perceptions?"

"Yes. But I don't feel fearful."

"Really? Try this. Close your eyes and just imagine that you know what your destiny is. How do you feel?"

"Argh! You're right!" I said after a few moments. "I still feel like I did when the unicorn mentioned my destiny and purpose like I'd been kicked in the stomach."

"That's perfectly normal. You remember your old reactions to the question. Although you now have new answers, your body hasn't caught up with what your deeper self knows to be true. This feeling of panic is remembered, not real at the moment. What we need to do is bring you a new memory to take its place."

I thought about that for an instant and exclaimed, "OK, I'm game. How?"

"Close your eyes. Breathe deeply. Feel the magic you felt last night. Breathe into that sense of infinity that you experienced. Good. Keep breathing and ask to see your destiny." She put something into my hand. Immediately I knew it was the antique key from around her waist. I started to open my eyes.

"Don't open your eyes. Keep breathing. This key is a symbol to remind you that the key to your destiny is within you and that you only need to ask to unlock and see the truth. You won't see your entire future all at once; that would be too overwhelming for anyone. However, you will see the parts you need to know to take the next steps to begin making it a reality."

I was amazed at how easily I tapped into the feelings experienced the night before.

Thoughts flickered briefly through my mind, visions too quick to see.

"Breathe." Joy prompted as she placed her hand gently on my back, over my heart.

My breathing deepened. A picture formed and cleared; I was traveling, telling stories, writing, dancing, but mostly sharing from my heart to the people around me. Whole auditoriums of children, adults, or a combination of both, listened intently to what I shared. I tried to see what threads they had between them. I was speaking before groups of tweens, and they appeared fascinated by what I was saying. There were even rooms filled with adults equally engaged in what I was saying. The thread, what was the thread? Ah, I was teaching. I was teaching! Laughter, joy, and tears abounded. But the main message and sharing was love."

I opened my eyes and looked at Joy. "A teacher!? I'm supposed to be a teacher!"

"Really?"

"Well, definitely not a traditional teacher. I seemed to be doing an awful lot of play, but we were learning about magic and love and creativity within

233

that. We were learning to trust ourselves and our feelings. We were having a wonderful time."

"How lovely, Zemma," Joy said, meaning it. "Perhaps you will find that work can be play and joyful, as well as fulfilling."

"Wouldn't that be something?"

"Yes, it will be."

"I feel there's more to it, something I'm not quite grasping."

In her calmest voice, Joy said, "Don't worry, it will come to you. Think about all the people you will be meeting and influencing and the many opportunities you'll have to help others stay connected to their hearts. Imagine yourself continually connecting to and pulling together all those threads you saw in your vision. Remember, sometimes you must go down the path a distance until you can see the next part of the journey. That is what our journey together has been, hasn't it? This is where your trust comes in. Hold the vision of your goal and allow your inner guidance to direct you. There may be changes and shifts along the way that you hadn't anticipated. If you flow with it and keep refocusing, it all eventually becomes clear."

"Oh, no! More waiting!!!" I groaned.

Joy looked at me and laughed again. "Will waiting be so bad if you continue to have adventures?"

"Ha! Maybe not! What if there's not a specific goal! What if I simply need to stay in my heart and through that help others do the same?"

"Zemma, that is the gift the unicorn gave you. Yes, it was the gift of communication, not of words but of the truth of love and the magic that lives in all of us when we allow it in."

Joy reached out her hand, pulling me to my feet. We twirled around in circles, dancing under the ancient trees.

CHAPTER 29

Up the Rainbow

During the next few weeks, we traveled faster than we had before. Previously we'd gone slowly, savoring each tiny little adventure on the way. Having Flicka and Swanee certainly helped, but now I felt we were being drawn onward towards something.

We met people and listened to their stories, shared our love and magic with them. We delighted each time we saw that spark awaken in someone. The beauty of that never lessened, but now, each time someone connected, I could feel the weave of the Love of the Universe vibrate even more clearly with love. Our encounters became briefer and briefer as we went, yet still meaningful. It seemed that part of our journey was to connect with more and more souls along the way.

I've tried to recreate those last few weeks in detail in my journals. For some reason, the fine points continue to elude me. I remember that Joy and I had many long talks around the campfire at night and as we walked. She shared more stories with me and reinforced many of the lessons and understandings I'd gained along the way. It was with surprise that I realized summer was coming to an end and that it was almost time for me to go home and reunite with my family.

It was all I could to not despair over the thought of leaving Joy.

One morning I woke slowly, cautiously opening my eyes. Something felt different. I crawled out of my sleeping bag, wishing I'd put on my sweats before going to bed. The weather had turned chilly, and I was shivering.

Outside the tent, everything was quiet. There was no fire, no Joy. It was unusual for Joy to go exploring in the morning before breakfast, before coffee. I shrugged and decided that must be what she'd done. I started a fire and put water on for coffee. I figured that when the coffee perked, Joy would smell it and come running. She didn't. I drank my coffee alone, shivering, a little from either the cold dread or something else I couldn't quite place.

I tried to shrug off a strange feeling of portent. My senses heightened; colors were brighter, the coffee tasted better than I remembered. I noticed every detail around me, how the tent flap folded back, the sputtering flames, and the wind blowing through the trees. Every aspect is still clearly imprinted on my mind.

Finally, I set out to look for her. I stood on the path listening for direction. I heard the sound of a creek and felt sure that was the right direction. I walked for some time. The trail became steep as it wound down into a canyon. I slipped and slid, dislodging small pebbles on my way down. The trees grew close together, sheltering the path from the warmth of the sun.

I reached the floor of the canyon and looked up; sheer granite cliffs towered over me. The stream I'd heard earlier gurgled at my feet. I turned and followed it upstream. Then I heard roaring water in the distance. I must be approaching a waterfall. I edged close to the wall, trying not to get my feet too wet. I rounded the bend.

Sun streamed into the canyon, catching the spray of the waterfall as it fell practically at my feet. A rainbow arched from the stream on the canyon floor and reached skyward over the waterfall and beyond. I blinked my eyes. I'm sure I stopped breathing.

Spread out in a wide flat area beside the stream were all our Crystalline Heart Family members! I was dumbstruck. I'm sure I was smiling like an idiot and looking baffled at the same time. That summer, this did seem to be my default look.

How did they all get here!? It seemed impossible that they'd passed by our campsite without me noticing. They would have had to do so because there was only one path I could see to get here. Someday I might finally get used to impossible things happening. But that day had not yet arrived.

I looked around happily at the delighted smiles beaming from Justin, Jackie, Jeff, Uni, Sonya, Willie, Sally, PP, Josh, and nearly another dozen people who had joined us in the last couple of weeks. I was speechless. Seeing them all together made my heart overflow with love, wonder, joy, and a strange humility that I'd been part of bringing this incredible family of beings together.

Joy motioned for me to stand beside her. I was in a daze as I touched hands with those closest on my way to Joy's side. We stood arm in arm for a full minute before either of us said a word.

Joy opened her arms wide. I swear I could feel the love emanating from her heart to each of us. She spoke softly, but somehow her voice was easy to hear and understand.

"My darling family, thank you from the bottom of my heart for joining us. It means more than I can say. You've all agreed to step in to help humanity in its evolution. By working together, we will keep the wonder, love, and magic alive here on Earth and throughout the Universe. I wanted you all to meet in person today to get to know each other and create bonds that will help you work together in the future.

"You are each here because you have a deep desire to share the love of your soul with others. You all have strong hearts, unique gifts, and generous natures. You have many gifts already and will gain many more over time. Zemma has already experienced this; in time, your gifts will manifest and continue to blossom as you grow. Be patient and be open to what shows up for you. Connecting along the way can help you stay focused, grounded, and in your heart. I hesitate to call what we do work or a 'labor of love' because it's so much more than that. Our English language doesn't have the words to convey the true meaning of what I want to share with you."

Then Joy began to sing. There were no words to her song, but her tone was crisp and clear and so beautiful. It was as if pure love and joy were transferring from her heart directly to each of us. My heart opened in ecstasy. I could feel everyone's heart coming together in a vast spiral dance as all the love and magic of the Universe joined us with All That Is. I felt beyond any human love, but I'm at a loss to come up with another word. Light, energy, joy, love, wonder, magic, Creation, and Source combined into something so pure and beautiful that it was impossible to contain. My heart, indeed, my entire soul expanded into the Universe and the All That Is. I was one with all of Creation – pure Love.

I don't know how long we were within this spiraling expanding phenomenal field; I could have stayed forever. Slowly, we came back to 'normal' consciousness. My 'normal' seemed lighter, more expansive, and more wondrous than before. I could tell, looking around, that I wasn't alone in my experience.

Joy smiled radiantly. "Welcome all as you live the world that you have come to live—one filled with love and magic.

"I have a vision I'd like to share with you. Close your eyes again and see if you can see it for yourself. Your life is a path connected with thousands of people. Can you see yourself at the front of a massive group of people that fans out in long lines that form a V behind you? Can you see that? There are more than a thousand people in this formation, all people who in one way or another you'll touch in your lifetime.

"Look more closely. Each of those beings has a similar group behind them—each of those, and so on into infinity. Can you get a feeling for how many people that is? Just that first thousand with their own thousand is a million. If you care to do the math, go ahead, but the answers may be a bit overwhelming.

"Focus on the Love; it's that simple. You Are Love. Together we are that and more. I encourage you to find ways to stay in touch; phone, email, Skype, Zoom, gather, dream together. I may even pop in from time to time.

"You may, in time, find yourself drawn into small groups. These "pods" or clusters are natural in that all work together in the dream time. Some of you have been working together for many lifetimes, perhaps even since the beginning of Creation. Each pod has a specific way of operating or areas of influence; working together helps you strengthen your work and keep your energy clear and effective. Each of you has a role to play. Never forget that you're important, whether you're working alone or in groups."

I could see many thoughtful expressions and nods as her gaze swept over us.

"One of the most powerful tools for connection is the talisman you wear, your heart pendants. If you find someone is on your mind, in your dreams, etc., then most likely, there's a purpose for you to get in touch. Don't waste time wondering and doubting; pick up the phone, email, text, or connect in whatever ways you've decided on ahead of time. If you don't know the purpose immediately, just spend some time, chat, share stories, etc. I guarantee you within a short time, something will click, and all will be clear. Now let's eat!" Swanee and Flicka flew over the trees towards us. Both were laden with large baskets.

It didn't take long to get blankets laid out and heaped with a large variety of food and drink. I don't know how Joy did it, but people were exclaiming as they each seemed to discover some of their favorite foods.

As twilight began to fall, dozens of fairies showed up, each carrying a glowing orb that gave off a warm light. They lined up alongside a path, beckoning us to follow them. Curiously one by one, we followed.

As we rounded the corner, many colorful tents dotted the meadow. I took a peek inside; bedding and pillows, enough to accommodate from one to four, filled each tent. It was a sleepover! Once again, everyone sorted themselves out and got comfortable for the night without much discussion—laughter, talk, murmuring, singing, and giggling lulled me to a peaceful, happy sleep.

I woke to the sound of singing. First one voice, then two, then three, sang *Morning has Broken* by Cat Stevens.

"Morning has broken like the first morning…….."

Those lyrics and the sunlight created a magical start to the morning.

One by one, as we arrived in the meadow, we were greeted by fresh coffee, juices, fruit, croissants, yogurt, and several varieties of cereal and granola. Talking, laughing, and more singing filled the valley for about an hour.

I heard singing in the distance. Was that *Somewhere Over the Rainbow*?

Gradually all heads turned towards the music, and we started walking back towards the waterfall.

Joy wasn't standing on the canyon bottom or even at the top of the water-fall. She was hanging mid-air as if she were riding up the rainbow.

"Zemma, everyone, good morning!" She waved, smiling.

"Uh, good morning, Joy. Come here often?" I asked.

"Not nearly often enough." She lowered her hand and slid back down the rainbow, landing gently at my feet.

"You've all got to try it. It's like nothing you've ever experienced before."

"I'm sure of that," I said.

"Oh, you. Don't look so serious. It's easy, Zemma; you go first." Joy assured me.

"Okay. So, do I just go over to the waterfall and say 'up' or something, like in an elevator?" I asked, disbelief thick in my voice. When was I ever going to learn?

"No, you don't have to say anything. You just know that you can do it, and you will."

She took me by the hand and pulled me closer to the rainbow. I waved my hand, passing it through the rainbow colors, feeling the damp mist on my skin. A quiver moving through my body let me know this was no ordinary rainbow. I smiled to myself at the thought.

"Oh, good. Smiling is good, Zemma."

I closed my eyes and willed myself to rise; I didn't. I opened my eyes and looked at Joy for instruction.

"Zemma, stop a moment and think about everything you've learned. Trust. Believe. Know that you are magic and love!"

I closed my eyes again. Joy's words evoked the magic I had felt in the forest. I opened my eyes to smile at her, but she was below me. I was halfway up the rainbow! In my surprise, I must have let go of the possibility because I plummeted into the water.

"Try again."

What a journey: talking fish, trees that trip passersby, women-who-are-hippos, or was that hippos-who-are-women, unicorns, Jeff and Jackie, magic wand gardens, flying bicycles, golden wishbones, magical mirrors, talking birds, flying like an eagle, and so many other adventures I'd had recently. I only had to look around to be reminded of yet another story. But most of all, I thought of all the Love I had found along the way. I moved effortlessly up the rainbow.

"Joy, this is incredible!"

"Well done, Zemma!"

Joy turned and looked at the small gathering before her. "We will all keep in touch. I thank you all for joining me and for coming together here. Go up the rainbow, everyone! We will follow! It's a marvelous way to travel."

"What's there?" Many mouths were asking.

"I don't know yet. It's something different for each of us."

"Have you been there before?"

"Many times." Joy replied.

"Then why don't you know what's there?"

"Well, because it's different each time, for you and me both," she said patiently. "Each journey to the rainbow's end takes you to the next step in your destiny's journey. Destiny changes as you go through your life. It's not until you breathe your last breath that you see the pattern of your travels and how everything is interconnected. In the meantime, the rainbow contains all the possibilities in one, and it's possible to allow my inner guidance to connect to the next step in my destiny's journey and take me there. It's always exactly perfect, so I simply let myself go with the flow. Tap into the love all around you. You've all felt the wondrous alchemy of love recently. The goal of alchemy was to turn base metals into gold. The alchemy of love transforms everything into crystal clear energy. The magic of love connects and lifts all hearts and souls."

"So, if it goes to your destiny, how do you know if you've gotten there or not?"

"Oh, you'll know."

"How?"

"You feel it in your heart. There's a rightness to it. And this time, each of you will go where you need to be, and you will do what you need to do."

I looked around and could see the same realizations on other faces as well. One by one, they all came to the foot of the rainbow and hugged Joy. She whispered something in each person's ear that seemed to delight and amaze them.

I've asked her many times what she said, never getting a straight answer. She did say, "It's different for everyone. I share the words that will lift their hearts and help them know that they are fully ready to step forward into the next part of their destiny."

Will and Sally stepped up first, holding hands and looking both excited and nervous. Whatever Joy said to them made them turn red from head to toe and start laughing. Will didn't have his entire "band" with him, but he did have a small drum and a guitar. As soon as Sally put her elbow through, Willie's drum started playing as he strummed a bright Flamenco tune, accompanied joyously by the drum and Sally's castanets. They looked up with happy, delighted faces, eager for whatever their lives had in store.

Jeff and Jackie looked at each other quizzically as if trying to settle something between them. Finally, Jeff bowed down, and Jackie leaped onto his back, reminding me of a cowboy of old. As Joy whispered in their ears, I could almost see glittery magic around them. It was there, and almost not there, as if it was a mirage. Jeff let out a mighty roar, and Jackie said, "Never doubt the love you feel or what you know to be true, no matter what anyone else says."

They didn't just rise; they spiraled around in merry flight, singing, "Jeff the Magic Dragon, was with his lifelong friend. They could both be brave and frolic in the rainbow as they rose. Fearlessly they set off to live the world and explore under the sea." Then with a final roar, they were gone!

I laughed when I saw that Josh had donned his jester's garb for the occasion. His face was solemn when Joy leaned in, touched his arm, and spoke her words of wisdom and encouragement. I swear I heard, "Don't fear the Unmaker; he can't stand against the sureness that is Love." Josh put his hands on his heart, his back straightened as if he'd stepped into a suit of armor; he felt so strong. Then he reminded us all that it's possible to fight and have fun simultaneously; it's not only possible, but it's also necessary. Josh twirled his hat, bells ringing merrily, juggling spinning stars, legs dancing in the air, Josh rose in pirouettes. How he managed to rotate in space and keep those stars going is still a mystery.

Sonya walked up calmly, looking quite elegant and sure of herself. Something seemed different. I'm still not sure if Sonya had lost weight or if the difference was that she was now entirely herself, in her body and no longer allowing other's opinions to take her smile away. She stepped boldly into the rainbow, throwing her arms wide as if welcoming and rejoicing in what was to come.

I had the strangest sense that at the end, there was a ghostlike image of her hippo form, separating from her and fading entirely away, just before she reached the top. She poofed into her future on her own but open to new possibilities.

I forgot to mention – the men and the donkey were here acting up and having a gay time. I was curious to see how they would choose to go up the rainbow and if their future would continue as they had in the past, or if perhaps they'd make new choices.

I was astonished when the donkey came first and began to climb up the rainbow. About 5 feet up, he turned, neighing at the men. It took them a moment to shake off their shock and follow him. It was quite a sight to see the donkey leading the way. I wondered what was in store next.

I'm sure you can guess how PP, our friendly neighborhood purple people eater, made the journey. Yep, he was blowing his horn and going to town.

It was quite a sight watching the entire boisterous, fabulous, loving family go up the rainbow, each in their turn and in their unique way as they moved forward to the next step in their destiny.

Finally, it was just the two of us.

I floated up the rainbow a bit but hesitated. "Joy, it just now occurs to me that I need to see my folks soon. How can I just go off willy-nilly and follow the whims of a rainbow?"

"When you reach your destination, your parents will be there. I can't explain how the magic works, but a message has already gone out to them, and they are on their way to meet you. We'll meet again and work together sometime in the future. I can't predict when or where. In the meantime, you just need to think of me, listen and feel our connection, and it'll be almost like we are right now."

"Do you know where I'm going?"

"No, Zemma. I don't know where any of you are going. I don't even know where I'm going. But I trust the process."

I slid back down and stood in front of her. "Why do you look sad?"

"Sad? I'm not sad," said Joy.

"Well, you don't look exactly your normally chipper self. What's up?"

"I'm going to miss you. Everything changes all the time. Nothing stays the same. It's simply our time for the next change. Zemma, it's been a delight and pleasure. I may even get a cell phone or learn to text just for you."

"I would like that. I hate to think of not being able to hear your voice."

Joy hugged me, a wonderful bone-crushing, dancing-around-in-circles hug. Laughing, I let her go.

Before I knew what was happening, Joy was gliding up the rainbow right behind Swanee. She smiled and waved. I started to call out to her, but she disappeared.

I don't know how long I stood looking at the rainbow. I knew Joy was gone, and yet I half expected her to slide back down laughing and splashing into the creek. I could swear I heard a tinkle of laughter and a Swan's honk!

I looked around, imprinting the canyon indelibly in my mind. Even as I did so, I knew it wasn't the canyon or that particular rainbow that held the magic.

It didn't matter anymore that I didn't know how it would all work out. I trusted that I would figure it out as I went along. I breathed deeply into my heart. I began to move slowly up the rainbow, Flicka right behind me.

I breathed deeply once more, and I knew myself as love and magic. I was Zemma. I wanted to roar to the world, "I am Zemma. I am love. I am magic. Hear me roar!" But that seemed too much like a folksong I heard once and was afraid it was too corny.

I knew the magic had only just begun. I was ready for what was next in life's grand adventure. I was living the world now and forever.

The end of this story – and the beginning of my destiny!

Appendix

My childhood and teen years (1952-1970) were enriched by cartoons, stories, and songs that filled me with imagination, wonder, and fun. These memories remain vivid in my mind and continue to remind me life can be wonderous and magical.

You may not have these same memories and experiences, in which case, my references may have no meaning for you. A situation that I'm happy to remedy.

I found both historical information and videos to fill in these gaps in your education. I hope they speak to your heart and imagination as they have mine.

APPENDIX A - Chapter 7: Hair, Stars & Magic Wand Gardens

"Help Mister Wizard" was inspired by a 1960 cartoon series *"Tooter Turtle,"* in which Wizard Lizard would send Tooter Turtle back in time. When he got in trouble he'd, cry, "Help me, Mr. Wizard, I don't want to be X anymore!" (X is whatever persona he had entered in his adventure.)

Mr. Wizard called him back with the incantation, "Drizzle, Drazzle, Druzzle, Drome; Time for this one to come home," and Tooter would come twirling back to "the real world."

Through these absurd adventures, I fell in love with the idea of time travel. I also came away with the idea that it's okay to explore many ways of being and yet always come back to who you are, but perhaps a bit wiser.

Books have always been my favorite method of exploring lives, worlds, possibilities, and ideas, both realistic and fanciful. I believe story can be a way to get lost and found at the same time.

    ∞   Wiki entry - bit.ly/helpmrwizard

I found a full list of videos of the series. I was shocked at the poor quality of these cartoons that shaped my early years. It just shows how much things have changed. I hope you can enjoy and look past the shortcomings.

    ∞   Video list - bit.ly/mrwizardvideo

Appendix B - Chapter 14: Doubt Kills Dragons

Puff the Magic Dragon – Written by Peter Yarrow Story names changed to prevent copyright issues. I couldn't get a response and permission from Peter Yarrow, but I hope he'll see and enjoy my tale.

I was always moved by this story of friendship and loss and deeply sad for Puff. I couldn't imagine how Jackie could have possibly left Puff for other games. As I wrote, I laughed and cried as the rest of the story came to light.

    ∞   Video Performed by Peter, Paul, and Mary with lyrics bit.ly/puffthedragon

    ∞   Hardcover book bit.ly/puffthedragonfbook

    ∞   Wiki Entry - bit.ly/wikipuff

Appendix C – Chapter 18: Zemma's Eagle Flight

From A Distance Things are not always what they appear to be! Everything changes if you can get some distance and perspective. That message in this song written in 1985 by American singer-songwriter Julie Gold has given me comfort, guidance, and inspiration.

    ∞   Video by Bette Midler bit.ly/bettedistance

Although Bette Midler's rendition is the one I'm most familiar with, it's been sung by many over the years. In looking for videos, I came across this video by the Byrds, and I fell in love with the way The Byrds seemed to feel every word and their moving imagery.

    ∞   **Video by the Byrds** bit.ly/distancebyrds

Appendix D – Chapter 19: Purple People Eaters Do Exist

One-Eyed One-Horned Flying Purple People Eater – Sheb Wooley, June 1958

- ∞ **Video** - <u>bit.ly/ppeatervideo</u>
- ∞ **Wiki entry** - <u>bit.ly/ppeaterwiki</u>

I was six years old when this song came out. The radio was on loud, and I remember dancing around the house singing it with my mom and little sister as my baby brother bounced in his bouncy swing giggling. It was one of those infrequent fun, silly, happy moments.

I stopped dancing, when it hit me, I was a purple person! I tugged at my mom's skirts fearfully. "Mommy, will the Purple People Eater eat me?"

She looked at me disdainfully, "Of course not; he only eats purple people." She answered dismissively, turning away to go back to folding clothes.

I cocked my head and tried to believe her; she was always supposed to be right. But I knew deep down I was a purple person. "But mommy, I *am* a purple person. Maybe he only eats purple grown-ups, not purple kids. That would be okay; I don't know any purple grown-ups."

She turned, "What? What makes you think you are purple?"

"Oh, that's easy. When I close my eyes, I see everything in purple. It makes me feel happy, and my heart feels warm."

Although she just harrumphed and turned away, I always held onto my knowing that I was purple, and that was an incredibly good thing.

As I was looking up references to the Purple People Eater, I came across this book and am glad I ordered it immediately.

- ∞ **"The World Needs More Purple People"** by Kristen Bell
  <u>bit.ly/purplepeoplebook</u>
- ∞ If this touches something deep in your heart, maybe you're a purple person too.

Appendix E - Chapter 26: Cricket Call, a Warning in the Night

In discussing the Internet and computers, Zemma says, "Did you know that electromagnetic radiation and radio waves can injure our physical bodies and affect our thinking and moods? I bought a shield with a matrix of crystals inside to help me stay clear, and I was careful about how I used the Internet. I guess I just paid attention."

I didn't make the Shield up for the story; I've been wearing a BioElectric Shield since 1994. As an empath and energy sensitive, it's made a huge difference in my life - even helping me deal with energy vampires.

Please read my story bit.ly/empathstory

While you're on the site, I suggest taking the empath/hsp quiz. bit.ly/alchemyquiz

I co-designed the quiz to shed light on five areas of sensitivity and give you tips and techniques to help you create more ease in your life. The info you get back is invaluable and doesn't require a purchase. Over 10,000 people have found the quiz helped them understand their sensitivities and feel more empowered in their lives.

Just learning that you're an empath or HSP (Highly Sensitive Person) can help you deal with the energies, negativity, and fear around you. I hope you get some insight into your sensitivity and gifts and learn something here or in the quiz of help. Once you do are no longer at the mercy of the energies bombarding you, like Zemma, you begin to step more fully into the truth of who you are.

&#x6A❦&#x6A

Be part of the ongoing adventure. . I have so many ideas I want to share with you and a host of others bubbling up inside me; quizzes, meditations, blogs, games, giveaways, and possibly some actual future real-life adventures, and so much more than even I can imagine.

Sign up for the mailing list at www.earthtostarsadventures.com

I promise not to overload your inbox, but will share promotions, news, special announcements, merchandise offers, upcoming books, and so much more.

Let the Magic Begin....

The Alchemy of Love

Poem by *Mewlana Jalaluddin Rumi*

You come to us from another world
From beyond the stars and void of space.
Transcendent, Pure, of unimaginable beauty,
Bringing with you the essence of love.

You transform all who are touched by you.
Mundane concerns, troubles, and sorrows
dissolve in your presence, bringing joy
to ruler and ruled.

To peasant and king
You bewilder us with your grace.
All evils transform into goodness.
You are the master alchemist.

You light the fire of love in earth and sky
in heart and soul of every being.
Through your love existence and nonexistence merge.
All opposites unite.

All that is profane becomes sacred again.

I have an unquenchable thirst for the Wonder and Magic that connects us all heart to heart. I'm a visionary, writing magical realism, sharing the wonder, love, and magic I experience in the world and beyond. I've always felt something was missing in the portrayal of magic; it's not all about hocus pocus or witches and warlocks. Another magic goes deeper, right to the soul of the Universe and who we are as humans. Despite a lifetime of reading, I haven't seen a single book telling this particular story.

Sometimes all it takes to believe in yourself is to see that you aren't the only one who feels there's something more. I write to help you discover what that might be for you. I infuse my writing with mysticism, wonder, love, and my rather off-beat humor that I hope will speak to your joyous heart.

I am a gemstone empath and Guardian of the Stones, co-creating with a person's soul energy a piece of jewelry that is meant especially for them. Each stone is infused with love and its original purpose in creation to assist the wearer in living their original intended purpose. www.gemstonealchemy.com

My wandering nature has led me to live all over the United States, though I am now back in Oregon to stay... maybe. My adventurous spirit will take my readers from the Earth to the stars and beyond.

I have a unique perspective to add to the "worlds of magic." When you are in tune with the space of magic, anything is possible, and you can feel grounded in the Earth and expanded into the stars and beyond. From this perspective of magic, I began to write...

 беる ♥ ೲ

Join the unfolding adventure of our Crystalline Heart Family. Sign up for my mailing list at www.earthtostarsadventures.com Be the first to get promotions, news, announcements, quizzes, and merchandise offers. *Let the Magic Begin....*